THE BEST MAN

Alisa Allan

Bon Voyage Books
An Imprint of Travel Time Press

Bon Voyage Books
An Imprint of Travel Time Press

The Best Man
Copyright © 2005 Alisa Allan, All Rights Reserved

ISBN: 0-9761480-2-1

The reproduction or utilization of this work is strictly prohibited. This includes not only photocopying and recording but by any electronic, mechanical, storage and retrieval system or any other means hereafter invented, in whole or in part without the written permission of our editorial office.

This is a work of fiction. Any names, characters, places or incidents are products of the author's imagination or are used in a fictitious manner. Anyone bearing the same name or names is not to be construed as real. Any resemblance is entirely coincidental.

Visit us
www.BonVoyageBooks.com
www.TravelTimePress.com
www.AlisaAllan.com

Publisher SAN# 2 5 6 – 5 7 9 X

Dedication:

To my Mother and Father, Elizabeth and Harry... You taught me the important things in life, showed me the world, and then gave me the reins. And even understood when I let go of those reins a few times, barreled straight ahead, and ran into things along the way. I thank you and love you for your continued support for anything I choose to do in life.

Books by Alisa Allan

WINDS OF CHANGE - ISBN: 0-9761480-0-5
Release Date: July 29, 2005
Cruise to Bermuda with a young woman who is forced to choose. Rekindle a past?... Or set it free?

AFTER MIDNIGHT – ISBN: 0-9761480-1-3
Release Date: August 31, 2005
Cruise to the Mexican Riviera and the Canada/New England coast with two strangers who marry and clash in a blaze of differences.

THE BEST MAN - ISBN: 0-9761480-2-1
Release Date: September 30, 2005
Cruise to Hawaiian Island paradise with a woman caught up in a tailspin of revenge after a failed wedding attempt, and finds herself in the middle of a bond that could not be broken.

BEYOND THE HORIZON - ISBN: 0-9761480-3-X
Release Date: October 31, 2005
Cruise to the Caribbean with three friends who are taken away by balmy tropical breezes and become vulnerable to its magic, then discover a web of lies and deceit underneath its beauty.

ONE LAST TIME - ISBN: 0-9761480-4-8
Release Date: November 30, 2005
Cruise to the Caribbean with a single mother and her son as they set off on a journey of adventure. Immersed in exotic ambiance, a woman lets go of a battle that threatens to drown her, but must eventually return and face it, and she must risk all she found to face it alone.

ANGEL MIST - ISBN: 0-9761480-5-6
Release Date: December 31, 2005
Cruise to Alaska as a young woman discovers a calm to the haunts of her past, but she finds she would truly have to go home again before she could find real peace.

Visit our website for more details and to join our mailing list:
www.BonVoyageBooks.com
www.TravelTimePress.com
www.AlisaAllan.com

CHAPTER ONE

"Has anything changed? Can you come with me tomorrow?" Cassie asked as soon as William walked in from a long day, she'd been anxious to know if things had gone better than the last few days and maybe plans could possibly be different now.

"I'm afraid not, if anything, I'm busier."

"You're not trying to get out of this, are you?"

"I'll be there." He assured her with a kiss.

"If I didn't know any better, I'd think you were making up work to avoid going."

William took her in his arms. "I promise I'll be there in a few days. I can't wait to meet that sister of yours you complain so much about." He added the last with obvious sarcasm.

"Well, she won't like you, she doesn't like anyone."

"That makes me want to go even more." He spoke with sarcasm again then continued as if he were worried. "And how do you know your parents won't be the same?"

"Because I told you," Cassie snuggled closer as he wrapped her in his arms. "They'll love you, I'm sure of it."

He pulled her tight to him. "And you? What do you think of me?"

"I'm marrying you, aren't I?"

"It's about time. I thought you'd make me wait forever."

"Not forever, just long enough."

"And you're still making me wait because we still haven't set a date."

"Maybe I wanted you to go home with me first."

William cocked his eyebrows up with suspicion. "Worried? I thought you said they'd love me."

"They will, it isn't that, maybe you coming home with me just make's it official."

"It's already official now, and you can't back out."

Cassie looked at him coyly and asked once more, still knowing the answer wouldn't change. "Are you sure you aren't making up work just to delay coming with me?"

"I know how important this is to you and I promise that isn't what I'm doing."

"I've just been so anxious for you to come to Lakeview, I'm losing patience now."

"You could wait and fly down with me." When he had to delay going, he thought she would too but she'd insisted on going the day she planned for, regardless.

"It would be perfect if we could go together, but this is an imperfect world, isn't it."

"It was a shot, anyway." He chuckled, knew she wouldn't delay leaving.

She often went by herself, and in the beginning of their relationship William wondered if Lakeview had something, rather someone, that he should have been concerned about. But William knew it was simply the matter that it was her home, where her family was, and her family was important to her, he knew that.

For as long as they'd had a relationship, it was odd he hadn't met them before now but something always got in the way. It was always Cassie to go home for visits alone. Finally, he was able to join her and she thought he would come up with an excuse, but he couldn't put it off any longer, they were engaged now and it was mandatory he go.

Cassie never felt as if he really didn't want to, one thing or another always prevented him, always got in the way. And although she thought he was trying to delay it, or back out, William was anxious to go, wanted to see the little town she talked so fondly of, and visited so frequently.

There was no question in her mind that her parents would love William because he was everything they wanted for her, the kind of man they'd always talked about. Loyal, devoted, a good strong head on his shoulders, someone stable and trustworthy. They'd only gotten their opinion of him from what she told them, but she knew meeting him wouldn't change that opinion. He was all of those things and more. All of those things they wanted for her.

So she left him to finish the project he'd been involved in, and went alone with the promise of picking him up at the airport when he could get there. The drive was smooth and easy, her only stop was for gas and if it was light, which it was since she'd left early, she always stopped midway at a little country store just off the highway. Only for a quick stretch of the legs and a few bags of fresh boiled peanuts her father loved, then she wouldn't stop again until she was there.

As she pulled the Lincoln Navigator into the gravel drive, a light snow began to fall. It was nice and picturesque, but she was thankful it hadn't started earlier in her long drive from Virginia to Lakeview, North Carolina. It was bad enough she had to get used to driving William's large SUV, she couldn't have done it in the snow, even though it was built for that. She didn't want to drive it at all but he was insistent because the weather called for possible stormy winter conditions.

The snowflakes made it a perfect homecoming. Ever so lightly it fell as if it wanted to whisper 'welcome', and she wanted to whisper back 'I'm home'. She had been restless during the drive, anxious to get there, anxious to get home, and a fulfilled emotion replaced her restlessness as soon as she turned off the interstate. Now as she drove towards the house she felt the comfort it always gave her to see it there.

Although she lived and worked in a big city now, Lakeview was her true home, the place she wanted to be, where she'd grown up and belonged. It was always that comfortable solace, that place she could come to for rest or rejuvenation. Although William was always hesitant to get away from work for anything, she had no qualms leaving her job in Washington, often doing so for a quick weekend visit.

It already weighed on her that it would only be for a few short days then she would have to rush back and resume her hectic life. You haven't even pulled up to the house Cassie, she told herself, don't start thinking about going back yet. You have four days to be here and you would enjoy every single moment, even if it meant putting up with your sister.

The spirits that soared by just driving down Main Street and making the turn into the gravel drive began to diminish just slightly when she saw Mel's car parked in front of the house. She should have known her sister would be there. Maybe this time would be different. Maybe her sister would be different. It was far from assured, but she could hope, couldn't she? She pushed the negative away and didn't let thoughts of Mel bring her mood down. With work behind her, she saw the house and let it ease what remained of her stress and tension out of her system.

"Cassie!" Her mother squealed from the front door she'd rushed to as soon as she saw the car. She waved quickly then turned to the inside again. "George, Cassie is here!"

She saw the welcome smiles of her mother and father, then Mel came onto the porch and just the look on her face told her things wouldn't be any different this time than they always were.

"I hope I haven't missed dinner." After she retrieved the bag in the front seat, Cassie closed the car door.

"I've been holding it for you." Her mother said.

"Yes she has, and we're all starving." Mel had to add to show her displeasure.

Her sister had to put in an immediate jab, blamed her for not being able to eat when she was hungry, Cassie only smiled and hugged her mother close when she reached her. "Hello, Mother."

"Where is your coat?" Helen asked with quick motherly concern.

"Mom, I just came from the car less than twenty feet away, I'm not going to get pneumonia," Cassie hugged her sister quickly whether she wanted it or not, then her father. "Hey, Daddy!"

"Ah, my baby girl, you look wonderful as always. Where's William? I thought he was to come with you." He looked with concern towards the truck but it was obvious there was no one else with her.

"He couldn't get away and I couldn't wait, so he's flying in. I have to pick him up at the airport, hopefully tomorrow."

"Oh yes, I'd forgotten he was coming. Mother did mention it." Mel refused to make it a big deal that her fiancé was coming to visit for the first time.

"Let me see the ring." Her mother took her hand the first opportunity she had. "It's beautiful dear. Your description didn't do it justice."

"I'd forgotten about the ring too." Mel glanced quickly away then went back inside.

Cassie wanted to ask if that tampon she'd gotten stuck in the ninth grade was still there. If she expected her older sister, her only sibling, to be any different than she'd been towards her since she went away to college six years ago, she didn't know why.

They used to be so close and Cassie hadn't been able to figure out what had gone wrong. All she'd done was gone off to college then stayed in the Washington area to start a career in marketing. Mel had barely spoken to her since. A few phone calls over the years resulted in arguments and hard feelings, so they stopped trying to keep in touch. Any visit she made home resulted in arguments, but that wouldn't stop, she would just have to endure Mel until she left.

Cassie suspected she wasn't happy with her life, hadn't been in a long time, but there wasn't a thing she herself could do about it. So she bit her tongue as much as she could, often suffered literal wounds, and went on about her own life. She had missed what they used to have, but it was just something Cassie stopped thinking about after so long.

Unlike Mel, her children were ecstatic to see her, each waited patiently for their turn to greet her with a large warm hug and a kiss, and as always, Cassie made them feel she'd come home just for them. It irritated Mel she was so close to them, another thing her sister felt jealous about. As distant as Cassie was from her, she always remained close to her two children.

"I hope you didn't eat anything on your way, I've made a feast," her mother took her purse and coat. "Why don't you get settled and wash up and then we'll eat early. Ricky can carry in anything else you have."

"Hey, Ricky, can you move the truck to the side drive? I don't want to leave it in the way right out front." Ricky, a young teen, looked shocked and more than pleased when Cassie threw him the keys to the truck.

"Really?" He asked with wide eyes.

"Yeah, really, you can drive can't you?"

"Way cool."

"He doesn't have a license." Mel protested.

"It's no more than twenty feet away, he's going to the side of the house, not to town."

Ricky had stopped and waited for his mother to object, was sure she would, but she huffed and told him to go on so he bolted through the door before she could change her mind, towards the vehicle he would have charge of, even if only for a few moments. Marie, Mel's ten-year-old daughter, followed close behind and helped her carry her things up to her old room. She was Cassie's shadow whenever she was in the house and with her help, Cassie unpacked her few things.

Her girly room hadn't changed since she lived in it long ago. Cassie often told her mother to make it something else, to use the space, but it was still furnished with her canopy bed. White lace curtains hung at the window, stuffed animals adorned the bed, and various teenage paraphernalia cluttered the room.

Marie set the small case she carried on the floor, plopped on her bed, and grabbed the stuffed football that was there. Then she began talking with excitement and animation about what she'd been doing, Cassie wanted to hear everything and she was more than happy to tell her. The girl talked about her friends, her school, Bobby Jacobs who went to her church and would be in the church play with her.

"Marie and Bobby, sittin' in a tree..." Cassie playfully teased as she began to sing the childhood song and Marie blushed and stopped her.

"Nooooooo... he's cute, but he likes Rachel."

"How do you know that?" Cassie questioned with raised eyebrows.

"Rachel told me."

"Of course she did, because she likes him too and she doesn't want you to like him." Cassie hung her few things up in the closet.

"Really?" Marie questioned with a scrunched face. Why would her friend tell her something that wasn't true? That she didn't know for sure?

"Just don't take Rachel's word for it." Cassie answered without going into explanation.

"I love spending the night in this room, I stayed with Grandma last weekend."

Cassie wondered for what reason, Mel didn't go anywhere often, not for fun anyway. Her and their mother must have had something to do, but before she could question it, Marie confirmed it.

"Grandma and Mom volunteered at the downtown square for that Christmas thing. Ricky went, but she said it would be too late for me so I had to stay home with Grandpa and was asleep when they came home so I stayed here. I love spending the night here on Saturday's, because Grandma has pancakes on Sunday morning."

Cassie smiled at the memory, she hadn't forgotten it, just hadn't thought about it in a long time. Her mother had fixed pancakes on Sunday probably every day of her life. If they asked for it on Saturday morning, they'd be denied, that was a Sunday breakfast. Then she thought about the event they volunteered for.

"Don't tell me I missed Silent Night in the Square."

"Okay, then I won't tell you."

"Oh." Cassie groaned. "I was so hoping it would be this weekend."

"Wish it was, you'd take me with you, even though Mom didn't."

"Mom didn't what?" Mel asked as she entered.

Marie looked a little guilty and Cassie answered. "Didn't like my canopy bed when you were small."

"And still don't." Mel sat down on the bed. "Marie, quit bugging Cassie and go help Grandma set the table."

"Okay." She sighed with disappointment but did as she was told.

"Does mom need me to help with anything?" Cassie asked when Marie left.

"I've been over here helping her all day. Everything had to be just right because you were coming home."

"I don't know why she goes to so much trouble."

Mel huffed. "Neither do I, not like you're anyone special. This time she's gone above and beyond because the boyfriend is coming for the first time."

"She didn't have to, we'll only be here a few days."

Mel didn't voice her pleasure at that. Instead, asked about her job for menial conversation purposes, a tinge of jealousy burned the edges of her words. "How's that city job of yours?"

"It's a paycheck at the end of the week." Cassie pulled her makeup bag out and sat down to brush her hair in the mirror.

"It's more than a paycheck, it got you out of Lakeview, didn't it?"

"Not everyone wants to be out of Lakeview."

"And not everyone wants to stay here. I think our genes were mixed up at birth." Mel saw her own reflection in the mirror beside her sisters. Although she was only five years older, she looked at least twenty-five years her senior.

"No one forced you to stay, you had all the opportunity I did."

"You make it sound like we had equal grounds, you didn't get pregnant at seventeen."

"We all make our choices Mel, don't hold the choices you made against me." Cassie should have just ignored her, but Mel constantly baited her.

"Are you saying I should have had abortions?"

"Mel, don't put words in my mouth, I said nothing of the sort. You can't hold the choices you made against me, I didn't do a damn thing to

you. It sure as hell wasn't me that got you pregnant." Cassie always felt on the defense for a life she had, one that Mel didn't.
"No, but you throw your life in my face every chance you get."
"I do nothing of the sort, you're the one who always brings it up. Do something about your own life and stop being jealous of mine."
Mel huffed with exasperation. "It certainly isn't jealousy, I just don't like that you make a point to drive down here in your fancy car, wearing your fancy clothes, and showing off. You probably paid more for those boots you're wearing than I did for my house mortgage last month."
Cassie looked at her leather Alaia boots she'd paid six hundred dollars for on sale. It had been her biggest splurge when she received her promotion and raise one year previous and didn't feel the need to apologize for it.
"I probably did, but I'm not throwing them in your face, they're my boots and I bought them because I wanted them. I don't wear them for you, I wear them because I like them and they go with this outfit. Not everything is about you, Mel."
Mel pulled her legs up underneath her. "No it isn't, we all know it's all about you. Every time you grace us with your presence you like to throw it in my face how wonderful everything is for you."
"I never said anything about my boots, I never said anything about my life, you're the one who brought it up. Deal with your issues Mel, and quit blaming me for them. I'm the one who tried to talk you out of marrying Eddy, remember? So you can't blame me for the miserable life you ended up with." Cassie wanted to bite her lip, her sister did this to her every time and she knew she shouldn't have stepped into the defensive role she always put her in. Why should she have to defend herself? Rationalize her life to someone who never saw past high school and regretted it now, took it out on her.
Cassie didn't say another word as she left the room and left her sister sitting on her bed. She remembered a time Mel sat on her bed and giggled and talked about pleasant things, like two sisters did, two friends. She hadn't seen those days in so long the memory was fading into oblivion. Often thought maybe she'd just imagined them in her mind. Maybe those times never really happened at all.
It never helped when her father gushed over her. At dinner, he constantly talked of her accomplishments, her degrees, her career, her travels. He seemed to want to press to his grandchildren what kind of life there was for them to seek out, didn't say the words but wanted them to look at Cassie as their role model.
A position that embarrassed her and she changed the subject as often as she could but could see the slow burn on Mel's face. Afterwards, she

had to deal with more of her sister's anger, when they were alone in the living room Mel didn't wait to start in.

"I don't even know why you insist on coming back here as often as you do, it isn't because you love Lakeview so much, this hole in the wall town, I think it's because you just can't pull yourself away from daddy's strings. You might as well be the only child in his eyes."

"Maybe I can't. But I don't see you trying so hard to pull yourself away from mom's strings."

It wasn't a secret which parent each felt the closest to, for different reasons they were pulled in opposite directions. Cassie loved her parents equally, but always felt pulled towards her father, they seemed to share the same strong personality traits, whereas Mel reminded her of their mother so much, they could have been the same person.

Cassie often felt both her mother and sister desired something more from life, but neither had the courage to go for it. Both loved and enjoyed their children, and with her mother at least, she loved their father and would go to the ends of the earth for him. But Cassie always felt she was unfulfilled, sometimes discontent to be wife and mother and nothing more. Although now she did involve herself in more things, and she included Mel, which Cassie often thought was for the specific purpose to give her some kind of outside life than the one she was stuck with, something to take her sister's mind off her loveless marriage.

George encouraged her mother with anything she desired to do and Helen volunteered, helped with organizations and formed a ladies library group, but her first priorities were always her family, and she was still so involved in Mel's life, only phone calls to suffice where Cassie was concerned. She and Mel exchanged recipes, shared mother/daughter shopping trips, and lingered over coffee or long lunches at times. They shared a bond Cassie never felt part of. They had so many things in common at that time in their lives, things Cassie wanted for her life eventually, but in between had so many other priorities. Even when they were younger, it was her mother Mel clung to, while Cassie was drawn to their father.

Cassie's main priority always seemed to be making her father proud. Always felt he'd wanted a son and she felt obligated to prove her worth in a son's place. It was her father she listened to when it came to her college choices, her father's advice she took when he suggested her major and persuaded her in the direction of her life. He often brought her back down to earth when she had notions that seemed lofty, notions he called frivolous and risky.

"Daddy, I think I might go to Europe to study for a year. My professor is taking a few people over to study international marketing and..."

He'd laughed at the idea. "You haven't even mastered marketing in the United States first, doesn't make sense to me. Keep your feet planted where they are and you'll grow strong roots. Don't get ahead of yourself Cassie."

As always, she listened to him, and regretted missing a wonderful year in Europe. Often regretted when she listened to him and squashed her ideas of anything else she desired to do. He was big on stability, make yourself a road and stick to it, he always said. One direction would take you down the straight path of life.

Cassie often dreamed of other paths but never acted on her desires because she couldn't risk his disappointment. Every time she thought she was stronger than that, would go her own way regardless, she'd hear his voice and become the child who tried so hard to please. After college, all she wanted was to move back to Lakeview but it was highly discouraged.

"There's nothing here for you Cassie. You can't find here what you can in the big city."

"But I can get a job in Morristown and..."

Her father laughed and shook his head as if it were out of the question, as if she joked. "That's almost as bad as Lakeview. It would take you an hour each way to commute. There's nothing here in this dried up old town for you young folks, the only kind of life you'll have is one like Mel's. Nothing wrong with Mel's life, but I wanted more for my children."

Maybe I don't want more for myself, maybe Lakeview is enough for me, she often thought, but of course didn't voice her feelings out loud. Cassie often wondered if her sister hadn't gotten pregnant, Mel could have been the one to leave and Cassie taken the role of staying in Lakeview and pursuing another direction. Why did she have to be the one to prove something?

Mel's role had become mother and wife. Even if she wanted something more, Cassie knew her sister would never pursue anything else, and she felt sorry for what she'd turned into. The once vibrant and beautiful girl had become a bitter, empty woman. Cassie often tried to find the girl she once was, the one who sat with her in the middle of the night and talked of the bright future each of them would have. Mel wanted to be an actress, then a model, then a writer, always something she wanted to be. Now felt as if life had passed her by and left her unfulfilled. She loved her children, Cassie had no doubt of that, but deep inside she felt her husband left her wanting.

But he was her version of security. Cassie knew her well enough to know she wasn't strong enough for anything else, and she felt sorry for her, felt Mel would waste her life because she thought she needed a man she didn't love. Cassie wanted her sister back. The one she shared her dreams with, the one she could turn to, talk to, confide in. She'd been lost so long ago but she often wondered if there was hope in the future. If Mel would ever let her jealousies die and become a loving warm sister again.

She knew it didn't make it any easier on her sister when her father constantly praised her. Cassie cringed but her father was proud.

"So when are we going to be invited to see that big fancy window office of yours?"

"You don't need an invitation."

"Can we go, Mom?" Marie asked with a glow in her eyes. "Can we go visit Cassie sometime?"

"You went not too long ago."

"That was years ago, and I barely remember."

Cassie didn't want to bring up the fact she'd often invited Marie and Ricky to stay the weekend with her, but Mel always had one excuse or another why they couldn't.

"If you're too busy, Mel, your mom and I can take them for a weekend, I think it would be good for Marie and Ricky to see what it's like in the business world."

"That's a great idea, let's plan it." Helen smiled broadly and Mel discouraged all.

"They're busy with all the activities they're involved in, maybe next summer, we'll see."

Cassie wondered how proud her father would be if she gave it all up and came back home, knew it was one of the reasons she didn't. He often voiced his opinion on how foolish he thought her dream of moving back to Lakeview was, opening a business in this small town wasn't a way to make a good living, wouldn't be enough for her future security. It was something she could think about when she retired from her career and needed something to keep her busy.

Cassie long ago stopped voicing her dreams out loud, they were never words her father wanted to hear, so she pretended to be happy in the life he wanted her to have and remained silent to her true desires. It made life easier.

Chapter two

Marie talked excitedly about being in the play at church the next evening and Cassie assured her she would be in the audience to see her. Later she sat down with Ricky who kicked her butt in checkers and quietly revealed a crush on a girl when Cassie asked. She always teased him because he was so handsome that surely he would have a slew of girlfriends, and he was now at the age where he did.

She enjoyed her sister's children immensely. It gave her a little taste of motherhood to be close to them, yet she could be the fun mother, the one who didn't have to discipline, or make them do their homework, or tell them they couldn't have ice cream. It was a taste that merely scratched the surface, a taste of motherhood Cassie certainly wanted more of one day.

Mel's husband, Eddy, stayed away from her for the most part, that was really the only way they got along, neither one cared for the other. So she wasn't upset when he left just after dinner, said he had a poker game with the boys. Mel would have gone home just after but the kid's insisted on staying so she simply sat on the couch and watched television, while Cassie played and took advantage of every moment with Marie and Ricky.

"Christmas is around the corner. What did you ask for from Santa this year?" Cassie asked Marie as she rolled the dice and moved her game piece along.

"Aunt Cassie." The girl sighed and rolled her eyes. "I'm much too old to believe in Santa."

Cassie looked at her almost in true shock. When did they stop believing? What age did that happen? She hadn't even had kids yet to begin the magic of Christmas tales and she sat across from Marie who no longer believed. As if on queue, she could hear her time clock inside ticking away.

"What did you ask for, Aunt Cassie?" Then Marie smiled teasingly. "From Santa."

"You little smarty." She laughed and tousled her hair. "I didn't ask for anything."

"Aunt Cassie already has it all." Mel piped in. She smiled and said it with a joking tone as if it wasn't a personal jab, but the two sisters knew it was.

Mel thought she knew so much about her life. All she saw was the fashionably modern Cassie with the latest clothes, the career as a highly paid marketing executive, and a cool apartment in a busy city. The freedom to live as she pleased, do as she pleased, everything Mel wanted for herself.

What she didn't know was that Cassie would hand it over to her if she could, in exchange for returning to Lakeview and opening a little shop on Main Street U.S.A.. A place where everyone waved, greeted you by name when you passed, asked how your life was going, and really cared about the answer.

Her ideal would be to buy a little house in Cape Point that overlooked the lake. A husband she loved, two children, one girl and one boy, all complete with flower garden and picket fence. After Cassie pulled off her imaginary rose-colored glasses she sneered at Mel when no one was looking. Juvenile, she thought to herself, but she drove her to it.

****

Lakeview was one of the rare places left on earth you could walk to town and not feel it was a dangerous thing to do. Cars passed and drivers waved, and it was a true wave, they weren't giving you the finger because you weren't fully on the sidewalk. Actually, there wasn't even a sidewalk on the road to town, just an old road with gravel and stone on the side. A few neighbors stopped and talked to her out of the window as Cassie walked the familiar route. One in particular surprised her, it was Mr. Grane and his daughter who she babysat on occasion, but it was the daughter in the driver's seat. He and his wife had been older when they had their only child, and he actually looked closer to being her grandfather rather than father. Then Cassie thought the full head of gray hair had maybe come with the teenage years.

"This can't be." Cassie exclaimed and the girl smiled proud.

"Just got my learner's permit yesterday."

The girl's grin took up her entire face, but the father's face was more of a grimace and Cassie had to laugh that he tried hard not to make it look so obvious. "How could you have let her get so old so soon?"

"I tried to stop it," he said.

"Want a ride to town? We were going to go out to the highway, but I can…"

"No thank you," Cassie answered quickly with a chuckle. "I'll wait until you've mastered it a little more, I remember you on a tricycle."

"It's no trouble." Mr. Grane encouraged it, he wasn't anxious to get on the highway with his teenage daughter.

"Maybe some other time."

Cassie waved as they went off and shook her head, still unable to believe she'd gotten old enough to drive. The older people in town had watched her grow up, now she supposed it was her turn to witness the younger generation grow into adulthood. An odd feeling it gave her. Also a sad feeling when she thought that she wouldn't actually be witness to it. She would get a card or it would be during a phone call with her mother when she would tell her that little Lewis Hanes had gotten married, or little Susie Brown had her first child.

Cassie thought about the next generation to come after that, a generation that wouldn't know who she was, she would become the 'visitor', the woman who came to town on occasion, they wouldn't know she was one of 'them', one of Lakeview's own. By that time, who would she visit? Her parents wouldn't live forever, and she couldn't imagine cozying up on Mel's couch for a weekend, Mel didn't even like her anymore. She almost panicked she would have no one to come and see, but remembered Marie and Ricky would be older then, they would have their own families, their own homes. And Mel may not want her, but she knew they would, no matter how old they got.

The people who lived here had been doing so for generations, but now quite a few of the younger generations were forced to go outside of Lakeview to make a good living. The promise of riches in the big city beckoned them, and it saddened her to see some old familiar houses now occupied strangers who'd made their riches, now wanted to retire in the old fashioned way of life that was her home.

Her mother always kept her up to date on the happenings and as Cassie passed the old Masterson homestead, she knew inside it was now occupied by a couple who ran some sort of internet company from their home and had five children. Two of them, bundled in snowsuits to ward off the cold, rolled down a small hill on the side of the house and Cassie laughed as they ran into each other and rolled as one.

The town had changed over the years, not largely, just little changes here and there, but most important was that it kept its charm intact. This she was reassured of as she walked down Main Street to see the Christmas lights and decorations that had begun to adorn the businesses that lined the street. Windows festooned with snow scenes, ribbons, bows, candles and Christmas trees. A few new fancy boutiques caught her eye and she imagined they bustled with activity during the summer months when tourists clambered to rent the best houses on the lake for either a short week, or the entire summer.

There were some families she'd met over the years who came every summer and she'd missed seeing them since moving away. Cassie used to work at the Marina Deli and often met the regular tourists who came year after year without fail, could remember vividly summer crushes with boys that seemed worldly because they lived outside of Lakeview.

She often thought of them over the years, the summer friends that eventually faded from her life, and wondered where they were and what kind of lives they now lived. Were they as frantic and harried as her own? Had they ever come back to Lakeview? Did they now bring their own children to vacation?

It was a town that went unappreciated when she was younger, and now that she was older she understood what they had all come for. The serenity, the peaceful way of life, the slow pace of how things were done here, the way it forced you to relax and forget about pressures of a busy city life. It rejuvenated your spirit. The residents proof there were people in the world that spent time to talk to you and not pass you on the sidewalk everyday and look through you as if you didn't exist.

In Lakeview, everyone mattered. It made no difference where you came from, who you knew, what you did, or what kind of bank account you had. Strangers and residents alike treated with the same respect and gracious hospitality.

Cassie stopped into a few stores along the pretty street. Spent more time than she intended talking to old Mr. Callahan whose wife gave every child in Lakeview piano lessons, while he operated the small bookstore. It saddened her to hear him talk of closing the store, retiring after thirty years in business.

"No children to pass it on to," he said. "And people tend to buy their books over the Internet or at the big blockbuster book stores in the city I can't compete with. Full time fishing is what I plan to do. That and the Mrs. has a list of things that need fixin', says it's about time they're fixed."

She talked for a long time and was saddened when she left, knew it was probably the last time she'd see the bookstore as the store she used to know, in the back of her mind wondered what it would be replaced with. She was uplifted a bit when she stepped into the deli and bait shop that still did enough business in the wintertime from locals to keep afloat, and found Susan, a dear childhood friend, had taken over for her retired parents. It was always good to see her, and though their lives were separated by distance and time they kept in touch by phone and email when they could. It was as if they were teenagers again when they saw each other.

Susan hugged her in greeting. "I was wondering how long you'd make me wait for you."

"You knew this would be one of my first stops."

"But it wasn't, you stopped and saw Mr. Callahan first, if I didn't like him so much, I'd feel slighted." She smiled and revealed how she knew. "Betsy Warner stopped in and said she saw you there, I knew you were on your way."

"Can't make a move in this town, can you?"

"If this were summer I'd put you to work, but we're slow, so it's the perfect time for coffee and a chat." Susan poured two cups as they sat on worn and broken wood stools behind the cashiers counter.

"If this were summer, I'd love to work. This was always my favorite job."

"It was certainly the one with the best view. Not only of the lake, but of all the cute guys that came in for bait. They didn't even fish, but they'd come in to buy a soda and bait."

"Remember those twin brothers? James and Jason I think their names were. Their family always rented the Lowman place, the biggest house here until they built that monstrosity a few doors down from it."

"That old eccentric rich guy still lives there too. He just holes up in that big old house by himself. Someone said he was a writer, been there for five years now and I can't find a person who knows much about him." Susan looked out to the house she spoke of and remembered when both of them used to see the boat coming across the lake that held the gorgeous twin boys they dreamed of marrying in their girly childhood fantasy. "You had the biggest crush on James and you never said a word to him. Every time he came in you froze."

"It took me two summers to get the courage up to say a word." Cassie remembered how crushed she was to find out he spent quite a bit of his time with Paula Glass who lived close to their rental. She'd always envied Paula's long blond hair and perfect little face.

Susan laughed. "Then all you said was... 'you want bait?'"

Across the other side sat Crystal Lake Resort and Cassie noticed it looked fresher with some improvements and new paint. "The resort looks nice."

"Since winter is their slow time, they've been working on it since the summer was over. Mark and I went there for dinner a few weeks ago for our anniversary. The inside looks great too, all new carpet and fresh paint, and they added a sunroom. Still the best place in town for a celebration meal."

It was Lakeview's only resort and it catered to summer tourists but stayed busy with residents that had anything to celebrate. It was always the best place to go. The pier in front was now empty except for the water taxi that made very few trips across in winter, but most of the richer tourists who stayed rented their own boats in summer and the pier would be filled to capacity.

Cassie could remember sitting in the deli and marveling at the wealthy people, wealthy by their standards anyway, who spent a week or two at Crystal Lake. The women wore crisp resort attire with hats and scarves and they'd come across and spend time on Main Street, called it 'quaint' and 'cute', while their spouses golfed or fished.

"How is Mark?" Cassie asked about Susan's husband who she was close to also.

"He's wonderful. Surprised me with a short romantic trip away for our anniversary, but we'll go at the end of January when this place is the slowest. My dad will come in while I'm gone and mom will keep the kids. It will be heaven just the two of us for once."

"I still can't believe your parents are retired, I never thought they'd leave here."

Susan hadn't either, but knew it had finally become too much for them. "I always include them in major decisions that have to be made, and keep them up to date. Makes them think they're still involved. They just couldn't do it anymore, and it's perfect for me, the kid's come after school and they help out quite a bit in the summer, and they'll be able to help out more when they get older."

"And another generation trained." Cassie could already see her children running the store in years to come. It's what kept Lakeview the prize it was. Many generations had started and ran the businesses there for the last several centuries, and most seemed content and comfortable to continue without change.

"Hey." Susan shouted, she'd just remembered something. "I thought your mother told me that boyfriend of yours is finally coming to town."

Cassie looked at her watch but had plenty of time. "I'm picking him up at the airport later today."

"Are you going to be here long enough for me to plan on dinner? Why don't we set up a night for you two to come over, Mark can make his famous seafood lasagna and the kids would love to see you."

"I don't see how we can make it. We're only staying till Monday."

"Maybe when you come back for Christmas. Why don't we do New Years Eve?"

"We'll leave the day after Christmas." Cassie moaned.

"I should have known. Probably have your New Year planned, some big party where you have to dress formal and the champagne flows out of a fountain. The life of my 'city friend' is one I envy. I can picture you in a red satin gown, maybe sequins, shaking hands and kissing cheeks of dapper gentlemen in tuxedos." Susan sipped her coffee and laughed. "Me, on the other hand, will be in my brand new flannel pajamas the kids will buy me for Christmas, huddled on the couch with a tin of cookies and trying to stay awake to see it on television."

"It isn't all it's cracked up to be." Cassie looked out to the lake, Susan's vision was very close to what it would be like. She wished she could be here instead, huddled in front of a fire with her own flannel pajamas.

"Anything wrong?" Susan asked with concern.

"No, I know you tease me about my life with love, and it doesn't bother me, but all I've listened to since I've been home is Mel talk about it with venom. She's so jealous about something she doesn't know anything about."

"Mel's not happy with herself, she can't be happy for you or anyone." Susan was quiet for a moment before she continued. "I heard something about Eddy, I don't know if it's true and I hate to pass on gossip, but maybe you should know."

Cassie raised her eyebrows in question then smiled. "It could be good news. Are you going to tell me he's fallen in love with someone else and is going to leave her? I know that sounds horrible, but Mel won't leave him, I can only think it would be good for her if a divorce was forced upon her."

"Could be possible, I've heard some things along those lines. Seems Eddy has taken up with a married woman who's here by herself most of the time while her husband is working in the city. From what I hear, the husband's doing the same to her, but again, probably just vicious rumor. It's a small town and people talk, and you know how some people around here love to talk about others. Sometimes I think they make things up in the winter because there's not much else going on."

"Let's hope it is true, and let's hope it would make a difference to Mel. But I'm not sure it would even if she knew about it. Rumors about him and other women aren't rare, but it hasn't done anything before."

They didn't spend too much time talking of Mel and her problems, and caught up quickly on their own lives. Cassie helped out when a few customers came in, reverted easily into the role of deli worker. Because time was short, she didn't make any promises to see Susan again but would do her best to try and work something out to get together before she left, if not this trip, then the next. And as always, Cassie encouraged her to visit her in Virginia but knew it wouldn't happen until her kids were much older and she felt she could get away easily.

When she stepped out of the door and onto the pier she heard a holler from Mark who'd just stepped onto the pier and saw her. She saw the broad smile on his face and the evil streak in his eye as he began to run towards her.

"No Mark, not today, I have to..." Cassie ran back inside and tried to hide behind Susan but it was no use.

Mark grabbed her, picked her up easily and ran back out the door and straight off the pier, they both came up laughing.

"Can't you ever give me a simple hello?" Cassie wiped her face and stood up to see Susan laughing at them.

Mark held out his arms for a hug and she went to him. "I've been working on a boat all day, I figured you wouldn't want to hug me dirty."

"Who said I would want to hug you anyway?" Cassie hugged him and laughed. "You're impossible."

"Plus you looked a little too un-mussed, you forget that we're simple folk here in Lakeview."

"Un-mussed? I don't think that's a word."

They climbed the ladder back onto the pier and Susan held out towels for them. "Still a child at heart," she said about her husband and although she'd handed Cassie her towel, she threw Mark's.

He wrapped her into his arms and gave her a wet hug as she squealed. "Hey honey."

Susan pushed him away playfully. "Dry yourself while I go get Cassie some dry clothes."

Mark held his hands out. "Cassie? What about me?"

Cassie playfully stuck her tongue out at him and he pushed her into the water again.

She changed into the dry clothes Susan gave her and was there another hour or more catching up with Mark. Cassie loved them both dearly, could still see the love they had for each other after all the years together, since they'd all been children together. It was refreshing to see such a marriage after being surrounded by Mel and her unhappy attitude because of her own.

"So where is this boyfriend of yours?" Mark asked.

"He'll be here."

"Does he drink whiskey?"

Susan swatted him. "Mark, you're going to leave him alone."

Cassie chuckled. "He's been warned, and he doesn't really drink whiskey anyway."

"What kind of man doesn't drink whiskey?"

"The smart kind." Susan teased. "At least they're smart if they stay away from you and Cassie when they're drinking it."

"How did I get into this?"

"You're just as bad, you're the one who started it." Susan teased her friend with a smile then turned her attention back to Mark. "You might have to wait till the next trip anyway."

"I won't meet him this time?"

Cassie looked apologetic. "We're only here a few days and things are hectic."

"Is there something wrong with him you're not telling us about? You've been dating him how long? Now engaged? And we still haven't met him?"

Cassie did feel bad they hadn't, but it was through no fault of her own. "You will, I promise."

When she finally left, Cassie walked down the water edge that ran behind the stores, noticed that the eating deck attached to Vince's restaurant was barren but knew the bustle of activity when the summer tourists waited up to an hour for an outdoor seat to enjoy their meal. She walked up the small hill to the town square where a gazebo sat in the center. Chatted with a few more people she saw and quickly caught up on lives as much as she could in the short time, then continued back through Main Street. It was then that a dark vacant building on the corner caught her eye.

It stood lonely and empty. A dark window and facade that stood out among the other vibrant one's that twinkled with lights. Cassie pictured it occupied, pictured it as she did in her dreams, as a bakery and coffee house. She knew business and marketing and Mel knew baking, they could be the perfect pair. The back of it faced the lake, and a deck like Vince's could be built and summer tourists would flock to enjoy their morning coffee as they watched the world go by on boats. A few tables could be placed out front if they wanted to watch the foot traffic.

Cassie pictured it painted white with a red and white awning above the door. Windows painted with bakery delicacies, as crisp white curtains hung on the side. Ricky and Marie could help out and eventually she could bring any children she might have, like Susan and her family, it could be something for generations to come.

She took a peek inside the empty space with the 'For Sale' sign on the door. It was the old small library, they'd built a new one a little outside of town where they had more space and parking. It made it even more perfect. She could sell used books from the built in shelves, set up a little reading area customers could enjoy coffee and a piece of pie. Big, overstuffed furniture one could linger comfortably in. It could become a town gathering spot, the perfect meeting place.

Cassie thought about all that would have to be done in order to accomplish it. Not only leave her job, give up her stable and steady career, but the thought of going into business with her sister who didn't even like her, would be a huge obstacle to overcome. Mel had no desires or dreams, her only goals were to get through the day. But Cassie knew if she were to get away from her husband, she could become the person she used to be. Would that ever happen?

She leaned against the window and sighed. Maybe in another lifetime, maybe her father was right and she would have to wait until she was old and it would be something to keep her busy.

As Cassie walked home it was the only thing on her mind but she eventually let it fade away and concentrated on what was before her. Her fathers words, 'lofty dreams', rang in her mind. Perhaps he was right. There was more involved than the simple task of renting a space and creating a business. Various factors would prevent her from seeing that sort of dream for a long time to come. If she didn't think about it, it made it easier to let it fade into the background.

CHAPTER THREE

"How was practice?" Cassie asked Marie about her play rehearsal then whispered close to her ear. "Did you see anyone special?"

"He gave me a Christmas card." Marie giggled and her smile lit up her face.

"What are you two whispering about?" Mel asked suspiciously.

"Nothing, Mom." Marie sighed and rolled her eyes.

Marie wanted to go with her to the airport, but she would have to get ready for the play and wouldn't have time. Cassie grabbed a quick snack of coffee and a piece of the delicious cake Mel made, and then left to pick William up. After, they would go directly to the play from the airport then have dinner afterwards.

William didn't seem that impressed with either the town when she drove him down Main Street, nor the childish play that didn't compare to a Broadway production. But he put on a smile and went along. She was the only one who noticed he seemed to want to be somewhere else.

He chatted amicably at dinner, and her mother commented on how polite he was, how well mannered. She liked him, and her father gave his approval in private before she went to bed.

"I think he's perfect for you. Has a great head on his shoulders and he knows his road in life and won't wander from it." He smiled. "You'll be happy with William."

She thought about his words as she lay in bed that night. She was in bed alone and William wasn't happy to be put up in the guest room, but he respected her parents enough to understand. She was restless as she tossed and turned and thought about the lives in Lakeview and her life so far from it. Thought about her father's words and how she'd be happy.

When morning came and she woke to find William in the kitchen, it was odd, him being in her family's home. It was the first time in her life she realized how the two worlds differed. How her two lives were separated. The hometown girl, and the career oriented one who lived in the busy city, with William in her kitchen she saw the two merge together, whereas she'd always viewed them as separate before, but it was a merge that didn't actually fit right.

Cassie realized her two worlds would never converge. The road ahead of her had to be free from 'lofty dreams' but she could hold onto the dreams of her reality, of sharing her life, having children, creating a family. It would be with William, but it wouldn't be in Lakeview, she couldn't picture that.

With William there, her mother talked more of the upcoming wedding. Wanted to find out details, what each of them wanted, and she chatted on continuously about making plans. Mel took her engagement as another stab to her personal life. Her voice was full of jealous sarcasm when she caught Cassie alone in the kitchen looking at her ring.

"Quite a ring, tops your life right off, doesn't it? A wealthy handsome man to add to your possessions, you're the epitome of perfection now."

"I don't want to fight with you this morning, Mel, it's too early to start the day off like shit, don't you think?" Cassie placed her empty cup in the sink, contemplated getting another cup before Mel came in but decided against it now.

"My day starts off dealing with shit every day, why shouldn't yours?"

"Your adult life started out like shit." Again, Cassie should have kept her mouth shut but took Mel's angry bait.

"Aren't you leaving today? As early as possible would be nice." Mel huffed.

"When are we going to stop this?" Cassie asked as she turned and looked her sister square in the face with no animosity, no anger. It was a question she often asked herself, now voiced it. "What happened to you Mel? You used to be strong, why don't you just leave Eddy so you can find a life again."

"Oh, I should have known. You became engaged and now you're an expert on marriage and husbands?"

"I don't have to be engaged to know you're miserable with your life. That didn't happen yesterday, it happened the day you married him, and each day that passes pushes you deeper and deeper into a shit hole you feel you can't get out of. Just leave him. You have two wonderful children that need a mother."

"I'm a good mother." Mel said defensively.

"You don't do your kids any favors by staying with a man you don't love. Marie asked me if I thought you would ever get smart enough to get a divorce. Don't you find it a little strange your kids can see the truth but you can't?"

"How dare you assume you know something? The kid's love their father."

"I don't doubt that, but even they can see the two of you don't work. They can see how miserable you are." Cassie felt sorry for the kids, they had never known the fun, loving person Mel truly used to be.

"Go back to the life you know something about, your own, because it isn't mine."

As she slammed out the back door, her father entered from the living room.

"What was all that?"

"Mel."

He shook his head. "I don't know what it is with her sometimes. You two used to get along so well."

"She has a lot to get through." Cassie looked through the window to see her drive away.

"Didn't I tell you that college career would get you places?"

"What?" She was confused as to what he spoke of.

"I told you. The right college, the right career and it would all pay off one day."

To him, everything she'd done had been to get to that point. To be engaged to someone like William. Wasn't it enough that she'd accomplished so much on her own? Did he see William as the prize to all her hard work? Cassie didn't say anything, simply smiled. It was everything he wanted for her life, his dreams for his daughter come true, and she didn't want to burst his bubble.

When they left, Cassie knew they all loved William, thought he was a good choice for her. Excited and anxious to see him become part of the family.

"I knew mother would start right away with the plans." Cassie said when they were finally able to leave. Her mother kept bringing up different things still, insisted they needed to get together again soon, said they needed at least a whole week together to go over details.

"She's excited. Her baby is getting married. And it's about time we started planning something, don't you think? You didn't plan on staying engaged forever, did you?"

It crossed her mind. "I didn't want all of it to get out of control, and the longer I put my mother off, the better it would stay in control."

Marriage loomed before her, motherhood after that, starting a family, wasn't it everything she wanted? Why was she now hesitant when it came time to plan? As the car drove away from North Carolina, it was as if her real dream slipped further and further away with each mile marker they passed.

Her dream was in Lakeview. William's life, the life he offered, was somewhere else. In the back of her mind her father's words rang clear... 'I'm proud of your life Cassie, the life you've made, the life you'll have.'

Cassie looked to the diamond that shone on her finger, the beautiful three-carat solitaire she would have picked out for herself if given the opportunity. It represented her future, the stable one everyone seemed to want for her, the kind of life Mel was jealous of.

"You want to pick out another?" William asked when he took her quietness as one of second thoughts on his choice.

"No, this is just what I would have picked out."

"I thought it suited you."

"How did Lakeview suit you? Did you like it?" It was important for her to know.

William started to speak, then stopped, then started again. "It's quaint."

"Meaning it isn't someplace you could see yourself living?"

He laughed then saw her seriousness. "I guess I never thought about living there, why would I?"

Cassie shrugged her shoulders but didn't say anything else. It wasn't just the question of whether she would marry William or not, which she already said yes, it was the question of where her life would go. She was at a crossroads of sorts. The engagement represented two paths, one towards William's life and the other back to Lakeview alone. Cassie was smart enough to know she would never be able to have them both.

When they returned, at William's urging, wedding plans proceeded quickly. They agreed on a fall wedding and Cassie found herself busy with choices and decisions to make. Her mother moved into high gear with suggestions and Cassie's head spun around in circles and things didn't get any better when William's mother had her own ideas.

"I know it's where your family is, but you have to consider how it will accommodate all your guests. Lakeview isn't equipped with the things the city has, such as decent hotel space, efficient caterers. My dear, the church is so small, how are you going to fit all the guests?" Jill sat before her with magazines and brochures of things that would be suitable. Suitable for her choices.

Cassie looked at her with disbelief. "How many guests do you think I'm having?"

"Well dear, our family and friends alone will tally at least two hundred, then of course William's friends, your friends, which most are combined, then your side of the family."

"Jill, I was looking at a much smaller affair, keeping it to mine and Williams family and friends. I don't expect people to travel all the way to Lakeview, except for maybe William's immediate family and a few special friends. I was looking at maybe fifty people total, certainly not over one hundred."

Jill's face fell. "There are two hundred on my list alone. We have many people who would be devastated if they weren't invited."

"If they're not invited, they won't feel obligated. If people are told it's going to be a small intimate affair they'll understand I'm sure."

Cassie would stick to her guns, even if his mother looked completely shaken at the thought.

It didn't help that William wasn't supportive to her decision and sided with his mother's choices. Cassie got angry and refused to talk about it for a week and when their second fight ended with angry words back and forth William could take it no more. When she locked herself in the bedroom he went out and returned several hours later to find her a little calmer as she lay across the bed.

The fights and arguments over the last few weeks had taken its toll on her, the stress more than she suspected it would be. When he returned and found her in bed, he sat down next to her and rubbed her back with tenderness.

"Let's elope," he stated.

Cassie huffed. "If only we could."

"Why can't we? I mean it, let's elope. We'll fly to Vegas, do it quickly and painlessly then we'll go off on our honeymoon and everyone will be happy." He smiled slyly as if it was what he'd planned all along.

Cassie looked at him with question then laughed. "For a moment there, I could see it happening and it honestly perked me up."

"It could happen. All you have to do is say yes."

"You're serious?"

"I have our tickets right here, including our honeymoon." He pulled an envelope out of his pocket but when she reached for them he pulled them away teasingly. "A kiss and maybe I'll tell you."

She kissed him quickly but he held it higher. "You said a kiss, I gave you a kiss."

"A real kiss," he said.

"A real kiss, huh? I'll show you William Sampson." Cassie pressed hard into him, closed her mouth on his and seductively bit his bottom lip, let her tongue sweep over his upper lip, then slowly, his arm began to lower and she quickly snatched the envelope away.

"Hey!" He protested and laughed.

"It's mine now, you told me all I had to do was give you a kiss."

"I'm upping the ante." He held her arms down and kissed her neck.

"You can't do that, that's not playing fair." Cassie laughed and held onto the envelope. "Besides, we don't have time, we're supposed to go to Lakeview this weekend, remember? Mother wants to go over some wedding things."

"We don't have to. We're going to Vegas tonight."

"Tonight?" Cassie sat up quickly. "You said elope, I didn't know you meant now."

William laughed and pulled her close to him. "Now. In your hands you not only hold our flight tickets to Vegas, you hold our flight to

Honolulu Hawaii where we'll board a ship and sail away for seven full days."

"William!" Cassie didn't know what to say. Thought she'd have time to think about it, certainly wasn't expecting to elope that evening.

"Your mother wants final decisions to be made this weekend. Do you want Lakeview or Las Vegas?" He snuggled into her neck and kissed it seductively. "Lakeview or Las Vegas? Now or later?"

It didn't take either of them long to get ready and pack. The thought of no more decisions, all control thrown to the wind and taking the easy road he offered seemed like the easiest thing to do until they got to the airport, only then did she question what she was about to do. Cassie was sitting in a row of standard chairs held together with metal, the boarding gate a few feet away, and she began to have second thoughts.

"I don't know, William, do you think we're doing the right thing?" Cassie looked at her watch that told her it was ten minutes till boarding time.

"Do you think we're doing the wrong thing?" He put his arm around her and pulled her close to him.

"Not that it's the wrong thing but... is it the right thing?" She knew she wasn't making any sense.

"It's right for us. All we want to do is get married. Your mother wants certain things, my mother wants certain things, and I don't even feel like it's our wedding. I guess if you get married when you're young you take their word for it. Maybe because we're not teenagers, they forget we've formed our own opinions about things and all I can see is four months of battle ahead with no one being pleased in the end."

Cassie lay her head down on his shoulder. Put that way, he was right. They'd lost control. "Tell me how much you love me again."

"I love you till the end of forever."

Within five minutes of being called to board she felt she had to call someone and tell them. The only person she could talk to at that moment was Mel, feared actually talking to her mother or father who'd been so excited over preparations for the big day.

Mel picked up on the third ring.

"Mel, I'm at the airport. William and I are eloping."

"Are you crazy?" She gasped.

"Probably. We're actually doing it the old fashioned way too, Vegas. Then a honeymoon in Hawaii." She looked over to William who was on his cell phone also.

Mel laughed. "I can't wait to tell mom this one."

"Good, that's what I called for, so you could pass on the news."

"I'll be happy to, I can't wait to see how mad they'll be."

"I knew I could count on you." Then she hung up quickly. Felt better that at least someone would know where she was and what was going on.

Cassie knew the disappointment both her mother and father would have, but she wasn't cut out to be mediator between the two families when no one would listen to what she wanted. She'd spent her whole life listening to what others wanted for her, this time she was doing it her way. Or was she? She didn't have time to contemplate further thoughts as the plane was about to board and now that she'd made her decision she wouldn't turn back.

"You have the honeymoon tickets, don't you?" William asked for the fifth time as they were getting settled into their seats.

"William, I have the honeymoon tickets. Packed nice and neat right here," she patted the side of her carryon bag before she slipped it under the seat in front of her. "You don't even care about the wedding, all you want is the honeymoon."

He grinned as he put his arm around and pulled her close to him with a kiss. "A week on a cruise ship sailing through the Hawaiian islands with my beautiful new wife? How can I think of anything else?"

"You were thinking about work, I saw you on the phone earlier."

"Oh, that wasn't work."

"What was it? Who did you call?" Cassie looked a little nervous, "You didn't call your parents, did you? You did and they were angry as hell and you just don't want to tell me about it." She rambled on with her assumption until he stopped her.

"We'll tell them after the fact, no sense bursting my mothers planning mode bubble earlier than I have to."

"Then who did you call?"

"I called my best man." William fastened his seatbelt and settled in.

"What best man?"

"He lives in California so I thought it would be easy for him to meet us at the last minute and he didn't disappoint. He's going to meet us in Vegas."

"You've never mentioned anyone in California."

"I should have. I haven't seen him in quite some time, we don't keep in touch like we used to." William didn't say anymore as they prepared for takeoff, but he was excited for the two most important people in his life to meet.

CHAPTER FOUR

She fell asleep during the flight several times, woke to snuggle closer to William, and then fell asleep again, but it wasn't very restful with the movement, a little turbulence and the noise. When they reached Vegas she felt as if she hadn't slept at all. They checked into the room at The Venetian and Cassie showered and fell into bed.

It was 5:00 a.m. Vegas time, and 2:00 a.m. their time so she was surprised William didn't join her for sleep.

"Where are you going?" She asked sleepily when he showered but dressed to go out.

"If I lay down with you, I may never get up. Clay will be here in a few hours so I'm going to play a little poker then I'll take a cab to get him from the airport." He bent down and kissed her but she was already half asleep.

Cassie didn't see William the rest of the day. He called and said he'd made arrangements at the wedding chapel there in the hotel for the next day at noon and said he already rented a tux for him and Clay and he hadn't forgotten the rings they already purchased at home. She was glad to be marrying someone so responsible and thoughtful, someone who didn't leave all the preparations to her.

She went shopping for a dress and after several stores finally found a simple white dress that suited her perfectly. A crystal adorned V-neck that was low cut and form fitting and fell just above her ankles. It was casual, yet elegant. Not too much and not too little. The woman in the store held her dark hair up and pulled a few tendrils down to show her how she should wear it, even made an appointment with a friend of hers who could do it in the morning.

"Is this crazy?" Cassie asked out loud as she looked at herself in the mirror.

"If it is, you're among the thousands of other crazy people who come to Vegas to get married." Then she looked at Cassie's figure in the dress. "And it doesn't look like you have to be in a hurry. Doesn't look like a baby in the oven."

"I guess you see quite a few of those?" Cassie turned to the side and was pleased with the dress. It was beautiful.

"We have an entire rack of maternity. They've even come out with an expandable line that can be rented. One size fits all. Great rentals." The woman looked to Cassie who'd become extremely quiet. "You love him, don't you?"

She hesitated for a moment. "Yeah, I do."

"Then it isn't crazy."

When she returned to the room, there was a note from William that said he went out to gamble a little. They'd missed each other several times that day and each of them left notes when they were in the room. They also tried to call each other's cell phone but only left a message on voicemail. Cassie finally gave up on seeing him that day and wandered down to the casino, lost a few quarters in a slot machine then went outside to enjoy the last rays of sunshine by the pool.

She found a quiet chair to watch the activity around her and when a waiter brought over a Pina' Colada she looked at him confused.

"I didn't order that." She stated as he tried to hand it to her.

"No ma'am, the gentleman over at the bar did."

Cassie looked over and a nice looking man smiled and raised his beer bottle to her in toast.

"No, thank you." She told the waiter who placed it back on his tray.

A few minutes later he returned with a strawberry daiquiri from the same man who smiled and raised his beer bottle. Again she refused but next came a martini, and again the same routine as she sent it back. Only this time, she had to laugh a little at his persistence. Finally he walked over himself with two cold beers in his hand.

"I really hate to drink alone." He said as he tried to hand her one but she wouldn't take that either.

"Then you probably should have stayed at the bar." Cassie smiled at him, she couldn't see him clearly because of the position of the sun, but she thought he was cute, although as a soon to be married woman, she certainly wasn't interested. "No offense, but I'm afraid you won't find what you're looking for here."

He nodded pleasantly, took her rejection with a smile and left her alone. She lounged for as long as she could and looked forward to seeing William when she returned to the room, but only found yet another note instead. He'd meet her for dinner in two hours. Even though she was disappointed not to see him, she thought about what they were doing. Nothing about it was traditional and Cassie decided she needed something to make it seem real, so she sent a note to the restaurant that said he was supposed to have a bachelor party the night before his wedding and not see the bride the day of. She would see him at noon the next day when they were to be married. He called as soon as he received it.

"My bride to be is standing me up?" He playfully teased her. "You didn't get a better offer from a high roller I don't know anything about, did you?"

"I'm too old for the sugar daddy's, they like em' just out of high school. By the way, not only am I not meeting you for dinner, I've sent your things over to Clay's room. You left his room number on one of your notes today and that's where you'll be this evening."

"Cassie, you don't have to go that far." William immediately objected.

"It's the only thing I have that will be traditional. I'll see you when I walk down the aisle tomorrow. Besides, it'll give you more time to catch up with your friend, you two have kept yourselves busy all day long, I'm sure you won't find it difficult to spend more time together." It would be hard but she stuck to her guns.

"But I was looking forward to introducing you to Clay." He tried to think of all the objections he could. "He's sitting right here waiting with me, we're both waiting for you."

"I'll meet him tomorrow. I've already made plans, I'm going to the spa in a bit and getting the works then I'm ordering room service."

"So you're leaving me to my own devices in Vegas? You're awfully trusting." William said slyly, hoping it would give her incentive to change her mind.

"Enjoy it tonight, don't think you'll get such liberty's after tomorrow, I may be an understanding girlfriend, but I may not be as understanding and trusting when I'm your wife."

"You're giving me your blessing for a last night of freedom?" William asked it jokingly, but when they got off the phone there were thoughts that began in his mind. The words seemed simple at the time, it was the meaning of them that sunk in much later that evening.

Cassie did just as she said, went to the spa and had the works. By the time she returned to the room she was so relaxed dinner was the last thing on her mind and all she wanted to do was fall asleep. Before she did, she dialed Mel's phone number.

"Mel?" Cassie asked when she picked up the phone but didn't say anything.

"What are you doing? Do you know what time it is?" Her sister's throaty voice was one of sleep.

Then she realized she was forgetting the time difference, it was well after midnight in North Carolina and Cassie apologized. "I'm sorry, I wasn't thinking about the time."

"You were only thinking of yourself." Mel said in haste, and then softened just a little, her voice tinged with slight concern. "Are you okay?"

"Everything's fine." Cassie sighed. "For a minute there, you sounded concerned about me."

"You have the world in the palm of your hands, what's to be concerned about when it comes to you." The jealous tinges to her voice were obvious.

Cassie couldn't get over the fact that as horrible as her sister thought she was, Cassie remembered a time she wouldn't dream of getting married without Mel by her side. It was too late to reminisce of things that wouldn't be. As much as she wanted to chat like the girls they once were about her dress, about the evening at the spa, about not seeing William until tomorrow, everything that had been going on in her mind, she knew it wouldn't happen. Knew it wouldn't be a lengthy conversation, but Cassie wanted it to at least be civil.

"We're getting married tomorrow at noon. I picked out my dress today, I think... I guess it will do. The woman at the store said it looked great but I had no one else's opinion but my own. And you know how I'm not the best decision maker at times."

The other end of the phone was quiet and just when Cassie thought she'd fallen back asleep her sister spoke quietly. "It wouldn't matter what you wore, Cassie, you'll look beautiful in anything."

"Was that a compliment?"

"Of course not, just a fact that goes along with your perfect little life."

"How did mom and dad take the news?"

"How do you think? This was perfect for you. Just run off and expect everyone to be happy for you. If I had done something like that I'd never be forgiven, but you don't have to worry. As mad as mom was, I'm sure by the time you get home she'll be ready to invite the whole town for a formal reception. And I think dad was just happy he wouldn't have to go through all the bullcrap anyway."

Cassie didn't know why she asked the question, but she did. "And you Mel? Do you think I'm doing the right thing?"

"No one that gets married is doing the right thing."

"Not all marriages end up like yours." She wished she hadn't said it but Mel equated all marriages with what hers was like. She hadn't known happiness since the day she wed, and Cassie knew she wouldn't until the day she divorced.

Mel sighed. "And I already know that yours won't. Your life always works out."

On the eve of her wedding night, Cassie hoped she was right.

****

The girl at the dress shop recommended a wonderful stylist. When she finished, Cassie looked in the mirror and had to admit she would make a beautiful bride. Dark hair was pulled atop the crown with loose large curls held with a million bobby pins and the tiniest of tendrils cascaded down the sides. Although she worked on it for an hour, it didn't look overdone, not stiff or tight with too much hair spray, just enough to keep it in place. The make up looked natural also, just the slightest hint of blush, a neutral shade of shadow that showed off crystal blue eyes, some mascara, and a glossy neutral lipstick that almost matched perfectly the color of her lips.

When asked about doing her makeup, she almost refused, Cassie didn't want to look like a Vegas showgirl with sparkles and glitter, and she didn't, when she looked at herself she was more than pleased. Lucia did a wonderful job and both of them admired her work in the mirror.

"A beautiful bride you will be." Lucia smiled at her in the mirror but noticed a look in Cassie's eyes. "You don't like?"

"No, it's great. I guess I'm just a little upset no one will see me. My family won't know I've made such a beautiful bride. They're not here to see it." Cassie chalked it up to wedding jitters that made her sentimental.

She remembered the day Mel got married and she served as Maid of Honor. They giggled as they dressed, cried when Mel handed her the bride's bouquet to hold while they exchanged rings and danced the night away and cried together again when Eddy passed out drunk.

Now Cassie sat alone on her wedding day. She fought the urge to call William so she wouldn't feel so alone, and the urge to call Mel again. And even though she was being sentimental and wanted to talk to her sister, wanted her sister there with her, Mel's marriage wasn't something she needed to think about when she felt the jitters. Someone like Eddy as a husband scared her to death.

The thought of feeling trapped in a loveless marriage subconsciously haunted her. Again, the wedding jitters gave her a few doubts about William, even though he was nothing like Eddy, she questioned if she were doing the right thing. But when she dressed in her hotel room, and looked at herself in the mirror, all her fears seemed to dissipate and it was replaced with excitement. She couldn't wait to see his face when she walked down the aisle. She did look beautiful, and she didn't care that he would be the only one to see it.

A limo would be waiting for them to take them to the airport as soon as the wedding was over, so she had packed her bags that morning and sent them with the bellhop who would make sure they got into the car when it came. William was supposed to do the same and she hoped he would remember. She continually fought the urge not to call him, even though she wanted to as soon as she'd gotten up that morning and every hour after. Not seeing or talking to him heightened her anticipation, and as she looked in the mirror one last time, she smiled at the new life that would begin for her that day. Was confident she was doing the right thing, and pushed the jitters away.

As she made her way down to the chapel she received many compliments, stares, smiles and early congratulations from people in the halls and elevators. The butterfly in her stomach had turned into a mass of butterflies as the excitement grew. Cassie didn't think about questions that ran through her mind, only thought of William's face she was now so anxious to see.

She timed it perfectly and walked through the doors at five minutes till noon to see the minister and a woman holding a bouquet of flowers, but William was nowhere in sight.

"Ms. Mitchell?" The minister looked to her and asked even though it could be assumed.

"Yes." Cassie answered with a catch in her breath caused by nerves.

"Welcome. We're almost ready to get started, we have a few more minutes, but don't worry, it isn't uncommon in Vegas for the groom to come rushing in one minute before the time. You look breathtaking by the way."

"Thank you." She smiled, wondered if he looked like Elvis on purpose with his dark slicked back hair that surely had been dyed. He must have been over sixty years old.

The woman handed her a dusty, plastic bouquet and claimed it beautiful. "This is our favorite bouquet all of our bride's seem to choose. It is our most expensive rental at $30.00, but if you'd like to see something else we have a few that are less expensive."

Cassie took the prickly plastic stem. She hadn't thought of flowers, maybe that was where William was, he'd taken care of scheduling everything, maybe he'd thought about the flowers too and would bring her a real bouquet. "This will be fine."

The minister smiled as if he felt he had to apologize before asking for money. "To save time, if you wish to take care of it now, I'll need the credit card to secure all the charges, unless you want to wait for your fiancé'. He made all of the arrangements, but this is the only thing left. This and the marriage certificate to sign after the wedding."

She reached into her small white purse with crystals along the top edge she purchased to match the dress and handed her card over. The excitement of before now faded a little having to take care of items like this only moments before she was to walk down a wedding aisle.

When she heard the door open, her heart lifted, only to be disappointed to see it wasn't William but another man in a tuxedo. Even though he looked familiar, it wasn't the face she wanted to see.

"The groom has arrived." The minister stated with an assumption.

"No, I'm not... I'm not the groom. I'm Clay."

"Clay?" Cassie looked instantly worried. "Where's William?"

"I was running late, I thought he was already here."

Now she really worried. "Didn't he stay in your room last night?"

"Yes, but I overslept and after my shower this morning I didn't see him in bed, so I assumed he had already left." Clay looked casually unworried. "I'm sure we just crossed each other somehow."

Cassie finished taking care of the expenses and instead of sitting, stood quietly as they waited. The longer she held onto the plastic bouquet the tighter her grip became, the sweatier her palms became, the more irritated she became as the minutes ticked by. Five minutes passed, ten minutes, fifteen minutes, and then twenty minutes had ticked by on the clock. Ten more minutes and the limo driver would be ready to pick them up and they wouldn't even be married.

Both Clay and Cassie used their cell phones to call the room and to call William's cell phone, but there was no answer at either, and neither left a message. They all stood in uncomfortable silence. Everyone wanted to speak, but no one sure of exactly what to say.

Clay sat down, then stood up, then paced, nervously fidgeted, and then sat back down again. With each moment that passed, Cassie became more agitated, a slow simmer in her gut indicated something was wrong and when Clay mentioned going to check on him, Cassie decided it best she do it herself.

"Maybe I'll go..."

"No, I think I'd better go check on him."

"I'm sure he just..." Clay tried to talk her into waiting there but she wouldn't listen.

"I can't be sure of anything right now, I'm going to see for myself."

CHAPTER FIVE

Cassie practically ran and Clay had to hurry to keep pace, but because he got stuck in the middle of a crowd he missed her when she got into the elevator and he had to wait for another. "Damn!" He said as he pounded the button on the wall.

Cassie reached the room and pounded on the door several times until it was finally opened. Just as it did Clay's elevator reached the floor but he couldn't do anything to stop what was about to unfold. Standing before Cassie was a bleached blond tan girl with a sheet wrapped around her naked body. Hair a rumbled bed mess, eyes a slit to the hall light, it was obvious to all but the true ignorant what had been going on.

"What?" The strange woman screeched, angry at being woken. She had a hangover and hadn't gotten to bed but a few hours before.

Cassie brushed past her and entered the dark room. The curtains were totally drawn and she could barely make out where the bed was, when she did she turned the bed side light on and there was William, sprawled out naked. The sheet the two had shared now wrapped around his bed partner.

"You shit!" Cassie screamed and whacked him hard across the back with her plastic bridal bouquet, wished he'd been lying on his back and it would have been his pride and joy she'd whacked.

William jumped immediately. Just like his newfound girlfriend, he too shielded his eyes from the bright light and was confused. "Wha...?"

"You lousy shit! How could you do this?" She never would have guessed she could resort to physical violence but she whacked him again, this time so hard the fake thorns on the stem scratched her palm though she wouldn't realize it until later. She couldn't feel it, couldn't feel anything but the searing anger and pain.

He opened his eyes and his arm came up to cover them from the light. He was still drunk, not only was he naked, he was still drunk. They had partied all night. "Oh God, Cassie, what time is it? I... I can be ready in a minute. Shit." It didn't even register that he'd been caught, literally, with his pants down. Just thought he overslept.

"Ready for what? I'm not marrying your sorry ass."

When he adjusted his eyes, he saw his beautiful bride to be like a vision in white, then the naked blond who stood next to her with a sheet wrapped around her and makeup caked and smeared on her face. It was a vision that sobered him quickly. "No, Cassie, it looks bad but... but I can explain, it isn't what you think."

"And you can't even think of a decent thing to say, how stupid and clichéd is that? You're naked, she's naked, and it isn't what I think?" Her voice reverberated loudly across the room, even angrier now that he thought she would be so stupid to think something other than the obvious.

William stuttered with explanation. "She's... she's a friend of Clay's, he met her and..."

"And you're taking his leftovers? Because he managed to get to your wedding on time while you were too busy, don't hand me bullshit, I'd need a dump truck to hold that load of crap!"

"What the hell is going on here?" The girl piped in then, with a total blank look on her face as if she couldn't figure it out for herself.

"Nothing is going on here. Cassie, listen to me, I..." William seemed to be wide-awake now but when he tried to rise quickly there was a pounding in his head and sparkly spots that twinkled, but he saw her heading for the door. A beautiful vision of her back and his voice pleaded. "Cassie wait, please."

"Come on." She grabbed Clay by his jacket sleeve and literally dragged him down the hall with a tight grip that wasn't letting go.

"Maybe you should..." Clay tried to talk but she stopped him quickly.

"Don't try to give me shit, I'm not going to believe anything, if she was sleeping with you then why did you manage to make my wedding and he didn't?"

"I think..."

"Don't think, don't talk. You'd just stick up for him anyway." Cassie still clung to his sleeve and pulled him with her into the elevator then pushed the button for the lobby.

"Where are we going?" Clay asked, didn't know why he had to be dragged into the mess.

"I have a honeymoon I'm not missing and you're coming with me. All my bags are sitting in a limousine and in a few more minutes I'll be in it. So will you."

"Me? On your honeymoon? Oh, that isn't going to happen. I'm telling you, if you just go back with me..."

"The only place I'm going is Hawaii and you're going with me." Her voice was stated as fact and she saw it no other way, he wouldn't be given any other option.

"Why am I going with you?" He looked at her astonished, thought she was crazed.

"Because if that son of a bitch doesn't think two can play at his game he's sadly mistaken. Right now the only thing I can even think of doing is taking advantage of a honeymoon he paid for, and doing so with someone else. And right now all I have is you, so you're coming with me."

"I'm not going. I can't go." Clay said as he got out of the elevator and stopped in his tracks, refused to go further.

Cassie shrugged her shoulders. "Fine, then I'll just walk into the nearest bar and grab the first man who looks halfway decent. I'm sure I'll be able to find someone willing to jet off to Hawaii."

"You won't take a stranger." He laughed, thought the idea absurd, but saw the determination in her eyes.

"If you leave me with no choice, I'll have to." She turned quickly but he caught her arm.

"Just hold up a minute. Calm down."

"Calm down? I was supposed to be married less than an hour ago. While I was waiting at the chapel, William was screwing a whore, and you want me to calm down?" Cassie turned towards the door again and he followed.

For whatever reason, Clay knew he couldn't just let her leave in the state she was in, so he followed as she quickly got into the car and barked orders to the driver who smiled and was ready to greet them with well wishes.

"If you can get me to the airport in record time, there's a hundred dollar tip in it for you."

"Yes ma'am, there's..." The driver was about to explain what was inside the car but she quickly stopped him.

"I don't need to know what's inside the car, I don't need to know about any special touches or where the music is, all I need is a ride to the airport and as fast as you can get me there."

They climbed inside and Clay's cell phone rang, it was William, and Clay almost fell to the floor as the driver took off. "I'm trying to tell her but she won't listen. Yeah... I know... She wants to drag me along on your honeymoon, what's supposed to be your honeymoon... I tried... okay... what if..." Clay sighed and hung up the phone. "William doesn't want you to do anything rash. Wants me to stay with you until you've calmed down."

"Well, looks like we'll probably be spending the rest of our lives together." Cassie huffed and talked to the driver through the window. "If you can go any faster, I'll throw in another hundred dollar tip."

"Cassie, it..." Clay started but again was shot down.

"Don't talk to me." She demanded gruffly. "Don't look at me, don't speak to me and above all, don't lie to me. I'm not going to believe anything you say so just shut up. Give me your drivers license, you do have one, don't you?"

"What do you..."

"I need to call the travel agent to make name changes and they're going to ask for information."

Without knowing what else to do at the moment, he reluctantly handed it to her. Cassie used her cell phone to make all the name changes she needed to for their travel. It was all set and she would spend her honeymoon with the best man, a man she didn't know. The stranger sat next to her but she didn't think of him, she thought of the vision of betrayal.

She couldn't get hold of her anger, wasn't able to contain it and think rationally. She'd been excited about the wedding, and then had her second thoughts, excited again, then jitters again. Paid for it, bought plastic dusty flowers, and all for what? The roller coaster ride of emotions ended in a freefall straight down and her thoughts were a jagged mess. All rational thinking or feeling was clouded by the immense pain that engulfed her.

"You know this is childish and irresponsible, don't you?" Clay said as he stretched out his legs. He decided to remain calm, at least one of them should be.

"That sounds like something my father would say."

"Maybe your father would be right, did you ever think of that?"

"Well, my father also thought marrying William was the right thing to do. Wonder what he'd say now?"

Then Cassie turned even angrier if that was possible. At that moment, it hit her that she had been pushed into the direction everyone thought was the stable and responsible one. Now look where she was, in a limo with a stranger, while her fiancée' was probably taking seconds with his whore.

"And what's wrong with being irresponsible? What's wrong with doing something I want to do and not what they want me to do? From now on, I'm going to live my life for me and not them. It's obvious their version of what will make me happy is screwed!"

Clay was quiet. He knew exactly what she talked about first hand and couldn't answer because she was right. With that she was right, as for kidnapping him for her honeymoon, he thought it a little extreme but could do nothing but go along at that point. He planned to talk her out of it and things would be straightened out before they boarded the ship, or at least straight enough that she would see him going with her wasn't an option, he would leave her on her own if he had to.

His cell phone rang and it was William again.

"I'm on my way to the airport," he said to Clay.

"Hurry." It was a desperate cry on Clay's part.

"Look, I'm telling you, I'm begging you, if I can't get there go along with her, don't let her do anything foolish, Clay, just stay with her."

"Go how far?"

"On the plane, on the ship, whatever it takes. I'm begging you, don't leave her alone." William's voice sounded out of breath. He'd dressed and run after her as fast as he could, now impatiently waited for a cab.

Cassie grabbed the phone from Clay's hand and spoke briefly. "Don't bother coming to the airport, we'll be gone before you get there."

"Cassie, you don't understand, I swear I had nothing to do with that girl. I know how bad it looked, but baby..."

"Don't baby me, William. Go to hell." She opened the window and threw the phone out onto the busy street.

"Hey! That's my phone." Clay couldn't stop her, it was already gone.

"Was your phone." She corrected as she turned back to stare silently out of the window.

William didn't make it to the airport on time and Clay panicked at the boarding gate, it meant he would actually have to get on the plane and go with her. As much as he tried, there wasn't a thing he could say to talk her out of it and the travel agent arranged for a ticket so he didn't have that excuse. He'd have to wait until they reached Hawaii, was sure William would be right behind them. If not, he could catch a plane back, but there was no way he was going on her honeymoon.

They didn't say a word to each other on the plane. Cassie sat in silent torment, while Clay's mind tried to figure his escape. He couldn't possibly go with her, would have to leave her on her own. And he didn't know this woman and wouldn't feel guilty for doing so, let William work out his own problems, why did he have to be in the middle of it? Everyone that walked by them would give their congratulations and best wishes as they thought they were bride and groom. What else would they think of a woman in a wedding dress and a man in a tuxedo? The stewardess even brought them complimentary champagne. Cassie downed glasses of it but it didn't seem to faze her.

They landed and though he had conspired in his mind to leave her at the airport, he decided to ride in the cab and leave her at the pier, which would at least give William more time to get there. He began his protests once again.

"You're nuts. I'm not going with you." Clay shook his head and chuckled at the thought.

"Fine. Driver, pull over at the first bar please."

"You won't take anyone else. That's totally ridiculous to pick up a stranger and..." He wasn't able to finish his sentence as she completely ignored him.

"This one is fine. Is that a bar?" Cassie pointed to a small corner place with a tattered awning.

The driver pulled over to the curb and Cassie got out, her veil flew in the breeze as she ran inside. A broken sign read Barbie's. At night, the neon light was broken, and it read Bar. Old wood that was in dire need of replacement, chipped paint, a broken window with cardboard taped inside, and the sidewalk was cluttered with motorcycles. Clay knew right away this was not the part of town, or the type of bar to be in. It wasn't on the tourist track, that was a sure bet.

Clay stood outside for several moments and contemplated leaving. This was ridiculous, he thought, whatever she ended up with, she deserved. Then he felt a little guilty for the thought, he didn't know her, but she didn't deserve what she'd gotten that day. A day that was supposed to be one of the happiest in her life and now she was in a strange bar looking for a strange man, any man, to mount revenge.

He sighed, had no moral choice but to join her inside, knew his good conscious wouldn't let him leave her at that point. Not there, not in some bar where anything could happen to her. He finally walked inside and the place was dark, and with the windows painted black one would think it was midnight.

Cassie adjusted her eyes and saw the place crowded enough to be able to find someone, anyone, at that point she didn't much care because she knew Clay would run to William and tell him she ran off with a stranger. It's what she wanted him to know. She walked up to the bar and plopped down her credit card, actually, the card William obtained specifically for their wedding and honeymoon expenses. She planned to take full advantage.

"Hey, who wants to go on a cruise with me?" She got a few whoops of noise from a few who saw her walk in. It was hard not to notice a woman in a white wedding dress but only a few turned around when the door opened to see her. The bar was noisy so she said it again, this time louder.

Cassie stood on a chair and faced a crowd. "I said... who wants to go on a cruise with me? Single, beautiful, available woman! The man who stood me up at the alter is paying for everything!"

When she screamed it at the top of her lungs the whole bar cheered, howled and whistled. She'd gotten their attention and continued talking as she now walked towards the bar. "Here's the deal. Whoever wants to go, line up at the bar. I'm buying ten shots of whiskey for each contestant. Each person has to drink all ten in a row and the first person finished goes with me. Bartender, set em' up!"

Clay made his way to her side and tried to talk some sense into her. "This is beyond insane. Look at these guys Cassie, you wouldn't want to spend five seconds with any of them, how do you think you're going to spend a week?"

"You won't go. You've already told me that and I'm not going by myself. You may not go, but you'll tell William and he'll be wondering who I'm with and what I'm doing. Not that it would bother him, but at least I'll feel like he gets a taste of his own medicine."

"I'll go, I'll go. Let's get out of here." He would give in and not say another word about it, but it wouldn't be as easy as he thought.

"Bartender, we have another contender." Cassie slapped the bar area directly in front of Clay for him to line up the shots.

"You're not going to make me drink, are you?" He questioned it but saw the determination in her eyes.

"Whoever wins, Clay, drink up just like the rest of them."

He groaned and watched as the bartender poured his straight ten shots. "Cassie, I think this can cause brain damage."

"Men are already brain damaged, won't make a difference anyway."

The bartender got into the spirit of the competition and waited until everyone was ready then blew a whistle for the contest to begin. Cassie watched each one as they began in earnest but struggled after a few. Some dropped out at the fifth or sixth shot. One man made it to eight but had already had his share for the day and passed out right at the bar. As the winners shot glass hit the bar, Cassie wasn't sure if she was disappointed or pleased at the outcome. Then realized it didn't matter, nothing really mattered.

When the cab dropped them off at the pier she didn't have any problem getting someone to help Clay into a wheelchair, and a nice staff member was kind enough to wheel him to the suite. She explained he had to have emergency dental work done before they left and he'd be fine. They didn't know he was basically rendered incoherent because of ten shots of whiskey.

CHAPTER SIX

Clay remembered nothing. The only thing he was sure of was he must have passed out, but at least he was on something comfortable and not a strange floor. When he woke he felt like he was rocking as the whole room swayed. Slowly, with great care, he moved his legs over the side of the bed but had to take a few minutes to fully rise to his feet. When he did, he was still rocking, couldn't do anything to stop the motion. Where was he? And where was the Mack truck that ran him over? The cement mixer someone had thrown him in?

When he walked out on a balcony all he saw was sea and strange land. Oh my God, that was the rocking, it wasn't only in his head, he was on a ship. What time was it? What day was it? Where was he and how did he get there? He'd never been so drunk that he couldn't remember anything, but his mind was a complete blank, it registered nothing as he tried to get it to work. As if it were a clean slate, not only couldn't he remember the evening before, he couldn't remember the day before, or the day before that.

Then the nightmare began to seep through. William's wedding, the wedding and the honeymoon, then he remembered the bride, Cassie. He was on a honeymoon without a wife, not his anyway. Did they get married? Was it William's wife? His head pounded and it took too much energy to think. Why couldn't he have just died of alcohol poisoning? The way he felt, it would have been much better that way.

Clay found the refrigerator and water. Liquid, nice cool liquid to help his parched dry mouth because he suffered a desperate state of dehydration. As he walked back out on the balcony again he was impressed with what he found when he could focus. It was quite large with a dining area, lounges and a private Jacuzzi.

The verandah was at the very front of the ship and he felt like the Captain must feel on the bridge as he stood there and looked down to a cement dock the ship was pulling into, and then out to green hills. On top, lush emerald mountains seemed to disappear into clouds, and below the mountains, homes sat along rocky cliff edges that fell to blue water that crashed up against the stone. Palm trees swayed in the wind and it was beautiful. Wherever it was, hell, he didn't even know where he was, just somewhere in Hawaii. He remembered someone saying something about Hawaii.

The balcony was big enough to live on, he thought to himself. That was great, he probably would. The breeze and fresh air helped to clear his head and he could now remember a little more. There had been no wedding, there was a bride and a groom, but no wedding had taken place. He'd been kidnapped by a raged woman scorned. On a Hawaiian honeymoon with another man's intended bride, add that to the massive hangover from ten straight shots of whiskey in record time. Could there be any more hell than this?

Clay rubbed his forehead as if it would clear it more. Cassie's face came into view, the anger and rage he'd seen, and he was glad there was plenty of space outside and the suite inside gave them room to try and stay away from each other. They certainly wouldn't be cramped, but he didn't intend to be there for the duration, there had to be a way out. Clay wondered if William had planned it, or if Cassie upgraded to the most expensive cabin available for spite.

It was obviously one of the more expensive suites. Not only the massive deck, but there was a living room, a state of the art entertainment center, television, CD player, stereo and DVD player. A CD/DVD library that offered many choices, and he also noticed computer access with available Internet connection. Maybe he could send an urgent email, an S.O.S for someone, anyone, to save him. There was also the wet bar where he grabbed another water then investigated the separate bedroom complete with king sized bed and walk-in closet. He would find out later it was one of five Owner's Suites on the ship.

Only when he walked into the bedroom did he realize the shower was running. Without a moments hesitation he opened the door and went inside.

"Hey! I'm in here! What the hell are you doing?" Cassie screamed from behind the shower curtain.

"I'm taking a piss," he said bluntly. "You wanted this, you got it. I'm here under duress and by force so that means you have no privileges when it comes to privacy."

"You're a Neanderthal just like the rest of them. What did I expect?"

"You don't even know me, why are you grouping me with every asshole you've ever met."

"You're all the same, that's why."

"I could argue that point."

"Not with a clear conscious, I'm sure. That's if you have one, which I doubt, as I said, you're a man like the rest of them."

Cassie pushed the curtain aside and didn't bother being discreet. She stood fully naked and wet then simply reached for the towel and began drying herself as she normally would if he hadn't been in the room, wasn't going to let him intimidate her. Clay chuckled to himself and shook his head as he finished and left the bathroom. Well, that wasn't going to scare her into getting rid of him.

After he showered, Cassie had already left the room and he found a pile of clothes she'd purchased in one of the ship's gift shops the evening before. On top a note that instructed him to get dressed because they had to be on the pier in an hour.

This was wrong. This was so wrong and shouldn't be happening to him. He should have been home. Had a date this week with Kate, what would she say when he had to tell her he was in Hawaii with another woman? Let him try to explain that one, he didn't even know where he would begin. A phone call to William, that's what he would do, a phone call and he would be here and everything settled. Clay didn't care that it would cost both arms and both legs for ship to shore, it was an emergency.

"William." He sighed when he answered his cell phone, Clay thought it possible he wouldn't be able to reach him.

"What happened to your phone?"

"It's somewhere on the road between the hotel in Vegas and the airport. After you called she threw it out the window. You have one pissed woman on your hands, actually, she's on my hands right now and I don't like it. She doesn't play fair, there was lot's of whiskey." He held his still throbbing head.

"Whiskey? You don't have a tattoo do you?"

"What?" Clay froze for a moment and in his mind tried to see if he felt anything odd. Wouldn't he feel it? Getting a tattoo was needles, bandages, healing. Wouldn't he hurt somewhere? Had he gotten one? He wouldn't know, as both body and mind were numb anyway. "I don't think so, I don't know. I didn't know I'd have to make a body check this morning. What the hell have you got me into? I'm here on the ship and I don't even know where I am, Hawaii somewhere, so what am I supposed to do now?"

"It's going to take her a while to settle down." William hadn't slept since he'd missed them, waited anxiously for Clay to call.

"That's an understatement, she called me a Neanderthal a little while ago, and she hates all men right now but insists on me being here to make you jealous."

"Well that's not going to happen, but of course don't tell her that. I trust you explicitly, Clay, you're the only one I would trust in this, you know that. And if you don't stay with her I'm afraid she would find someone else and do something drastic to get back at me and I can't take that."

"Stay with her? The entire trip?" Clay lay back against the couch in submissive desperation. What little energy he had mustered had been zapped again at the thought of it. "Will, don't you think there's another solution? Think of one, something, anything, I can't think right now, I can barely keep my eyes focused and my brain is still so foggy. If someone asked me my name it would take a half hour to think of it. There has to be something else."

"It's the only thing I can think of. You can keep an eye on her till she calms down and can listen."

"Listen to what? What are you going to tell her, Will, the truth or your version of it?" Clay was exasperated and his voice revealed it.

"You know how much I love her, I've talked to you about her. This one is different, I really do love her."

"I can tell," he said cynically.

"Come on, Clay, you've always looked out for me and I really need you now." William paused on his end. Knew Clay wouldn't betray him. "Hell, enjoy the week on me, have a good time. She loves me, she'll come to her senses when she misses me this week and I'll straighten it all out when you get back. We will still get married you can count on it. When we do, you're still going to be my best man, aren't you?"

"Sure." Clay said quietly. He felt sorry for him, it was something he couldn't see for William's future, not at that moment when she still spit fire.

"Call me and keep me posted. Oh, and maybe you shouldn't mention anything about us, just let her think what she thinks. You're a friend from California." There wasn't a question in William's mind Clay would do as he asked.

As he hung up the phone there was a light knock on the door, then the butler let himself in and was surprised to see Clay.

"Oh, I'm sorry sir, I can come back if you wish." He apologized and began to close the door again but Clay reassured him.

"No, come in."

"You were not so well last night, your new bride say you were sea sick. Are you better this morning?"

His new bride, the nightmare was getting worse but it wouldn't get any better if he tried to explain. Clay didn't bother correcting his assumption that Cassie was his new bride. Why explain something that made him nauseas just thinking about the story. His mind was not clear enough to explain anything to anyone.

"Yes, I'm feeling much better, thank you."

"I am Hernandez, your butler. Your new bride, Ms. Cassie, requested champagne and strawberries every morning, have I missed her?" He held up the bucket of champagne he'd brought with a worried look on his face.

Just then she entered the room. "Hernandez, I almost forgot you were coming this morning."

"Ah, good morning, Ms. Cassie. You wish I should pour?"

"Please. Could you also do me a favor? I'd love a picture of us, maybe on the balcony."

He was more than happy to oblige and after he poured them a glass, adding strawberries to the bubbly liquid, he took several with her camera.

"Thanks, I appreciate it so much." She smiled grandly, played a role well.

"Will there be anything else?"

"No, thank you." Cassie stated without consulting Clay but Hernandez made it a point.

"And you, sir? Along with the champagne every morning, is there anything special I can get for you?"

Clay wanted to answer... 'A way out of here', but he didn't. "I don't think so, but thank you for asking."

"I see you slept on the couch, you will not need it made up for this evening, will you?" The butler looked at him with question and concern that two newlyweds would sleep separately.

Clay smiled broadly, he would make it as miserable for her as possible, and then she would want to get rid of him. "Of course not, with the seasickness last night, I didn't want to disturb my wife. I'll be sleeping in the bed this evening."

"Very well sir." He smiled knowingly as if he knew they'd enjoy the evening.

Before Cassie could open her mouth to object, he was gone, so she objected to Clay. "What do you mean you're sleeping in the bed?" She shrieked when they were alone.

"Since I'm being forced into being here with you, I'll not put myself out, so I'll be sleeping in the bed with you. And I'll warn you now, I sleep in the nude." Clay waited for her scream or objection, but none came.

"Fine." She said just as matter-of-factly as he. Again, she wouldn't let him intimidate her. "I sleep nude also. Maybe we can get the butler to take a picture of that too. William will love that one, I'll get him a large print, maybe even poster size."

Clay laughed. Any other time or place, any other two people, and the conversation would have been flirtatious, enticing and seductive. Instead, it was two stubborn people who refused to back down, two stubborn people who would sleep nude together just to prove a point.

Cassie drank two glasses of champagne and with each sip, thought about William getting the credit card bill and smiled inwardly. He'd ruined her wedding but he would surly know how much she enjoyed their honeymoon without him. She enjoyed the glasses on the balcony while Clay was getting ready and enjoyed one more even after as he stood quietly against their balcony banister and looked to the island as people disembarked.

"You are ready to go, aren't you? We have to go get a cab." Cassie picked up her bag she packed for the day and started for the door without waiting for an answer.

Clay had been ready, he certainly wasn't the one enjoying the early morning drink with the hangover he had. "Aren't you the nagging wife. You'd think we were actually married instead of on this fake honeymoon. Can't I just sleep off my brain damage from the whiskey?" Clay rubbed his temple, had they really been married he would have suspected she took out insurance and planned on killing him.

"You're going to pretend to have a good time. I've got cameras and we're going to take lots of pictures together and William will see them all. Come on." She took him by the hand and dragged him along again.

He was a little surprised her anger didn't subside in the slightest from the previous day. Possibly just a smidgeon, she didn't look as totally wild eyed as she had when she opened the sunroof, screamed expletives, and threw her plastic bouquet into the road. By now it was probably in a million tattered plastic shreds, as cars couldn't avoid running over it. Maybe it had subsided just slightly, but she was still hell bent on revenge of some kind.

****

Dating back to 1897, numerous lighthouses over the years made Ninini Point home. The one that jutted out on the Point now dated back to 1932, Nawiliwili Harbor Lighthouse. It was off white in color due to an ordinance that stated buildings could not be white because it would be in stark contrast with the surroundings. Nawiliwili Harbor served as cruise ship base, named for the Wiliwili trees that were once abundant in the area. It would give them access to what was known as the Garden Isle, for Kauai was abundant with the sweet smell of the mokihana berry that permeated the air and lush green landscapes that held the power as if to intoxicate one's senses.

Kauai was not only the oldest of the primary islands in the Hawaiian chain, it was also the state's fourth largest island and most Western of the Main Islands, with the exception of the inaccessible and private Ni`ihau. It was an area that was mountainous and lush. Mount Wai`ale`ale`, often said to be the wettest spot on Earth with rainfall in excess of 450 inches a year, offered dense jungle that blanketed it's rain-drenched slopes. The highest, Mount Kawaikini, towered with its peak that rose 5,243 feet above sea level.

Canyons, gouges and rock formations abounded. Like other islands, volcanic action formed its base with peaks rising above. All surrounded by cobalt blue Pacific, edged with white surf as water crashed along its shores. The deepest canyon, Waimea, was almost 10 miles long and more than 0.5 miles deep. It brought together water, sunshine, and clouds, offered a memorable image as a rainbow of colors danced along canyon peaks. From a spectacular lookout spot one could view the Kalalau Valley and one of the most beautiful sights on the island.

Tumbling waterfalls and arguably the most beautiful and secluded beaches in the islands, Kauai was a tropical paradise that called to tourists and moviemakers alike. Dinosaurs of Jurassic Park were set amidst its scenery. Indian Jones outraced South American tribesmen in search of a prized golden idol in Raiders of the lost Ark. But perhaps the best known of Kauai's movies was the 1958 World War II musical South Pacific which was filmed near the quaint town of Hanalei.

Blue Hawaii in 1961 featured Elvis Presley and was filmed at the Coco Palms Resort. Just another of many enchanted evenings, love struck actors, shipwrecks, plane crashes and many other movie scenes that featured the island in more than six-dozen projects or television shows over the past 70 years.

What Cassie planned was a helicopter tour that would give them a glorious vantage point to experience the splendor of Kauai. As they boarded, neither one thought about the close confines of the space inside, and when they were settled there was no way to get around their bodies touching. Both in shorts, Cassie constantly shifted her legs so skin wouldn't touch skin. Eventually, the magnificence of the island took both their minds off the close proximity.

Unobstructed views from the open space without doors, and a system to talk to the pilot and ask questions, made the experience truly memorable. They started out the tour at Waimea Canyon, nicknamed by Mark Twain as the Grand Canyon of the Pacific. As they explored, the pilot was knowledgeable with his information about the formations as many different areas of the Canyon were toured. They proceeded to Kokee State Park area then on to the Na Pali Coast that was breathtaking as they went deep into major valleys.

They soared above it all. Verdant valley's, craters, brilliant waterfalls and lush jungle. Every view, anyplace you looked, contained majestic brilliance that made one feel a small fragment, a miniscule piece of a much larger thing.

Little had been said between each other, they spoke to the pilot, not to each other. And when they landed, the ride back to the ship was quiet. Clay looked over to Cassie's silent form as she took in the beauty along the way. She looked a little tired, pale, and he did feel sorry for her, but couldn't she just deal with it herself and not drag him into it? He knew his purpose would be to smile in the photos, create jealousy, or rather the appearance of it, but didn't she take into consideration he would tell the truth that nothing went on? Maybe she assumed it would become his word against hers. She couldn't know the deep loyalty between him and William, the one that bound them together.

Clay watched her gaze out the window. Inside he cursed William himself, as he thought about how she looked on her wedding day. So beautiful a bride she was, everything any man could dream of gazing upon to walk up the wedding aisle to meet him. Even though she looked hard and tough on the outside as she tried to deal with what happened, not in the most ordinary of ways he might add, he could tell the emotional battle inside of her was a bubbling turmoil of hot lava.

Just as he was beginning to soften, feel empathy towards her, she turned her head to him.

"What the hell are you looking at?" Cassie snapped, felt his eyes on her and now pulled her sunglasses off to better see him in the dark cab. Crystal blue eyes seemed to flicker with light flecks.

"I wasn't looking at you, your scenery is better on that side."

"That wasn't the case the other day. Don't think you can pull any kind of pick-up here like you tried in Vegas."

Clay looked sincerely surprised and she went on to explain.

"You don't remember coming onto me at the pool? I knew you looked familiar and I figured it out. You were the one who kept sending me drinks the other day, and my luck, I'd get stuck with you. I should have grabbed a stranger at the bar."

Clay straightened, he honestly hadn't realized it was Cassie by the pool, she had on a hat and sunglasses, he'd seen very little for such a short time of her actual face. "Had I been thinking clearly, I should have let you pick up any guy at that bar. I'm not sure it was worth the horrendous hangover I had this morning. Besides, I would have been laughing my ass off all the way back to California with the thought of you in that great Suite with an oversized sweaty old man with a hairy back who smelled like beef and beer." The thought made him chuckle outwardly, only making Cassie snap again.

"Please, you're only teasing me with reminders of what could have been."

The rest of the ride was silent, other than the driver who explained the scenery they passed and talked about his beautiful island. They stopped at a wonderful beach before returning and were lucky enough to witness two young Hawaiian Monk Seals frolicking around playfully along the waters edge and in the sand.

Kauai held the distinct notability as being a destination unlike any place else on earth where a marine mammal as endangered as the Hawaiian Monk Seal shared beaches with such a large number of people. Viewing had to be kept at a distance and no flashes could be used when taking pictures. And for the protection of both the animals and people, one had to keep a safe distance and not bother them, feed them, or try to touch them in any way.

A few were there to watch, and after they played a bit, they lay on the sand and it wasn't long before an older, much larger one, about 400 pounds, came to join them in an afternoon sleep. Cassie took several pictures from a comfortable distance underneath a shaded palm and was still snapping away when Clay joined her.

"I guess I was at least lucky enough he didn't plan a honeymoon in Alaska in the wintertime." He handed her a bottle of water he bought for her, surprised she would take it, but she did.

"I'm glad one of us is lucky," she said sarcastically. "But if one has to be miserable, as we both are, Hawaii is certainly the place to be miserable in."

"Did you want something else besides water? They have..."

"Don't be nice to me, Clay. Let's not pretend we'll become friends after all this, I don't need anymore friends, I have plenty so you don't have to bother. It would be a waste of your time." Cassie opened the water, grateful for the coldness of it.

"We don't have to be friends, but since you insisted on me being here and I'm stuck with you, I don't see why we can't at least carry on a conversation."

"We can't do that because I don't like you, you're probably very nice and charming, but you have a major disadvantage, you're a man. And right now, all men are shit in my book." She took another drink of water and her eyes were as cold as the liquid. "So don't talk to me, don't try to be nice to me because it won't be reciprocated, and you'd do yourself good to stay away from me unless I need you for a picture."

"So you plan to do nothing but use me." He tried to joke but she only shot him another venomous look.

"That's your only purpose for being here."

When Cassie walked away he watched her back, again cussed William under his breath for what he did to her.

CHAPTER SEVEN

That evening they were treated to the wonderful Hawaiian experience of a traditional luau on a beautiful beach. Under torchlight they were greeted with a flower lei and sat at a table with several passengers from their ship. The group of them became comfortable quickly. There were two older couples that traveled together, their third cruise through the islands of Hawaii, and a younger couple closer to their ages, Kyle and Lee, who left the kids at home for a romantic vacation. All of them together became a lively group.

They enjoyed the many drinks that flowed. Along with the wonderful food of Steamed Kalua Pig, Polynesian Chicken, Mahi Mahi, Beef Teriyaki, Salmon, along with sweet potatoes, poi, rice, fruit salad, coconut cake and much more to tempt their taste buds. A choreographed show bought out dancers in customary grass skirts, lei's in their hair, and some held torches they threw into the air in swirls of fire.

The drinks relaxed her and she pushed William from her mind and smiled into the camera as the others were kind enough to take their picture together when asked. Cassie found herself truly having a good time among the newfound friends. They talked and laughed as if they'd known each other much longer than a few hours. Even Clay couldn't ruin the festive mood by telling everyone when they asked, they were on a honeymoon. He knew she wouldn't explain the situation and he did it to get under her skin. She simply smiled and changed the subject.

With the encouragement of the others at the table, and then the crowd as they cheered, the four women got up when they were somewhat forced into volunteering for a Hula instruction lesson on the stage. The music beat with pounding rhythm as their hips swayed, then hand motions were added. Although it didn't take Cassie and Lee long to pick it up, the two older ladies struggled a little but took it all in good fun.

When it was over the four of them laughed hysterically as one of the older women said she was going to be using what she picked up that evening on her husband.

"What's so funny?" One of the gentlemen asked when they reached the table.

Not one of them wanted to answer, except for the woman who originally said it. She piped up right away. "I just told them you were in for a treat tonight, dear."

"Whoa Henry, did you bring some extra heart pills?" His friend teased.

"I might have to borrow some of yours." Then he looked to Clay. "You're a lucky man, Clay, your new wife can do the hula for many years of marriage now, I had to wait forty eight years for my wife to learn it."

"If she does the hula for me, I might need to borrow some of those heart pills from both of you." Clay answered and they all laughed, including Cassie.

The good mood lasted the rest of the evening. After they left the friends they made, Cassie became quiet again and Clay let her have her space. Nothing was said as each of them stuck to their word and went to bed naked. Neither budged in sleeping elsewhere, or not sleeping in the buff just to prove they weren't going to back down.

****

In the morning when Clay was still dazed with sleep, he felt the soft warmth beside him. Unconsciously, he pulled it closer and felt the smoothness of her back. As his hand moved slowly down, her body arched towards his and he felt breasts against his chest, then both of them almost at the same time opened their eyes and became fully awake instantly.

"Hey!" She pushed him quickly away.

"I was just responding to you, you were the one laying up against me." Clay nonchalantly pulled the sheet up to cover himself.

It would be awhile before he could get up, quite awhile, even more so when he watched her pull on the white robe. It hung off her shoulder, left it bare and all he could see was her soft skin. She called for coffee from room service.

"I'm going to take a shower, will you get the coffee when it comes?" Cassie left the room, giving him the opportunity to put his own robe on.

When coffee came, he took it out to the balcony and she joined him when she was through. Still in her robe, her hair wet and no makeup, it didn't change how beautiful she was. Natural and confident. As much as he resisted being there, at least she was attractive to look at.

Most of his girlfriends were done up before he even opened his eyes in the morning. Hair done, perfect makeup applied, there was a girl once who hadn't and it frightened him when he saw her morning face. Wondered how makeup could change a person so drastically.

He thought about Kate at home. Wondered what she was thinking of him for standing her up. Not calling her to change or cancel, he knew she wouldn't speak to him when he returned, she was that kind. And she'd probably have a real problem with him being in Hawaii, sleeping naked with a woman he'd just met a few days previous. Clay couldn't worry about Kate anymore, there was no explanation or rational reason for his predicament and he wouldn't even try to explain the unexplainable when he returned.

Both of them were quiet while they enjoyed the morning lost in their own thoughts. The previous night's revelry and laughter was not carried over to morning, but Clay didn't feel she was as distant as she'd been the day before.

Cassie leaned back in the chair, closed her eyes, and felt the breeze caress her face. She listened to the sounds of the morning becoming a day. After several long moments, Clay broke the silence.

"I am sorry about all this." Clay finally said, he didn't want to talk about it anymore than she did, but he felt an apology was necessary. And he was sincere with his words, knew it couldn't be easy for her.

"Don't get soft on me, I like hating you," she said without moving.

He could easily get a flight back, leave her alone in her misery, but he wouldn't. He knew she would be susceptible to any Casanova who would surely take advantage of the situation, take advantage of a beautiful woman in pain and on the rampage for revenge. Would she really pick up someone? Was she the type of woman who could have a one-night stand, actually have sex with a stranger? Clay didn't think she could really go through with something like that, but in her state of mind it left the question. Would she go that far for sheer spite?

Then he thought she probably would, and take pictures of it too. William's intention for him to go along with her was for her own protection, and he understood. Now he wondered if he was doing it for William, or himself? He didn't really know her well, even if he had slept nude with her, felt her breasts against his chest, watched intensely as her hips swayed on a stage, listened to her sweet laugher. Saw her beauty in early morning sun as she relaxed beside him now. He didn't know her well at all, but he did feel for her and what she was going through.

"I'm not getting soft, I like hating you too. There's a girl in California who will never speak to me again."

Cassie was quiet for a few moments. It never really crossed her mind about what kind of life he had. His girlfriend, his work, she knew nothing about him at all and now it dawned on her what she had possibly done in her quick rage that caused her to lose all of her normal senses.

"If it would make things better, I'll talk to her when we get back. Guess it isn't fair for your life to be ruined also. Then again, she'd be better off without you anyway."

"And you are assuming that because you're classifying me as what you now think of as a typical man. If I were to classify you as the typical woman I know, I would have thought you slept in the nude last night for sex. Was that the real reason?"

"Ha." She said loudly. "Don't let it cross your mind, don't even dream of the notion."

"Don't worry, I didn't." He lied. How could he not have thought about it when a beautiful naked woman was in his bed? Then he thought about Kate again, but it wasn't her he thought about last night. "I'll explain things to Kate, maybe she'll understand, maybe not. Guess I'll see how much she actually trusts me after I tell her... 'Yes dear, I did sleep with her, and in the nude, but I swear nothing happened'... that sounds credible," he said with a slight laugh.

Cassie thought about his statement and her situation. It was the truth, and she knew it because she was the other party to it. Could it possibly be the case with William? Had he told her the truth? No, she told herself. It was a different situation, wasn't it? She hadn't asked Clay to explain to her who the girl was. Whether she'd slept with William or with Clay, as William said. And debated it in her mind now but felt he'd just lie to her anyway. He was William's best friend, it would mean nothing for him to lie and say it was his girl in the room, even if he already had a girlfriend. What would she care that he cheated on her?

The ship stayed overnight in Kauai and would leave that day at 1:00 pm, so they had the morning left to enjoy island offerings. After the late night luau Cassie desired something more relaxing and wanted a great beach to explore for their remaining time. A cab driver they found promised them paradise and did not disappoint. The beach he took them was considered by many local residents to be the finest in the islands and not having seen the others, Cassie couldn't imagine she'd need to.

A 2-mile-long crescent of beautiful sand lay before them and was almost deserted on that early morning, giving them plenty of room to explore. As Cassie took to walking the edge of the surf, Clay relaxed. He fell asleep for awhile, took a dip in the ocean, then spent time watching the solitary figure of the woman who was beginning to haunt every thought in his mind, thinking of her at every turn. When she left the suite for a short time after they returned the evening before, all he could think about was where she'd gone. Of course it didn't make it easier to get her off his mind when she stripped naked last night and got into bed without any hesitation. It was a long time before sleep came.

The evening before, at the luau, he felt as if he'd learned so much about her in those few relaxed hours her guard was down. Some of her true personality was revealed. He couldn't remember the last time he'd had so much fun with anyone. She was bright, witty, and spontaneous, as her true character was revealed he knew he'd never met anyone like her. As odd as it was, had never met anyone he felt so completely comfortable with. Both had fallen into their natural selves and forgotten, even if for a brief time, what had brought them together. As he watched her approach him now, he couldn't stop his mind from thinking of what could have possibly been, had their circumstances been different.

Cassie sat down on the towel next to him. When she spoke it was more her thoughts aloud, rather than a sincere question. "What do you think, Clay? Think the world would miss me if I never went back to reality?"

"I'm sure there are plenty of people who'd realize you weren't around."

"My sister would celebrate like it was New Years Eve if she didn't have to see me again." She leaned her head back and closed her eyes to the glorious sun as if content to sit there forever.

He looked at her smooth body, she wasn't as thin as the women he dated but she turned him on like no other he'd known. And she wasn't doing anything to do so, didn't have to try as she simply sat there naturally. He had to turn his eyes away and look towards the ocean. "You two don't get along?"

"Well enough that we've never come to physical blows."

"What seems to be the problem?"

"I don't know, she's miserable with her life and thinks mine is better. All she could talk about was how perfect my life was. She's going to love the fact that my fiancé' ends up being a big asshole. The fact that I was stood up at the marriage alter will make her day."

"Surely she's not that heartless to take pleasure from your pain."

"She will laugh in my face and love every moment of my suffering."

"Were you ever close?" Clay asked, liked the easiness of the conversation without her rage.

"When we were kids, it didn't start until I left Lakeview and went off to college. I don't know what happened, she married, began having children, and after that became more and more bitter at everything around her. Not her children really, I know she loves them and doesn't blame them for the way her life turned out. But she's never been strong enough to make another choice. One of those people stuck in a miserable marriage and thinks there's no way out."

"Divorce isn't as ugly as some people think it is, sometimes it's the best thing for everyone."

"You divorced?" She turned to him and questioned. The girl in California could have been his wife for all she knew, he could be married, for all she knew.

"My parents. They were divorced when I was two and it was best for everyone. Some people just aren't meant to be together, no matter how much they love one another. Even after the divorce I think my parent's still loved each other."

"And now?"

"My father passed away. When they got divorced I moved with my mom who remarried and had another son, my brother. But just after I graduated high school, my father got sick and I moved back to the west coast to take care of him. He never remarried and didn't have anyone but me." Clay sifted sand through his hand. "She'd call all the time, of course would talk to me, then spend hours on the phone with my father. When he was really sick and we knew he wasn't going to make it, she came and stayed and took care of him the last month of his life. It meant the world to him."

"How long ago did he pass away?"

"Just after my 18th birthday. I moved back close to my mom for a few years, then rented an apartment with my brother and tried to do the college thing, but I wasn't into the frat scene. That stuff wasn't me. I tried to fit into the mold my stepfather wanted me to, but it didn't happen. I've probably lived twenty places since then."

"And you finally settled in California?"

"I'm there, don't know how settled, but I'm there."

Cassie sighed. "I couldn't do that. I have to have home base to make me feel grounded. I couldn't imagine what my life would be like if I couldn't go back to my parents in Lakeview. I hate living in the city, but it's where my career is."

Cassie told him about Lakeview. She found herself revealing her dream she had given up that one day when she had enough money as a cushion, she hoped to open a bakery and coffee house. To return to build her own life there, the small town life she'd grown up with, was what she wanted for her children. And of course someone to grow old with on the porch swing, to help her create a place in the world where their children could always come home to.

"Sounds like a fairytale, doesn't it?" She said amused. "Well, it is, it's something that will never happen."

"It's something that's possible." As he'd listened to her, he couldn't help but think about something like that for himself. Had traveled and lived so many different places he wondered if he would ever have the opportunity to settle down in the kind of life she described. It did sound like a fairytale, and he wasn't sure it even existed, not for him anyway, but she held the possibility for herself.

"Oh, and of course a dog, some mangy mutt rescued from a shelter that will lie on the rug in the kitchen. Dig up the flowerbeds, you know, just something else to add to the perfect little picture I've painted."

As Clay listened, he couldn't help but think that maybe what happened with William had been the best thing. He couldn't picture him living the kind of life she described, he was too business oriented, too city. He almost laughed when he thought of William chasing a mangy mutt around a yard to keep him from eating the flowers she described.

Cassie noticed the small smile that crossed his lips. "What are you smiling about?"

"Just picturing something in my mind."

She didn't question what, because when she looked at her watch she realized they would have to hurry back to the ship. They had been so relaxed neither realized what time it was, and the driver dropped them off with only about twenty minutes to spare.

"I guess you were probably hoping we'd miss it. It might have been your opportunity to escape back to California," she said as they boarded and showed their cards for entry.

Clay answered honestly. "I figure I'd stop bitching and complaining and just enjoy it. It's easier that way. Besides, the only thing waiting for me there right now is a very pissed off girlfriend."

Cassie pushed the elevator button and looked at him sincerely. "I am sorry about that, I'll do what I can to try and explain when we get back."

Clay could only laugh. "This situation my dear, is too bizarre for explanation."

CHAPTER EIGHT

The itinerary called for scenic cruising through the islands the rest of the day and Cassie couldn't think of anywhere better to view their passage then from the hot tub on the balcony. Their suite was in the very starboard of the ship and it was perfect.

Conversation flowed as Clay explained his line of work. He basically purchased houses, remodeled them, and either rented them as investments or sold them for profit. It's what allowed him to travel all over as he could basically do his work anywhere.

She could tell he was satisfied and thoroughly enjoyed what he did. The sense of satisfaction at a finished project and the challenge he faced with new ones. He talked about a small town once where history abounded. He'd redone two homes side by side and sold them both because he swore ghosts lived in them, but the people who purchased them were excited at the prospect when he told them.

"I could live with quite a few things, I'm not sure I could live with ghosts." Cassie found herself getting goose bumps just thinking about it.

"They were friendly ghosts. They'd move things around on me, shut doors, open windows in rooms. I pictured them all the time just laughing behind my back."

"And you're sure it wasn't a girlfriend you'd scorned along the way just trying to drive you crazy?"

"I'm not sure any one of my ex's would have been smart enough."

"I don't want to know how many that would amount to, nor do you have to explain their highest level of education. I think I get the idea."

Cassie pictured in her mind the type of person he was. Handsome, she couldn't deny. With his dark close cut hair and strong features, his muscular chest, stomach and arms were in clear view and she supposed the muscles came from his strenuous work instead of him having to work out at a gym to get that body. His most prominent feature was his intense blue eyes that looked brighter against his tan skin.

His physical assets were enough to draw the attention of many young single females. Cassie pictured him the type of guy who had no trouble finding dates, or sex if that's all he wanted. He was a few years older than her and it surprised her he wasn't married, but maybe he had been.

"Ever been married?" She asked.

"It's hard to settle when you travel so much, and the girlfriends I've had haven't been serious relationships, I've never had much time for that. Too much work and too much travel."

"Think you'll ever settle down one day?"

"I haven't found that place yet." He answered honestly.

There were many places he thought about settling in permanently, but nothing ever felt just right, there was always something missing. Funny, as he sat in the hot tub with Cassie, it felt all he needed. There was an odd sense of comfort, a strange silent feeling of closeness towards this basic stranger, something he couldn't explain.

Neither had the energy or the inclination to dress after they'd been in the hot tub all afternoon, so ate in their robes as the sun set into the horizon. They ordered room service for dinner and the butler made the dining table on the balcony up to perfection.

"I'm going to go to the late show this evening, someone told me it was great and I don't want to miss it."

He didn't ask to come, or indicate he wished to, and Cassie didn't offer for him to join her as she dressed and left.

Clay dressed also but didn't go to the show, he wandered the ship and came to relax in a night club on the eighth deck, a tropical room that gave one a sense of being at a beach party outdoors. He found himself sitting at the bar with a newly divorced mother of one. She was there with a few girlfriends and he found her attractive, and she gave off signs it wouldn't be difficult to become more intimate with her, but as he sat there, all he thought about was Cassie. Where was she? What was she doing?

"Do you have any children?" The woman asked politely, felt as if she had to gain his attention again every few moments.

"No, no children."

"Here with friends?"

Clay looked at her and wondered what to say. No, not exactly. What kind of answer did he give? It was easiest to keep up the pretenses of marriage they told people, even easier when Cassie entered the room.

"Here on a honeymoon," he stated, and waved Cassie over when she saw him. "There's the wife now."

The woman looked and smiled, but Clay saw her disappointment she'd been wasting time talking to a married man. Any other time he would have been more than politely interested.

Cassie walked over to them and was accompanied by Kyle and Lee she'd sat next to at the show.

"Hey honey." Clay said and put his arm around her then kissed her cheek. "How was the show?"

"Great." She smiled.

He introduced the woman and she smiled pleasantly, shook hands, and then made her way back to the table with her friends.

"I hope being introduced to the wife didn't scare her off." Cassie said it teasingly but he saw the edge in her eyes. Then she turned her attention back to Lee. "What was that drink we had at the show, I think I'll have another of those."

"A blue something. Blue Hawaii?"

They ordered then moved to a more comfortable spot at a table and talked easily, Clay and Kyle about sports and Cassie and Lee about other things. Cassie ordered several of the blue frozen concoctions, probably a few more than she should have, and she found her mind kept wandering to the woman at the bar when she'd walked in. She wasn't really married to Clay, they meant nothing to each other, but it reminded her clearly of the infidelities she suffered and Clay represented that.

Cassie wondered if she and Clay were a real couple, if they actually meant something to each other, if like William, he were the type of guy that could easily push it to the back of his mind and enjoy another's company without a second thought. She answered her own question and assumed he was.

Later, on their way to their room, they were alone in the elevator when he mentioned her mood. He'd noticed her distance and the edge in her eye that hadn't gone away. "Did I do something?"

"You were just being a man," she said and didn't look at him, stared at the lighted numbers that told them what floor they were on.

"What kind of answer is that?"

"I don't have to explain myself to you."

He should have kept quiet but couldn't, he was angry now too, because she was angry at him. "Maybe you do."

"I don't have to explain myself to anyone, least of all you, you're nothing."

"Nothing?" He almost shouted. "A little harsh considering I've been playing this game of husband and wife with you because it's what you want, maybe I deserve to know when something's bothering you."

"A typical man, you think you deserve something. And what have you done to deserve anything?"

"I've given up my life for a week. I'm here on this ship pretending to be someone I'm not, your husband. I smile when I'm supposed to and I spend the evening sitting with people I like and basically lie to them about what we are, and all because of you. This isn't for me, I never asked to be drug to Hawaii, I'm here because you needed to be saved from yourself, so yes, maybe I think I deserve an explanation why you're angry."

"To save me from myself?" The statement made her even angrier.

"You weren't in the best state of mind to make logical decisions."

"That's obvious now that I'm stuck with you. You make yourself sound like some knight in shining armor, you just happened to be there and I drug you along, you didn't come willingly to do your good deed for the day. And does it really matter to you that I'm angry right now?"

He glared at her eye to eye, frustrated she shut him out again. Angry she'd turned on him and now loathed him as she did every man, and there wasn't a thing he could do about it. "No, it doesn't matter to me. Go back to being the pissed off woman scorned. Treat me like I'm everything you despise. Hate me for everything you think William and any other man has ever done to you, I don't care. But don't confess your dreams to me in one minute then turn around and act like I'm the one who did you wrong."

"Save me from myself." Cassie repeated the words in a disgruntled huff. "I'm the only one I can trust."

Again, he cursed William under his breath for what he'd done to this woman who didn't deserve what she'd been handed. And he cursed himself even more, knowing then where her anger originated. It wasn't done on purpose, he didn't think anything of it when he sat talking to a woman at the bar, it was innocent conversation, but he knew it was the moment her anger began. Knew what she saw it as, even though they meant nothing to each other, and knew he should have been more considerate, given what she'd been through.

They didn't say anything more as each angrily got ready for bed. Clay took off his shirt, his pants, and his underwear and it didn't faze her as she did the same. A black lace bra and panties were the last to go and he glanced at her body as she easily slipped into bed, her back to him.

He stood for a long time, debated on giving in and putting his clothes back on and sleeping on the couch. Dammit. His head told him he should, but his anger wouldn't let him. If he did, she would see it as her victory. He would see it as her victory. Determined to make her as miserable as he felt, he slipped in naked beside her.

CHAPTER NINE

Flowing down the lower slopes of Mauna Kea, the old sugar town of Hilo offered Hawaii's largest historic core of buildings dating back to the turn of the century. It was a showcase of Hawaiian architecture, with splashes of varying degrees of Western, Art Deco and Renaissance Revival that made it a picturesque place along the tree lined bay front.

Hilo straddled a tranquil river leaving one with vivid memories to take home of waterfalls and lush vegetation fed by much rain as it was known as the rainiest city in the United States. Most happened in the evening, leaving days of lush tropical oasis to explore.

The evening before, Kyle and Lee offered them an invitation to spend the day and they had agreed then. Now, as Cassie stretched and woke, saw Clay's body beside her, she regretted her decision, should have spent the day alone, as far away from any man she could possibly get.

She faced him, watched his even breathing and a tinge of guilt at her anger the previous evening surfaced. She did blame him for everything, only because he was the easiest target to blame, he was the one there with her. Maybe he wasn't like William, maybe he wasn't the type of guy who would cheat, what did she know? Maybe he was the kindest, sweetest guy ever or maybe not. It would be easier for her to view him as an asshole.

Cassie rose and stepped into the shower, she heard him enter, but certainly didn't think he would get into the shower with her, when he did she screamed in protest. "What are you doing?"

"Morning, love," he said cheerily as he reached for a bar of soap. "We don't have much time, only about thirty minutes before we have to meet Kyle and Lee, so I figured we could save time by taking a shower together. No sense me waiting for you to get out."

Drive her away Clay, he told himself, drive her as far away as you possibly can. Make her uncomfortable to be around you. Make her run in the opposite direction. He spoke the words over and over in his mind, but he didn't know why he thought she would run from the bathroom, he should have at least known that about her by now.

Cassie had been facing him and never turned as she leaned her head back, closed her eyes, and rinsed the conditioner from her hair. Naked, wet, beautiful, and he was the one to turn in the other direction, had to busy himself with the soap and washcloth until she went away.

****

First on the agenda was a visit to the outdoor Farmer's Market that was held on Wednesdays and Saturdays on the corner of Mamo Street and Kamehameha Avenue in historic downtown. It opened early and closed when everything was gone. A market filled to capacity as over 100 local farmers and crafters offered tropical fruits and vegetables grown in the islands along with flowers and locally made crafts and gift items.

Hilo was the nation's orchid capital and Cassie fell in love with the flowers in such vivid colors. Clay secretly arranged for some to be delivered to their suite when she wasn't looking, along with a note for their butler to take the credit if asked about them. It was on impulse, his reasoning that of cheering her up. She hadn't really spoken to him at all and it was easy with other people around, each of them carried on with Kyle and Lee, they didn't have to deal with being alone or talk to each other, and it was only obvious to them how distant they were.

There were many things that had to be explained by their driver/tour operator who accompanied them to help with purchasing some things for their travel day around the island. Fruits included Cherimoya, Jaboticaba, Jack Fruit, Lychee, Rambutan, Soursop and some they knew such as Mango, Papaya, Pineapple, Strawberries and White Pineapple.

They purchased a few things to try and the driver had utensils and such he provided at their first stop of a beautiful waterfall where he prepared some of their fruit. Cassie loved the fresh pineapple but was reluctant to try the Cherimoyas because they were prehistoric in appearance. But when he sliced it for her she found it a delicious blend similar to many tropical fruits combined, its texture much like papaya, and it was said Mark Twain once characterized the exotic fruit as 'Deliciousness itself'. Cassie had to agree.

The driver was a local who like others among the islands, took great pride as he showed them everything beautiful he could in one short morning. They enjoyed several gardens, scenic overlooks out to the pacific, along the coastline, and inward towards the mountains. Passed several small quaint villages and stopped at Akaka Falls located on the slopes of dormant Mauna Kea volcano. Water plunged over 410 feet in a sheer drop over the cliff.

Then they had to be returned for a tour on horseback Lee arranged. Although she'd never been on a horse, Cassie was always up for new experiences, but when she saw the large size of the animal it was intimidating.

"This animal is huge." She said as she waited for help from their guide with instruction on how she was supposed to get on it.

"I take it this is new for you." Clay left his horse when he saw she would have trouble, laughed at her perplexed look.

"Is there a stool or something? I don't think I can get my foot up in the stirrup to get on."

He instructed her as he literally picked her up from behind to give her a boost and guide her leg over. The horse moved and she let out a little yelp of nervousness and he couldn't hide his chuckle.

"Oh, yeah," she huffed. "Laugh, Mr. Cowboy."

"You'll be fine, just relax." Clay stroked the large animal with practiced ease, his days in Texas once gave him many an opportunity to ride horses and he'd learned a few things, could tell this particular one was a docile animal, one she would need.

"You'll be fine, just relax." She mocked his words.

Cassie soon discovered he was right, her initial fears relaxed once the horse started moving and they were very well trained for their task of following along, there wasn't much she had to do but calm down and enjoy. She didn't really have to guide him because he knew exactly where he was going, so she sat back and took in the tremendous views.

The guide narrated as they rode along spectacular scenery. Considered by many to be one of the most beautiful places on the face of the earth, on a ridge high above the Waipi'o Valley, it was hard to disagree. They were led to some places restricted for years by sugar cane companies, some now accessible but only on horseback, and one could understand trying to preserve the serene and quiet setting.

They rode the rim of the valley to the top of Hi'ilawe, one of Hawaii's highest and most beautiful waterfalls. From there the falls, the valley floor and black sand beaches of the Pacific spread out before them. It was enough to take one's breath away. Cassie had never seen anything more inspiring, as if she'd found the spirit of Hawaii right there in that spot. At the lookout, gently rolling hills, Mauna Kea and the Valley Mountains came into full view and in a grove of Ohia trees they paused to relax awhile as the guide explained the trees.

"It's big fluffy pom-pom flowers are typically used to make Hawaiian leis. Said to be sacred to the goddess Pele, it is also said one must pray to the ohia flowers prior to picking or she would create a rainstorm. Or some say if it is picked on the way to the mountain it will rain." The guide laughed. "There must be many pickings. It rains almost every evening in Hilo, it is the rainiest city in the United States."

The group laughed and he continued. "Ohia trees are often the first life to form after lava destroys an area, thus it has sacred meaning to us. It is the promise of new life."

People dismounted their horses and dispersed about. Cassie had listened intently to the guide, but didn't dismount, and watched as the others wander elsewhere, relieved when Clay came to help her.

"I assume you can't get down on your own. Or are you just so comfortable up there you don't want to get down?"

"Your first guess would be the right one. You don't want a prize or anything, do you? I have no offering. I could pick you a flower but we'd just get rained on." She let him guide her right leg over, then he easily held her in mid air it seemed while she removed her left foot and he gently put her on the ground.

"The Hawaiians certainly have their stories to tell, don't they?"

"You don't believe them?" Cassie asked.

"I think most of them have grown in proportion over the years. Like the one about all the little people that built a ditch of stone overnight."

"But this one makes sense, the tree is the first thing that grows over lava stone, and it represents new life." Then she changed her words. "The promise of new life. Guess if one has to believe in anything, this would be my choice. Why not? Seems appropriate for my situation, don't you think?"

"Is that what you want?" He asked.

Cassie looked at him, then out towards the trees. "Who knows what I want. I'm the last one to ask."

What did she want? What was she feeling? Nothing, she told herself as she stretched her legs, bent them at the knees a few times and knew she was using muscles she didn't know she had as she'd straddled the horse and gripped on. She didn't have to think of anything right now, all she had to do was enjoy Hawaii and its beauty. Didn't have to think of her old life, nor any new one she might have to create. She was in a limbo, and it felt a safe haven, even if only for a little while.

"The promise of new life," Clay repeated. "It's a created metaphor, one that makes sense, associate new trees with new life. But I don't know about picking the flowers and it rains."

Cassie looked at him with a dare in her eye. "You sound awfully cynical. Pick a flower without praying and see if it rains."

"Are you serious?"

"I dare you," she teased.

He walked over and picked one, then stood before her and looked up into the sky. "It's still a beautiful day, not a cloud anywhere."

"You just wait, I hope it rains right over top of you."

He put the flower in her hair. "Now it will rain on you, but you'll look good when it does."

Cassie continued to stretch. "My muscles are already tight, I have a feeling that hot tub will be put to good use this evening."

Kyle and Lee walked up to them and had overheard the comment. "I'd be surprised if that hot tub hadn't been put to good use every night." Kyle commented quietly with a sly smile.

Cassie hadn't heard him but Clay laughed quietly, wanted to comment certainly not in the way one would expect newlyweds to use it, then he almost laughed out loud at the contrast of how people perceived them and what the truth was behind closed doors.

"What are you grinning about?" Cassie commented when she noticed.

"That's a new groom grin, I had one on my face for three years and it wouldn't go away." Kyle answered, assumed he knew what Clay's grin was from.

Lee took hold of his hand, the two had become like newlyweds again themselves as they enjoyed a second honeymoon on the cruise. "This time I'm going to have the grin, Kyle's been pampering me so much, and of course all the staff. I won't know how to act when I have to go home. The kids are going to think it awfully strange when I walk into the dining room and wait at the table for someone to bring me dinner."

"I think Cassie's going to kidnap the butler, Hernandez, and take him home." Clay said, and then added with a laugh. "I wouldn't put it past her, she's good at just taking what she wants and damn the consequences."

Of course only the two of them knew the silent innuendo, and nothing more was said as each enjoyed the quiet splendor spread before them as the four of them walked together, then Kyle and Lee ventured off alone. As they walked together, unconsciously, somewhere along the line over a few rough spots, Cassie had slipped her hand through Clay's arm to keep her footing stable. Only when she became aware of the feel of his upper arm muscles in her palm did she slip it away again.

"What'd you do that for?" Clay asked casually.

"I was just doing it for Kyle and Lee's sake, you know, keep up the pretense of newlyweds. I don't want to have to explain any of this, so we might as well act like it a little," she lied.

He wasn't sure if she told the truth or not but didn't question it. "They're a nice couple. Kyle mentioned they lived in Virginia, not to far from the border to North Carolina. Said we'd have to keep in touch and maybe get together sometime. I'll leave that up to you to decide what to tell him if he mentions it again."

"I don't know why I feel like we have to keep up any appearances in front of them, we hardly know them. But I feel like we started this farce and I can't tell them the truth. It wasn't on purpose, a simple comment and they have an impression of us."

"I guess we didn't know we'd become friends with them." Clay said then laughed. "Who gets the friends in the divorce? Do I keep in touch with Kyle and you keep in touch with Lee?"

"I don't know the proper protocol, I've never been married before, much less divorced."

"Had they met us the first day they would have guessed we were married and on our way to divorce, but we're not arguing as much anymore." Clay looked guilty as he added to his statement. "Sorry about last night, I had no right to question you on anything. Have your moods, I understand."

Cassie wasn't sure which she preferred. When she was angry all she saw when she looked at Clay was red, he was a man, so it made him the enemy. Now as she got to know him better, she found she really liked him as a person. As they prepared to leave, Clay helped her on the horse again, his strong hands gripped her waist, then after her left foot was safe in the stirrup one hand moved down to her rear as he seemed to hold her in mid air until she could get her right leg over.

"I think you did that on purpose," she laughed.

"What?" His look was pure innocence.

The horses descended gently through open pasture where cows grazed as they came upon sugar cane fields and wild flowers. Cassie stayed steady following the guide as her horse trailed along relaxed and knowing as its instinct kept her steady. On the other hand, Clay had been given a different horse since his experience on horseback was more than hers and she watched him as he freely galloped across open land, enjoyed much more freedom. She was envious as she watched his speed and skill, her slow horse merely putting one hoof in front of the other with no hurry to get anywhere.

When he rode up to her with a broad smile she could only imagine the thrill until he persuaded her to get on his horse. After protest she gave in as the guide took the reins and led her horse alongside him, and she joined Clay.

"Just hold on tight, I'll take you for a real ride." Clay said, liked the feel of her arms around him for security.

"I'm sure you will."

As the horse began a slow saunter she was fine, then he picked up speed once she was more comfortable. Before Cassie could object it became a full speed run across the wild flowers. It was exhilarating as the wind whipped through her hair, a sense of freedom enveloped her and she felt safe not only atop the powerful animal, but safe in his expert skills as a rider. Cassie was surprised she wasn't frightened at all, reveled in the feeling. When he finally slowed down she was barely breathing and she began to let go of her grip around his waist.

"Don't loosen your grip, I might take off any minute," he teased.

"It's a good thing I had a grip, I think you wanted me to fly off the back."

"That wasn't too hard a run, was it?" He was now concerned it had been a little much for her but she hadn't told him to stop.

"It was great." She sighed, now removed her hands completely as the horse rested and grazed. "Where did you learn to ride a horse so well?"

"I lived in Texas for a while once."

Clay's hand came down to his side to rest a minute, it casually lay atop her leg and her hand rested upon his arm as they quietly took in the view around them. They were an intimate silhouette against the sun that began its descent into ocean to close another day, a day both would hold onto long after it slipped away. They remained quiet and took in the surroundings that mesmerized them both, unsure how much time had passed, as if she were in a trance, Cassie finally broke the silence.

"We'd better get back." Cassie said quietly, not wanting to let go of the moment in time, but it wasn't hers to keep.

The venture over, they returned to the ship and Clay came up with an excuse of wanting to pick up a small gift for his mother. After he sent Cassie ahead, he called William, needed to hear his voice to remind him of the situation, he felt as if he were losing a grip on reality.

"Hey, Will." He said when he picked up his cell phone midway through the first ring.

"Clay, I've been crazy here. What's going on?" William's grip on his phone had become permanently indented into his hand. He held it constantly, waited for Clay to call.

"I'm just doing what you asked, just keeping an eye on her. Everything's fine."

"This is tearing me up, I can't stand being without her."

"I can imagine," he said, could hear the desperation in William's voice.

"What do you think, think she's coming around?"

"She doesn't seem to be as angry anymore if that helps."

"I'll do anything, Clay, I just don't know what. How am I going to get through this? Have you talked to her about it?" William paced the room with the phone in his hand, hadn't been able to stop thinking about her and wanted to rewind his life.

"She hasn't mentioned it, and neither have I."

"Maybe you could. I'm desperate here, Clay, and I don't know what else to do. I've never asked you something like this before, and I never will again, I swear."

The two were quiet. Clay waited and William took a deep breath and continued. "Can you tell her it was your girl in the room?"

"Oh Jesus, William," Clay sighed, raked his free hand through his hair in frustration.

"I know. I know it's wrong but you don't know Cassie, she'll never forgive me. This is my only chance."

"And what? You marry her and cheat on her again?" The even tone was gone and Clay's voice was angry now.

"It'll never happen, I swear to you, Clay. I don't know why it did in the first place. I'd been drinking, I got the wedding jitters. My last night to experience someone else as a free man, I don't know, it freaked me out and I don't know why I went through with it, but I did. I can't change that now but I can swear to you it won't be like that. I'll be true to Cassie till the day I die. I can promise you that."

"Will..." He began with hesitation but was stopped.

"Please, Clay." William pleaded now, it was his only chance and he knew it.

"I don't know if she'll even believe me."

"It's my only shot. You're the only one who can help me and I don't know what else to do. I can't lose her, she's everything to me, and if I lose her I have nothing. Please, it's my only hope."

Clay knew he was right, one lie from him and she'd probably be back in his arms.

William continued with his pleas. "I can't believe I just asked you to do that for me, but I'm desperate without her. See what it's doing to me?"

On the other end of the phone, Clay's palms were sweaty, it was a heat not caused by the sun that filled his body. As he looked out across the bay, white sailboats lazily dotted its surface, but beyond that nothing but a vast sea that looked as empty as his future.

CHAPTER TEN

After enjoying a few drinks at one of the bars with Kyle and Lee who'd already dined, they promised to meet them later, then went to dinner that evening at a restaurant inspired by Hawaiian Royal Families, one rich in history and pageantry of Hawaii Monarchy. The decor was intimate and exquisite. They were escorted to a table for two by the window and their view was of glorious moonlight as it danced along dark sea.

"Ah, the newlyweds, welcome. While making your reservation your butler Hernandez also arranged this bottle of champagne for you with his compliments." The wine steward presented them with the bottle, then opened and poured.

"How sweet he is." Cassie smiled. "I don't know what I'm going to do next week without him. I think this is proof that the only man I'll ever need in my life is Hernandez. He has the ability to take care of every need I can possibly have, even if I didn't know I needed it. How perfect is that?"

Clay envied the butler, wished he were the one she would allow to take care of every need she could possibly have, but of course he remained painfully quiet. As he watched her eyes sparkle over the candlelight, the soft glow it cast upon her face made her as breathtaking as Hawaii itself.

Stop thinking about her like that Clay, he inwardly screamed. Constantly struggled to think of her as William's fiancé', but the task was made more difficult as he sat so close to her. Romantic surroundings, soft music, champagne, and he could smell her sweet scent, imagined he would for a long time. He fought to pull his mind back to the way things were, and the impossibility of it all.

"Is there something wrong?" Cassie asked when he was extremely quiet.

"I was thinking of reality. After today on horseback again, maybe I'll move back to Texas, a friend of mine has been trying to talk me into it for some time."

Cassie didn't want to ask if the friend was male or female. "Ever get out to the East?"

"Some."

He said as little as possible for her not to make the connection between him and William, and it made him uncomfortable, he felt as if he were lying to her somehow, being deceitful. But in the beginning, William had asked him not to in order for her to trust him enough to be the one to drag along. Did it matter anymore? Actually nothing really mattered anymore. He was screwed all the way around.

"Maybe one of these years if you're ever close to Lakeview, you'll be able to stop in and have a cup of coffee at my bakery. It'll be right on Main Street, won't be able to miss it. Of course, you may not recognize me, by that time I'll be so old and decrepit I may forget to throw out the day old doughnuts and serve them for a month."

"So do it now." Clay said quickly.

"I don't have nearly enough money saved, and I don't want to be in debt for the rest of my life."

"You have a career you can always go back to if it doesn't work out."

"But I wouldn't want to after having a piece of a dream."

"Then there's your answer. You want it that bad, it can't fail. Going back to your career will be the driving force that will make you successful so you won't have to."

"But..." Cassie began to protest immediately with another excuse.

Clay straightened and looked her directly in the eyes. "There will always be an excuse. Not enough money, not the right location. There will never be a perfect time. Either you do it, or you don't."

"I have to..."

She tried to talk but he kept interrupting as if he knew exactly what she was going to say. "There's no guidebook or rulebook for dreams. The most important thing is to take the steps to realize those dreams."

"But what if..."

"What if a bus hits you tomorrow?" He pressed on. If she sought her dream out, took that direction, he knew William well enough to know he'd never survive in the small town. William wasn't cut out for it. "If the first steps don't work out, it just makes you grow and learn more. If something doesn't work out it isn't failure, it's merely the process that moves you forward."

Clay continued to stare at her, waited for her to say something, and Cassie smiled. "You seem to have an answer for things I hadn't even asked."

"The easy road is the career, the safe cocoon where someone else takes the risks. That's fine, very honorable. The hard road is taking on the challenge of following what's in your heart. That takes courage."

Cassie sipped her champagne. "You make me feel a little like my sister who doesn't have the courage to change her life."

"Is that what you want for yourself? To stay in your comfort zone and be miserable because it's more work to change it?"

"It isn't that I'm miserable, I do enjoy my job." She was good at what she did and she did speak the truth, she did enjoy it to a certain degree.

"But it isn't what's going to make you ultimately happy, it will never be enough."

"Okay, some very valid points." Cassie had to agree he started her mind working and she began to adjust her thinking. Maybe she could see it earlier than planned, maybe she wouldn't wait until she was old and it would be something to keep her busy.

"And?" He pressed.

"And what? Some very valid points, maybe I'll consider it earlier than I'd planned."

"Maybe isn't a very solid answer."

"My entire life isn't very solid right now, how am I supposed to make solid choices and decisions?" She raised her eyebrows as if she'd proved her point.

"Very well, but it is something you should be thinking about."

"Not right now when I'm starving." Cassie turned her attention back to the menu.

The meal was superb, the service flawless, and afterwards they walked up one floor to the Promenade deck and outside where the gentle ocean breeze blew softly. The sound of the wake against the boat was enough to soothe tired souls, an atmosphere one couldn't duplicate anywhere else. Cassie couldn't help but think how romantic and lovely a honeymoon the week would have been, had it been real. But she didn't let it bother her, she laughed out loud.

"I have to thank you," she admitted. "I can admit now you've made it a little more pleasurable then it could have been. I was so raged I couldn't think straight and I would have picked up the burly guy who smelled like beef and beer."

"It's not like you made it easy for me to be here. I'm still suffering the effects of that whiskey."

"I picked up some pictures yesterday from the photo shop. Our boarding picture was exceptional, I'm smiling away, the happy bride, and here you are in a wheelchair with a happy glazed look."

"A wheelchair?" Clay exclaimed with laughter, she'd never explained how he got on the ship.

"I told them you had to have emergency dental surgery and they'd given you something to ease the pain."

"That must have been a sight."

"Quite a sight. When I walked alongside the chair as you were being wheeled, you couldn't keep your hands off my butt. Once you even managed to pull me down into the chair with you and everyone clapped and congratulated us. You turned your lip up and impersonated Elvis... 'Thank you, thank you very much'. You made it a pretty entertaining show."

"I don't remember that part, but I'm glad you told me, makes it an even more unforgettable experience."

Cassie would admit to herself he was right. It was a week that would forever be embedded into her memory that was sure, and she was glad she could laugh about it after only a short time. Her initial anger could have harbored for so much longer, but the beauty of Hawaii, the relaxation, the pampering of ship staff all contributed to ease it away. And yes, Clay deserved some credit also.

"But I do sincerely thank you. You could have left anytime, and I know you stayed because of William, to keep an eye on me. But I appreciate that you did now."

"In the beginning it was because of William." Clay walked slowly beside her, wanted to reach for her hand, possibly put his arm around her, but stopped himself. "I could have left anytime, but other than loyalties to William, I also realized I wouldn't want it to be on my conscious if you did something rash you'd regret later."

"You and William have been friends for quite some time, haven't you?"

"The best of friends for years." Without explaining, Clay hoped she would see his reasons he wouldn't be able to pursue any further relationship with her even if he wanted to, he felt it was important for her to know. "He loves you, Cassie."

"I never doubted that before."

Clay looked out to sea, the darkness spotted only with the moonlight and the reflection of the ships lights, and he took a deep breath. Was now the time? Later? When would be right? Would there be a right time to lie? The words were on his tongue, he was about to say them, when Kyle and Lee opened the door and joined them.

"There you are." Lee exclaimed. "We were late and thought you two were waiting for us but saw you when we walked by the door. Or have you already been there and left because we weren't there?"

"No, we were just about to go in." Cassie answered. She looked to Clay, knew he was about to say something and she was disappointed they'd been interrupted.

From the Promenade deck all they had to do was walk inside to the lounge where the music pumped out rhythm and people took to the dance floor, everyone intent on having fun in the lively atmosphere. They easily found a table and ordered drinks, and then Kyle and Lee encouraged them onto the dance floor along with them.

The song was a fast one, the floor crowded, and they couldn't help but continually bump into each other. When it ended, Cassie was relieved but the Cruise Director encouraged all newlyweds to remain on the floor and at their newfound friend's insistence, who still didn't know it was a lie, they were playfully forced to remain.

As opposed to the first song, this was slow and melodic. Of course it would be something romantic for newlyweds, and although Cassie thought nothing of being close to him, when he held her in his arms, all of a sudden his proximity was something she was very aware of. She pulled away slightly.

"What's the matter, Cassie?" Clay asked knowingly with a sly smile.

"You don't have to hold me so close, this isn't real, you know."

That was a fact he was well aware of, regardless he pulled her closer again. He shouldn't have, probably shouldn't have been dancing with her at all, but Clay pushed the guilty feelings aside.

Cassie thought it would be easy, a simple dance she could get through, but it got complicated when the Cruise Director decided it was a game.

"Now that we have all you newlyweds on the floor, we're going to make this interesting. As the photographer is roaming around, he's going to be our judge and pick out the best one."

Cassie began to get a little nervous. "Maybe this wasn't such a good idea."

The Cruise Director went on. "Some of us old married couples might have lost the sense of new passion somewhere, so we have to be reminded how to get back in the swing of things from all you newly married. I want you to kiss your spouse in the most passionate way you know how." A roar went up from the audience. "This dance is actually a kissing contest and like I said, the photographer will be the judge because he'll be up close. The winning couple will receive a dinner in one of our special restaurants, along with a bottle of champagne."

"I think we've already eaten there, and had champagne." Cassie tried to pull away with more insistence but he only held tighter. "It isn't a prize we'd want anyway."

"You've been making me smile for pictures for days, isn't this what you want? A great picture?" Clay should have let her go, sat down at the table and watched the others, and he knew he was pushing it but he was angry with William for putting him in this position. Foolishly set in his mind there was no reason he couldn't enjoy it for awhile longer. An innocent dance and a kiss, wasn't he entitled to at least that much?

Before she could protest further the Director droned on, Cassie wished she would just be quiet and go away, far away.

"Everybody ready? When I say begin I want all of you to lay it on the line. This is an adult entertainment room so no holds barred. One... two... three... begin."

"This is foolish, Clay." Cassie said, but didn't make any attempt to pull away.

"It is, isn't it?"

Clay's hand slowly slipped behind her neck and pulled her to him. His fingers entwined in her hair as their lips touched softly, gently, and then she opened to him fully. Cassie could have sworn her heart stopped beating as something swelled inside her, something powerful that gave way as she sought out his touch. Then her heart must have begun beating again because she could hear it pulsate furiously, heard her breath catch between them when he parted slightly. It was only for a second or two, but it was enough to make her yearn for him again, and yearn for even more, much more.

Recklessly, she discarded all sense. Thought of nothing but his taste, his smell, and the way she wanted him. So lost they both were, they hadn't seen the flash, hadn't heard the applause and whistles or the words of the Director until she spoke again only louder.

"Whoa, I think there's no doubt we have clear winners. Can we get an escort please? Someone to carry these two back to their cabin? I don't think we'll be able to get them apart."

As she finally pulled away from him, she looked into Clay's eyes and for one split second saw sadness there.

CHAPTER ELEVEN

Because they were the winners, they had to go up on stage and the crowd cheered loudly. This was getting so out of hand, Cassie thought to herself. Less than a week ago she was home preparing for a wedding, now she stood on stage with a stranger she'd won a kissing contest with and the entire audience believed he was her husband. Clay held her hand tightly, she was glad he did because she would have bolted from the room had he not been.

"I haven't seen you two all week, no doubt you've been in your cabin the entire trip." The Director said as they became the spotlight on stage.

Cassie blushed out of embarrassment, the audience believed she'd blushed because the statement were true and they cheered again.

"How long have you been married?" She asked.

Clay answered all the questions because Cassie couldn't speak. "Just before the cruise."

"And where are you from?"

She droned on with question after question that Clay answered. Cassie squeezed his hand tighter and tighter and wished the moment would end, wished the woman would stop talking so she could delve back into obscurity. Before she stopped talking, she asked them to kiss one more time.

Clay kissed her softly but they wanted more, the crowd only cheered louder and louder as if they were at a soccer game and wanted a score. This was ridiculous, Cassie thought to herself. She stood on a stage and felt forced to kiss this man. Couldn't she just leave, couldn't he save her and refuse?

Neither happened as Clay pulled her to him, placed his lips on hers and in one second she was lost again. The crowd didn't matter, the cheers didn't matter, and Cassie heard none of it. She was lost in his passion, lost in his soft lips that were so tender on hers, yet held immense power as she seemed to burn from the tips of her toes to the roots of her hair.

It was what the crowd wanted as the cheers and applause were almost deafening, and more pictures were taken by the photographer. Wasn't this what she wanted? Wasn't she just doing it for her own needs of revenge? Was it the only reason she was ensconced in this man's arms and lost completely in his touch?

It had to be, there was no other explanation. Surely she couldn't be feeling anything for this man, it was only the fact that she had been jilted by another, left alone and vulnerable. The heat running through her was a natural emotion any woman would have experienced being in his arms. Because she was feeling it so intensely didn't mean anything. Did it?

When they finally were allowed to descend from the stage Clay placed his hand on her back and guided her through the crowd where strangers congratulated them and made playful remarks. But Cassie barely heard, his hand seemed to burn through the material of her dress directly to her skin and that was all she paid attention to, she even pictured red fingerprint marks on her back. Clay turned to her with a smile when they could speak privately.

"All for the sake of pictures, that wasn't so bad, was it?"

"It wasn't too bad. I ate a chocolate cricket once for a science experiment so I had the stomach to put up with that." She said casually and smiled broadly for Kyle and Lee who waited for them at the table, they even stood and gave them a standing ovation.

"That was a ten if I ever saw one." Lee laughed as if it were an Olympic score they'd gone after, then she playfully swatted Kyle. "How come you never kiss me like that anymore?"

"We've been married awhile, I'm out of practice. Come on, let's see if we can get back up to par." He took his wife's hand and led her to the dance floor.

"Are you two coming?" Lee asked behind her shoulder.

"I'm sitting this one out." Cassie answered and refused to get on the dance floor the rest of the evening.

They enjoyed the rest of the night until the place closed and she was really sorry to see it end, wasn't sure if it was because she was having a good time, or she didn't want to be alone with Clay. She realized it was the latter when they were alone in the elevator.

Each of them tried valiantly not to look at the other, not to have any sort of physical contact. When their hands accidentally brushed together Cassie thought she would come out of her skin.

"You're awfully quiet." Clay was the first to speak.

"I'm tired, it's been a long day and even longer night."

"I only did that because you want the best pictures. It isn't going to make you feel uncomfortable around me now, is it?" Clay watched her squirm a little, enjoyed it.

She laughed quickly. "Oh please. I hadn't thought about it since the second it ended. That little kiss didn't bother me a bit."

"I didn't think so. Like you said, you could eat chocolate covered crickets, that little kiss was nothing to get through." He laughed at her statement of earlier, knew she was trying hard not to show the affect it had on her.

Clay knew it had an affect, there was no doubt. No doubt it affected him, and he could sense no doubt she too was thinking about it that very moment. Without realizing it, he put his hand on the small of her back again to guide her out when the elevator doors opened and they reached their floor. It seemed a natural thing to do and he didn't give it a second thought until he almost took her hand in his. What was he doing? He shouted inside his head. This wasn't real, none of it was real, keep reminding yourself of who she is, he continued to shout to his brain, but his brain constantly fought hard not to be overridden by his heart.

So there was a passionate connection there, she was a beautiful woman and in the romantic surroundings of Hawaii it was hard not to be drawn into it. It didn't mean anything, it didn't mean anything, it didn't mean anything, the words repeated over and over in his mind as he constantly tried to remind himself of who she was, constantly tried to put William's face and voice to the forefront. As his emotions constantly battled to try and drown William out.

When they entered the room, he casually began to hang up his clothes and as soon as he could, went to take a cold shower. One of many he'd taken on this trip. Cassie came in, washed her face, brushed her teeth and applied moisturizer. She noticed there was no steam and smiled inwardly, knew it wasn't hot water he used.

She shouldn't have started it, but the temptation to flirt was much too great. It wasn't something she would normally do under normal circumstances, which this wasn't, but he'd made her feel like a wanted woman. Her self-confidence boosted after her cheating fiancé' shot it down by sleeping with another woman. She was desirable, she'd done nothing to push William into the arms of another woman, it was just his own stupidity, wasn't it?

"Hey, Clay, that kiss didn't have any affect on you, did it?"

"I was just doing my duty."

He turned the water off and reached for a towel but noticed it wasn't there. As he opened the door he saw her sitting on the counter holding it in her hands, then she threw it at him. She'd been getting ready for bed and sat with her bra and panties on, nothing else, but he pretended, as usual, not to notice what she was or wasn't wearing.

"What if I don't believe you?" She said coyly.

He shrugged his shoulders and laughed. "It was nothing."

"Prove it." What was she doing? Cassie screamed to herself.

Stop now, stop before it's too late, anything that happens will be your entire fault. You don't have to prove to yourself you're desirable. William didn't hurt you so bad that you'll never recover, and you weren't to blame for him seeking out affection from another. It had nothing to do with you. Cassie kept screaming the words in her head, and wanted her mouth to form the words to take it back, but it was as if it was frozen. Clay stared at her and she prayed, hoped, he wouldn't act on her words. He was standing there naked, she was in barely anything, and what did she expect would happen?

He'd wrapped the towel around himself, now remained motionless for several moments but she felt she couldn't back down now. She stopped breathing as he walked slowly to her, placed his hand behind her neck and pulled her to him. It wasn't soft and tender as before, this kiss was full of passion and fire. Their lips pressed hard together, tongues entwined as she buried herself in his warmth.

She pulled her mouth away and guided him to her neck where he softly caressed it with his lips, his tongue, as her legs wrapped around him, pulled him closer to her. She was overwhelmed at her reaction to him, the feel of his skin against hers made her lose all sense of control. Cassie's fingers spread wide as her hands took in every inch as they moved down his tight muscular back and slipped beneath the towel making it fall to the floor.

"Cassie," he said her name breathlessly, his deep voice barely able to speak, and it made her want him even more.

His lips touched her skin, her heart was about to explode, and anticipation of more made her gasp. Then suddenly he pulled himself completely away from her.

"See? I told you, just a kiss. No affect at all. Nothing." Clay tried to catch his breath as he leaned against the wall behind him and his hands raked through his hair in frustration. He remained there as still as he could possibly be with his eyes directly on hers.

She felt cold without him, but Cassie smiled as if she too were in complete control. "You might want to take another cold shower before you come to bed." Then she chuckled lightly, slipped down from the counter with ease and left the room.

It was a long time before he was ready to lie down in bed and Cassie was already asleep. She lay on her stomach and the sheet covered her lower part, but a good portion of her bare back was exposed as her arms reached under her pillow, her dark hair stark on the whiteness of the case as it spread out.

She was seducing him even in sleep, and Clay watched her in the dark as he sat alone in the chair. How could he have let this happen? My God, he was falling in love with his brother's fiancé'. Or ex-fiancé, ex-girlfriend, whatever she would be when this cruise was over, but he was falling in love with a woman he could never have. As much as he knew William had done her wrong, he also knew how much William loved her. As soon as he met her said immediately it was the girl he would marry and spend the rest of his life with, talked about her for a year. Now William's voice was desperate as he tried to hang on to her. Clay kept William's frightened voice close inside his own thoughts but his feelings that had begun to emerge tried to push the sound out.

William was the closest thing in his life. Clay from their mother's first marriage and William from their mother's second marriage, they didn't have the same father, they were half-brothers. But they were the closest two full brothers could ever be. There was a bond between them that nothing would break, and loyalties lie in Clay's heart at the sad realization that no matter what he thought of Cassie, she could never be his.

After his sleepless night, with the idea of spending as much time away from her as he could, he left the suite early that morning before the sun had risen, so Cassie was alone when she turned and shifted slightly, felt the coldness of the empty bed beside her and opened her eyes to see Clay wasn't there. When she rolled over she looked around the room but he wasn't there either, and when she listened for the shower didn't hear anything, realized she was completely alone, and then she lay quietly with a tinge of disappointment.

What was she thinking? The thought of Clay conjured up emotions. Emotions, sensations, feelings, she shouldn't be thinking, didn't need to think. She knew her sensitive state was fragile and weak, she'd just been stood up at the marriage alter by a man she thought she'd spend the rest of her life with. A man she'd invested herself in, built a relationship, formed a future, now the direction she would take was altered severely. The unknown lay ahead and she didn't know what the future would bring, but knew she didn't need it complicated by Clay.

Cassie stretched in the comfortable bed. Why couldn't she be like some women who could easily have sex, could easily be attracted to someone and think nothing of sleeping with him and moving on the next day free and clear? Because the mere thought of him conjured up a passion and her willpower would have to fight hard to defend her morality. If she could cast morals aside, Clay would easily be a choice that would satisfy her.

The ship docked in Kona at 7:00 am that morning and they'd made plans to again spend the day with Kyle with Lee. Cassie was relieved she wouldn't be alone with Clay. It wasn't him she feared, it was herself she couldn't trust. When he returned to the room from being gone there was no sign of any discomfort. No reminders of the night before when she practically threw herself at him and expected him to resist, which she was now grateful he had.

"Good morning," he smiled nonchalantly and began to open her bottle of champagne Hernandez had delivered. "I take it you're ready for your daily dose of champagne?"

"It was a good idea at the time, now I just feel like a lush drinking champagne every morning. Am I going to need rehab when I get home?"

"I can safely say I believe it's a habit you'll only reserve for honeymoons. And I can't imagine you'll have enough honeymoons to make you a rehab candidate."

"No, Mr. Walker, this will be my one and only for quite a long time." Cassie smiled and took the glass he offered.

"But promise me you'll keep this morning ritual special to us. Maybe your next one you can change to Bloody Mary's or something else appropriate. I don't know if I can handle the thought of my ex honeymoon partner sharing something so special."

"Out of respect for you, I'll consider it."

He raised his eyebrows. "Consider it? That's promising." He said it as if he were hurt.

"What time are we supposed to meet Kyle and Lee?"

"I had breakfast with them, I said we'd meet them outside in about an hour."

"Good, that will give me time to grab something to eat. I can't just have champagne, I need something in my stomach."

"I saw Hernandez and asked him to bring it up for you."

"What did you tell him to bring?" She questioned.

"Fruit. Lot's of fruit, especially pineapple, and those pancakes you like." Clay walked out onto the balcony and Cassie followed. As if they were an old married couple, he knew what her likes and dislikes were.

"Did you..." she began but he stopped her.

"Yes, I told him to bring the cinnamon syrup you loved too."

****

Kyle and Lee were both good company and good distraction. Cassie felt more comfortable not having to spend the day alone with Clay, not having to be alone with Clay. Her mind wandered back periodically to their few kisses the evening before and she had to stop herself from thinking about it, stop herself from daydreaming. It wasn't uncomfortable between them because of it, and Clay went on in his casual, carefree way as the small group set off for their day. He and Kyle deep in conversation and Cassie wondered if he too was forcing himself from thinking about it, or if he truly didn't think about it at all.

Lee had planned the day and both Cassie and Clay were all too happy to let her do so. Both had ended up in Hawaii spontaneously and hadn't prepared for the trip, but Lee had known for months she was going and had done extensive research, was one who liked to be prepared for what she wanted to see, so the four of them set off for a day of adventure.

Their first stop was a beautiful stretch of beach and an early morning surf lesson given by some of the island's most advanced lifeguards, and although Cassie was a little hesitant, she threw caution to the wind and jumped in without second thoughts. Clay was as excited as a small boy and it didn't take him long to be up and riding the waves like a pro, and

Kyle was right behind him. When Cassie and Lee required more help, Clay playfully blamed it on the fact their instructors were bodybuilding, tan lifeguards.

"I'm beginning to think you're not getting the hang of it, because you don't want to." Clay mentioned when they were on the surf once.

"What are you talking about?" She was truly innocent in not understanding his meaning.

He motioned his head towards her instructor who was walking towards them. "I think it's a little obvious he'd give up his lessons for the rest of the day just to teach you."

Cassie laughed. "He's practically a child."

"He might be young in age, but a minor he isn't, a man he is."

"So he might have a little crush, I think it's cute."

"Cute." Clay huffed.

"You're not jealous, are you?"

"Jealous? I think it's ridiculous he's hanging all over you."

"Come on, Cassie, no time to waste." The instructor said and Cassie didn't look back as she went off into the ocean again, leaving Clay inwardly fuming behind her.

It was an odd sensation for him, Clay had never been the jealous kind, confident in himself and self assured as a man. It was odder still that he was feeling it when he and Cassie meant nothing to each other, she was free to do as she pleased, and with whomever she pleased, so who was he to feel that tinge of jealousy that clouded the edge of his emotions. Later when they left, and Lee teased about it also, he laughed with the rest of them and playfully joked about it, but inside it still bothered him a little.

It bothered him because he wasn't confident and self assured when it came to Cassie, he meant nothing to her, and Clay realized that's what bothered him the most. His confused mind put them together, coupled them as everyone else did, and yet reality was far different. She had no loyalties to him, at that point, she had no loyalties to anyone, William's actions had set her free and she was obligated to no one at that point in time, but Clay realized he wanted her to be obligated to him in some way. With conscious effort, he pulled back a little and tried to remain distant from her, both physically and mentally for the rest of the day.

Their next stop was Punalu'u Black Sand Beach. It was one of the most picturesque beaches with jet black sand and tall leaning coconut palms that gave one a true sense of Hawaii. It offered the thrilling experience of swimming and snorkeling with the endangered green sea turtle that made its home there. Calm, sweet creatures that were used to humans, unafraid of them, and spent their days munching away on the green algae that grew on the lava rock around the shores and paid no mind to the people as turtles basked in the sun on the beach or on the rocks.

At night they would crawl onto the sand and lay their eggs, and tourists were advised by multiple signs they couldn't be touched or bothered. Cassie delighted in the experience and often while swimming had to move out of their way. Then they ventured off to Kealakekua Bay where Lee was advised that it was the best snorkeling spot for fish and they all agreed she was right. Calm, well protected waters gave them view to incredible marine life as it was home to over 150 different species of colorful reef fish. They spotted several moray eels, trumpet fish, trigger fish, puffer fish and others. It could only be accessed by boat and they'd taken a kayak from the boat launch to get there. On the way back when they were alone, Cassie commented on Clay's disposition.

"You've been awfully quiet today."

He shrugged his shoulders as he paddled, kept telling himself it was all surreal, Cassie wasn't a part of his life. That was difficult to do as they created memories together. "Have I?"

"You haven't been talking much, not to me anyway."

"What do you want to talk about?"

She was in the front of the kayak and stopped paddling and turned around. "Are you having a good time today?"

"Would it make a difference if I wasn't?"

She wondered if he was thinking of his girlfriend at home, the one who wouldn't understand his plight. Cassie thought that to be the case and wondered why it bothered her. "I'd feel guilty dragging you off to Hawaii and you didn't even enjoy it."

"I'm enjoying Hawaii."

"But not the company, you'd rather be here with someone else." The words came out harsher than she'd intended.

Clay stopped rowing as they were close to their destination and they lingered there a moment. "It's hard not to enjoy this, no matter who someone is with. I think we both understand it isn't the trip either of us planned."

She had a slight tinge of guilt for pulling him away from his life, away from someone else he'd rather be with. She smiled in a way that asked him forgiveness. "Things could be worse."

Clay thought about the light statement, he wasn't sure she was right, but she didn't understand what he was going through at that moment, though he too smiled. "I'll pretend as best I can we're having a wonderful honeymoon, I'll continue to smile and be the loving husband you want me to be, it will all be over soon anyway."

"Apparently, not soon enough for you."

"I'll get through it." He would get through it, and afterwards, he would have to deal with the consequences of what his life had become since she stepped into it.

Clay would have liked to have ended the day, get back onto the ship and distract himself with something, a pool game, ping pong, one of many activities the ship offered, but Lee had other plans and they continued on to a boat tour along the coast, one that would end their day with a sunset cruise. Cassie was delighted with the spinner dolphins that put on a show as if they were from a marine park and performed. Clay listened to her laughter ring through the air. A sweet sound of joy, and although the dolphins delighted him too, it was the sound that delighted him more. The boat then meandered through lava tubes and the guide pointed out dry caves that were abundant along the rocky shores. It was just the four of them onboard and it seemed like their own private tour.

"So are you two going to start a family anytime soon?" Lee asked.

"As soon as possible." Clay said as he stretched out his legs and smiled to Cassie who almost laughed out loud.

"I wouldn't be surprised if that kiss alone you two had last night were enough to make Cassie pregnant." Kyle laughed.

Cassie almost blushed, it was the first embarrassing mention of the incident, but Clay answered jokingly. "I can't control her in public, she knows how much I don't like any public display of affection and it was her chance to shine. I can't keep her hands off me most times."

Cassie playfully swatted him and he laughed and joked again.

"See?" He put his arm around her and pulled her close.

As she leaned into him she pinched his side and he let loose.

Next, the boat operator found a secluded beach and they went ashore. Walking through the water she and Clay got to fooling around as she splashed him in silent retaliation and he splashed her back. Then one thing led to another and as she tried to run from him he quickly caught her and scooped her up into his arms with threats of throwing her.

"That's not fair, you can't throw me because I won't be able to get you back in the same way. I won't be able to pick you up." Cassie pleaded with him to put her down.

"Who says I was going to throw you? Maybe I'm just carrying you ashore."

"Don't play Mr. Innocent, I know what your intentions are."

"And my intentions are not honorable?" He looked into her eyes that sparkled brightly in the sunshine, held her secure as her arm wrapped around his shoulder.

"I'm going to hang on tight, if I go, you'll fall down with me." She wrapped her other arm around him and it brought their faces much closer together.

Cassie could feel his breath on her mouth, could remember the way his lips felt against hers and the sensual emotion he aroused. Before she could stop herself she pressed her mouth against his as he pulled her closer to him. It was his intake of breath she heard this time when he pulled away.

"Is this all part of the act, Cassie?" He asked while fighting his desire to kiss her again, he had to wonder if she knew what he was going through and she only wanted to make him more miserable.

"Of course." She said lightly. "We want to look convincing, don't we?"

He looked into her eyes and knew she was lying, it would have been better if she weren't, it was only something that could never be. Clay couldn't stop himself if he wanted to as his lips met hers once more. This time it was much longer than they had allowed the first time, and this time neither one was willing to pull away, it was Kyle who interrupted them.

"Hey you two, come up for air," he said as he splashed them and laughed. "I'm no prude, but that's embarrassing me."

"I told you I can't keep her hands off me." Clay joked, but his eyes never left Cassie's as he could see that she too had been disappointed there were others present.

"Oh, Kyle," Lee hollered at him from the shore. "Leave the lovebirds alone, it's romantic he's carrying her to shore, you could have done the same for me."

"See how bad you're making me look, Clay? You have to stop being the romantic husband, my wife expects more from me because of it."

Cassie had let up her grip from around his neck. "You heard him, can't have Kyle looking bad." Clay said as he easily swung her out and threw Cassie into the water.

She screamed but came up laughing. "You…"

"Hey, no names," Clay said as he ran to shore and was there to pick her up again when she reached him.

"Put me down, you're not going to throw me in again."

"Don't dare me."

"I didn't dare you the first time."

"I saw it in your eyes, you might as well have." Clay held her tight and they weren't interrupted again because Kyle and Lee had taken off on their own down the beach.

"I didn't dare you, and I'm not now, put me down."

"I'm only playing my part."

"You don't have to," Cassie looked down the beach where the other two had walked and pointed in their direction. "They're gone, they can't even see us anymore."

"They might turn around."

"They won't."

"How do you know?"

Cassie didn't know, and she didn't care, so lost she became being in his arms and staring into his deep eyes she wasn't even sure there was anyone else on the same beach, wasn't sure of anything except the dangerous position she was in. In that one moment, there was no one else but them. It was Clay who broke the silence, had to talk to keep his mouth from going where it wanted to.

"We won't have to put ourselves through this lie much longer, one more evening and you'll be rid of me. Are you counting the hours?"

"The seconds." Cassie answered with softness as her voice had a hard time coming.

Cassie hadn't been thinking of the cruise ending. What did she expect to do? Sail the waters of Hawaii for the rest of her life? Lost in a farce and a life that wasn't hers? It was their last day, what would come in the morning? So many questions that had to be answered but she didn't want to think about the questions then, didn't want to think about anything that was to come, only wanted to stay lost in that moment for as long as she could.

Their captain supplied them with a bottle of champagne and poured them each a glass as they sailed off towards the port. All of them were quiet as the sun began its descent to end another day, all of them quiet as they waited for the phenomena of the green flash of the Hawaiian sunset. A fleeting splash of intense emerald light that would appear on the horizon in the blink of an eye and the boat captain explained one had to look away until only the very top of the sun's disk was about to disappear below the sea, it was only during this last instant, and only for a moment, the green flash was visible.

Kyle and Lee weren't sure whether they saw it or not, while Clay and Cassie hadn't even been looking. Cassie sat comfortably in the nook of Clay's arm as he held her and both of their thoughts were elsewhere. Both lost in thoughts of what was to come.

CHAPTER TWELVE

That night was formal night and they'd promised to all meet up for dinner and the evening together. Clay's tuxedo from the wedding had been cleaned and he would wear that as Cassie dressed in the black dress she'd purchased in Vegas the same time she'd purchased her wedding dress. A wedding dress that now lay in a jumbled mass at the bottom of the closet.

The solid black dress she wore now plunged deep in front. As opposed to the white ball of fluff that lay on the floor, this one did not emit a feeling of pure, innocent beauty. It was a halter style that plunged deep in front and left her full back exposed. A built in bra made her breasts seem at least four times bigger than they actually were as her cleavage bounded over the top.

Cassie had never worn something so sexy and revealing, and when she'd purchased it, she had second thoughts but decided to anyway, knowing William would love it. It was to be a surprise for her new husband, but William wasn't there to see it now, was he? And she didn't have a new husband to surprise, did she?

She would have worn something else, but had nothing else to wear. Had she thought of it earlier she would have been scouring every boutique and store on the islands to find something else less revealing and sexy, but it wasn't something she'd been thinking of. Now she didn't have a replacement for it and there was nothing else in her suitcase suitable for the formal evening.

It even crossed her mind not to participate in formal night at all, but then she'd have to make excuses to Kyle and Lee who were probably already waiting for them. They'd planned to have drinks before dinner and she looked to her watch, knew they'd be waiting on them and she couldn't back out now. She put the thoughts out of her mind, it was only a dress, she was probably putting more emphasis on it than Clay would, he would probably barely notice.

Clay buttoned his white crisp starched shirt and watched her as she stood with her back to him on the balcony. Her bare back that was tan, smooth, and flawless in its beauty. The dress was so low it almost reached parts that should definitely remain covered and his only thought was that she couldn't possibly be wearing any underwear. As he stared, lost in his thoughts, she slowly turned and in that one instant before she knew he was looking at her, he could see a sad vulnerability in her eyes. Like an innocent child wounded and now lost. Whatever she'd been thinking about vanished, because when their eyes locked it was gone.

"You're worse than a woman, how can it take you so long to get ready?" Cassie walked towards him, with each step the dress clung to different parts of her body.

"I have a ton of crap to put on." Clay put in his cufflinks. "All you had to do was slip that thing over your head. But I don't know why you even bothered with that, not like it covers much of anything."

He glanced to her once more but his eyes were drawn down to her breasts and he quickly looked back to the mirror. Cassie walked slowly over next to him, stood beside him and turned to face his reflection in the mirror, looked into the reflection of his eyes there.

Clay didn't see the sad vulnerability he'd merely caught a glimpse of before, he now saw seductive eyes that teased him.

"You don't like my dress?" Cassie's words low and sexy, her eyes never left his and it took all he had not to glance down again.

"Sure, great," he said casually.

"All men are the same, aren't they?" Cassie stepped closer to him. "I could have missing front teeth and a beard and it wouldn't matter. As long as my body looks decent you don't care about the face."

"Don't judge us all together in one group sum."

"Are you different? You'd look at me the same way if I was standing here up to my neck in flannel and granny underwear?"

He thought about her not wearing any underwear again, cleared his throat in nervousness. "That depends."

"On what?"

"What color flannel." Clay turned away from her.

He couldn't look at her again, probably not for the rest of the evening. Maybe he should picture her in flannel and granny underwear, it would certainly help him get through the night. It might work for a while, but he would only have to return to the suite and sleep with her in bed nude.

Or maybe she planned to pull another 'prove it' moment and he would have to fight his emotions and refuse her. How miserable was his life? Clay decided he would be the one to break down and wear something to bed that evening, knew he couldn't take it anymore. Maybe he'd have Hernandez make the couch up instead. Even better, he wondered if there was an empty cabin somewhere, anywhere, on the ship.

"You do look nice." Clay complimented her as they took the elevator up two decks.

"Thank you. And the answer is no." She said casually as she watched the lights change on the buttons.

"No?" He asked confused.

"I'm not wearing any underwear, granny or otherwise."

Clay moaned as the doors opened. "Why did you have to do that to me?"

Conversation flowed and they got into a lively conversation with their waiter who was comical as he emitted a wolf whistle directed to the two nicely dressed ladies, Cassie and Lee, every time he passed the table. They promised to return later that evening when he made a production of them leaving.

"The two most beautiful things in the room, and you will leave me now? What shall I look at?" He took the ladies hands and kissed the back of each of them. "Promise me you come back. I am here all night waiting."

"It will be late." Lee answered. "We're going to the show after dinner."

He threw his hands up. "I do not care! I am here waiting."

The restaurant on deck five was an atmosphere of bold tropical colors. It was vibrant and at the same time emitted an elegance of the islands and they dined on steak and lobster then went to a fantastic show that featured tropical dances and island music. Then as promised, returned to the lounge where Cortez, their earlier waiter, sat patiently by the door as if he had really been waiting for them.

"You have returned. I have missed your beauty." He kissed the top of their hands again as the men looked on with smiles.

"I think I'll come back here every night, he sure knows how to make a lady feel priceless." Cassie said as they sat down.

"Are you implying I don't?" Clay leaned closer to her and whispered. "I order the perfect breakfast, I carry you through the sea, I gave you a horseback ride you'll never forget. And I've served champagne to you as soon as you wake. And you imply I don't know how to treat a lady?"

"That doesn't count, that's all as Mr. and Mrs. Walters who don't exist. That's all in a pretend world that isn't ours." Cassie too leaned close to whisper, her voice low and provocative. The wine she'd drank that evening had gone straight to her head.

Her statement was one she'd been thinking about, now voiced. It was all pretend, she kept telling herself. Nothing was real about it. They weren't husband and wife, they weren't in love, they weren't on a honeymoon, they barely knew each other. Over and over she repeated it, but it seemed the more she repeated the more it faded into the distance.

Clay took her hand and led her to the dance floor where a slow song emitted through the speakers.

"Did you ask me to dance?" She looked playfully offended.

"I'm your husband, remember? I don't have to ask permission," he pulled her closer. "Besides, you'd have said no."

"No I wouldn't have. Maybe yesterday I would have said no, but not today, not now." Cassie looked into his eyes and thought she saw a hint of sadness, one she'd noticed on several occasions but was unsure of its meaning.

"Things aren't any different now." Clay said the words to try and convince both of them, but they didn't sound convincing.

As he held her and they danced, his mind wandered to thoughts of what could have been between them had they met before all this started. How cruel was fate to have thrown into his arms his brothers fiancé', and how cruel it was to give them this opportunity to be together. For what? What was the cruel intent and purpose for him to have this time with the one woman who had ever penetrated through to his heart and emotions? The one woman he could never have?

He was quiet as he thought of his brother now, the torture he'd been going through, fully understood the pain he heard in his voice every time they talked. The fear of being about to lose the woman he loved. Clay understood everything his brother had been feeling, shared his every emotion.

He should tell her now, he should have told her the moment William asked him to, he'd only prolonged his agony. Although he told himself to tell her, Clay didn't, he held her to him as she rested easily against him and they swayed to the slow, sensual music that surrounded them. When that song ended, neither was aware that another had begun, or another after that. They were quiet as they held onto each other.

There were no words between them, each of them lost in the moment that was to be theirs, Clay was the only one aware that it was to be their last moments together.

When the night ended, instead of going to their room as Kyle and Lee had done, they held hands as they walked along the deck and took in the starry moonlit night as the ship made its way back to its home port. There was nothing but the sound of the wake to disturb the silence.

Clay finally stopped and leaned against the banister, Cassie fit herself easily to him as she pressed her body to his and he couldn't stop himself from wrapping his arms around her and pulling her even closer.

"We have to talk," he said as he took a deep breath.

"Talk? Isn't it too nice of a night to waste on talk?" She'd given it much thought and she was prepared to throw caution to the wind come what may. "I think it's about time we got rid of this sexual tension between us. I've decided we should just sleep together to see if it's real."

"It isn't real Cassie."

She chuckled. "You can't tell me you don't desire me, I may be stupid in some things, but I can see you're feeling something just as I am."

"I am, but it isn't real Cassie, you're feeling vulnerable because of what you think has happened to you."

"That might be part of it, but I think there's more and I think we need to find out what it is."

"We can't do that." It tortured him to say the words.

"You don't want to sleep with me?" Her face was so close to his, one more centimeter and they'd kiss.

"It certainly isn't that." He removed his arms from around her and pushed her a little away from him. "For one thing, I think you've thoroughly enjoyed the wine this evening. You didn't take advantage of me when I had too much whiskey, I wouldn't take advantage of you when you've had too much wine."

"You passed out, I couldn't take advantage if I wanted to. And I'm not as bad as you were, I've had just enough wine, I still know what I'm doing."

"Do you?" His hands held her upper arms. "Aren't you doing this because you want to get back at William? That's what this is all about, isn't it?"

"Is that what stops you? William? What if I said I certainly have no intention of going back to him?"

"That doesn't make a difference. That may be your decision, but it wouldn't change things." Clay looked deep in her eyes and wanted her to understand even if he couldn't say the words, even if he couldn't explain his loyalties to William, he somehow wanted her to read his mind, to know why it wouldn't change things.

"Why? If I'm not with William why couldn't we see if this thing between us has any substance? Maybe it could turn into something. I'm not saying I want a serious relationship right now, but I'm wondering if I'll ever see you again after tomorrow."

"You're not thinking straight, Cassie, not emotionally."

"I'm thinking with all my emotion right now, that's the problem."

Clay wanted desperately to kiss her, to carry her back to the suite and make love to her all night long. The yearning he felt for her burned through every blood vessel in his body, but it was a thirst that couldn't be quenched.

Cassie moved closer to him again and kissed his neck gently, let her tongue flicker once seductively, and then reached his ear where her lips whispered tenderly. "What's stopping you, Clay?"

"Cassie, don't."

His hand became buried in her silky hair and he didn't stop her when her mouth moved from his neck to his lips and she kissed him. Small sensual touches of her lips ripped through him. She seductively bit his lower lip and he could have easily lost his senses but took her arms again and pushed her back from him before it was too late.

"We can't." His tone held sad regret.

"Why? We're on our honeymoon, we sleep nude in the same bed and we have a great time together. You can't tell me you don't feel anything. Give me a good reason why we can't take this any further."

Clay stopped listening to his own thoughts and had to concentrate hard to hear William's desperate pleas of love. He fought for strength and self control, fought hard for the courage to make the words come out of his mouth. He had to tell her, had to stop this before he went too far and it would be too late.

"It wasn't William's girl in that room, she was with me," he said the words quickly, they were out of his mouth, and he thought he'd feel better once they were spoken, but of course he didn't.

Cassie stood for a few moments without saying anything as the sound of the wake permeated the still sea air around them. Her mind fought hard to take in what he'd said, it was a jolt to her senses from one extreme to the other as they were just in each others arms and now the mood drastically altered.

"You're his best friend, you're lying for him." She didn't know if she was angrier because there was the possibility of it being true, or if she was upset because she thought he was lying to her.

He held her arms with soft tenderness, the words he spoke next would seal his fate. "William didn't cheat on you. All I had to do was keep my mouth shut, you already think William was unfaithful, so I didn't have to say a word. Cassie, I want nothing more than to take you in my arms, carry you to the suite and make sweet love to you all night long. I'm standing here in hell because I can't seem to hold you close enough and yet I have to tear myself away from you. Why would I lie and say it was my girl in that room when I want you so bad?"

Her mind whirled and she felt as if she had to struggle to keep her balance both physically and emotionally. "How the hell did she end up with him? It was him I found in that room, not you."

"William was passed out, didn't even know she was in my room. I took a shower and dressed and when I came out that morning, I didn't see him in the bed where he was sleeping and I assumed he'd left, and I thought I was the one running late. He must have been in the other bathroom and then just went back to bed. But the girl was in my bed, not his."

Cassie backed away from him as if in slow motion, as she did, Clay saw her eyes change instantly. There was a cold silence, a painful sorrowful look that ripped through him. She looked desolate and alone as if the rest of her world had just crashed upon her shoulders. The little piece of sanity she thought she'd found now slipped through her hands and the pain he'd caused her would stay with him for a long time to come.

When she walked away from him, he didn't follow. Clay remained for a long time in that one spot then sat alone in a deck chair on the top deck after getting a double shot of whiskey from a bar. He made himself comfortable, quickly downed the glass, leaned his head back, and cursed himself for answering the phone and agreeing to the request of what he thought would be the simple task of being his brother's best man.

A quick trip to Vegas, it sounded great at the time, how was he to know it would have such a dramatic impact on his simple life. The lie he just told cemented their fate. William and Cassie would work it out, she would forgive him, he would pretend to forgive her the supposed mistake she'd made, and things would be wonderful.

It would work out well for him that way too. Even if they hadn't worked it out, his silent brotherhood trust would still prevent him from having her. It was done, now they could get on with their lives and he could return to his own. But Clay had to concede, he had no life, admitted to himself even if he could never admit it to anyone else, that William had his life, and there wasn't a thing he could do about it.

CHAPTER THIRTEEN

Clay eventually returned to the room, and immediately worried when he didn't find Cassie there, could tell she hadn't been there at all, but stopped himself from going in search of her. He wasn't what she needed, wasn't what she wanted to see, he was sure. He lay on the couch and closed his eyes, but never really slept and as the sun rose he ordered coffee. Hernandez was surprised to see him still in his tuxedo he remained in from the previous evening.

"You have good night?" The butler smiled with misconception as he began to pour the coffee.

"No, Hernandez, I didn't."

Then he looked worried as he looked around the room. "Ms. Cassie? Everything okay?"

"No, it isn't." Clay sighed and took the hot liquid. "But it's a long story, too long to even begin explanation, if there is any simple way of explaining, which there isn't."

The butler looked even more confused but Clay didn't say anymore as the phone rang and he picked it up. When he did, Hernandez discreetly disappeared.

"Hello?" He said quickly, hoped to hear Cassie's voice but didn't.

"Clay? It's Will."

"Hey." Was all he could manage, even that was more than he wanted to say.

"I called last night but couldn't get you. I'm in Maui and wanted to let you know. Your ship gets in at 8:00 and I'll be at the port when you get off. How's Cassie?"

"I don't know, Will. I did as you wanted, I explained the situation, I don't know what she's thinking and I don't know what her plans are." Clay sounded impatient. He was tired of this game they played, tired of everything and wanted his normal life back.

William was quiet for a moment. He hadn't been sure if Clay would actually go through with it, now felt slight relief his work to get her back wouldn't be so hard. "Thanks, Clay."

Clay didn't say anything else, couldn't say anything else as he felt like he could feel life slipping through his hands, he simply replaced the phone in the receiver. When the ship docked, he was almost the first one off. Dressed in the tux he'd entered in, his wallet in his pocket, they were the only thing's he had when he began this journey, and the only things he had when he left.

William was the last face he wanted to see, but the first face he saw when he made it out the doors. Clay quickly lost himself in a crowd, slipped into a cab and slipped away. The only thought on his mind was Cassie as he wondered if she'd ever think about him, if just once, he'd ever cross her mind.

****

Clay went back to California and waited, waited for something. A call from William to tell him they were getting married after all, a call to tell him they weren't getting married. A call from Cassie, even though he knew he didn't need to talk to her, it would only hurt him more and it was only stupid hope she would think to call him anyway.

He felt the need to apologize to her. Maybe that would help the empty void in his heart to heal, but he didn't hear from either of them, no call ever came. Several months later, Clay packed his things and headed back out to Texas. Then he moved three more times before William caught up to him again.

"I've been trying to track you down." William said as he laughed. "If I didn't know any better, I'd think you were hiding from someone. You certainly know how to keep a low profile."

"Same stuff, moving around, keeping busy on the road." Clay was surprised but he didn't feel as much anger towards his brother as he had. It subsided to numbness, time was a healing factor.

"It's been months, Mom said you finally called and I got your number from her. I have some great news."

Here it was, Clay thought to himself, the news he'd been waiting for. He and Cassie would be living happily ever after and he could pretend to be so excited. Clay took a deep breath and closed his eyes, after all this time and he still dreamed something drastic would happen. Wasn't sure what it could possibly be, but held hope that things would work out somehow, for him, not William. But that was not to be the case.

"Cassie and I have worked things out, we're getting married."

The words shot through him, tore straight ahead to his heart, took away all hope. "Great," he managed to get out. Maybe he would move to Indiana, he'd never been there. It was an odd thought and Clay wasn't sure why he thought it at that particular moment, but before William spoke again it was already settled, he would move to Indiana.

"The wedding's in a month, and I want you to be my best man."

Clay looked out his window to the woods beyond, a deer and her fawn grazed on the edge. "I'm a little busy, William, I'm moving to Indiana."

"Indiana?" William questioned with surprise. "Why Indiana?"

"Some things there I want to get involved in. There's a city there that will be booming soon, it's as good a place as any."

"Haven't you made enough money yet?" William knew his brother was wealthy, he may not have a college degree, the only way his father thought one could make an honest living, but he'd proved him wrong. Clay was worth a hefty sum.

"It isn't about the money." Clay answered honestly. "Being settled is you, Will, what you were cut out for. I'm of a different stock."

"Are you going to leave me the only one in the family to give mother the grandchildren she's been screaming about?"

"I can't ever see them from me, isn't something that's in my future."

"Still looking for the perfect one?"

"No, I've given up on that." Clay had grabbed a beer from the fridge, now finished it quickly, didn't like the conversation that centered on him.

"Maybe as crazed as Cassie was when she dragged you onto that ship, left you with scars that make you leery of all women."

William laughed and Clay pretended to also. The scars were far different than what he spoke of. "Yeah, maybe."

"She wants to get married in her hometown, and even my mother and hers are agreeing to everything, so it's turning into the kind of day she wanted from the start."

"I'm happy for you," he lied. "I wish you the best, but don't count on me to be there."

"It's important to me, Clay." William's tone pleaded. "The last thing I'll ever ask of you, I swear."

****

After Hawaii, William was so attentive and supportive of anything she wanted, she eventually fell back into planning her wedding as if nothing happened. Too numb to think about what she was doing, too confused to make any drastic changes in her life, so she went along with every suggestion William made to where their life was concerned. They picked out a new place to buy, planned a honeymoon to Bermuda, and she had full reign over all wedding plans.

Cassie made simple plans. If no one approved, out of fear, no one said a word because they were afraid they would run off and really get married elsewhere. All that was said upon their return was they had second thoughts about eloping and decided on the traditional affair. No questions were asked, and nothing volunteered about what actually happened.

Cassie didn't talk about it to anyone, didn't even want to think about it herself. Every time she did mixed emotions sent her haywire and it was now as if it were some surreal dream from a distant life, a distant place. She told herself anything she might have felt for Clay was the result of circumstances, the result of believing William had cheated on her. Truly believed now that her flirting and desire for him had more to do with wanting to feel wanted as a woman, at a time she felt rejected.

Certainly real feelings weren't involved. She'd known William and planned her life with him over more than a year's time, certainly one stranger she spent a week with meant nothing to her. She questioned that once more when William informed her he would once again act as best man.

Cassie was packing for their honeymoon, wanted to get everything prepared in the few days they had left so last minute things wouldn't turn into chaos. Plus she wanted to be ready, everything organized and planned and all she had to do was relax and look forward to the day there was nothing to take care of. No phone calls, no choices, no arrangements, for the moment, it was the immediate goal ahead of her.

"I called Clay, he'll come." William said as he sat down on the bed. "He's going to be my best man again."

"I'm surprised. I would have thought the last time was enough to send him running for the hills," she continued to fold clothes neatly as if the name didn't cause her stomach to flip.

"I haven't brought this up, I don't know why, but there is something I want to tell you about Clay." William seemed fidgety and nervous. He wanted no secrets, and although he hadn't meant to keep it a secret, there really was no reason to, it seemed that way now.

"What's that?" She asked as she continued her task without missing a beat.

"He's my brother."

Cassie stopped packing, the skirt set she held in her hands remained there just above the suitcase she was about to put it in as she turned her head to face him. "Your brother?"

"I should have explained earlier, but we've been so busy with the plans and all. It didn't really cross my mind until now."

"How can he be your brother? How can I not have known you even had a brother?" She felt deceived by the news, as if they had conspired against her somehow.

"We have the same mother, but Clay never really got along with my father, his stepfather. Dad always wanted him to go to college, get a nice job in business, but Clay had other things in mind and they clashed. My dad didn't welcome him at all, so he never even came to visit unless dad was out of town..."

William tried to read a reaction, but couldn't. If he had to describe it, it would be shock and he continued talking, his voice on edge with nerves. "...He moves around quite a bit, but we've kept in touch over the years and I never really talked about him I guess out of habit. I couldn't talk about him at home because my father would get upset, so I never mentioned it to you. It just never came up, and I didn't think about it, till now."

She placed the clothes she held in her hand in the suitcase then left him alone in the room. Cassie felt angry, but wasn't sure why. Felt she'd been lied to, by William for not telling her until now, and by Clay who hadn't revealed his true relationship the entire time they were together. It also crossed her mind that his loyalties were even deeper to William than she'd originally presumed. Was it possible he had lied to her? The two of them conspired from the beginning to set the entire thing up for her to trust him? Then when he told her it was his girl she would be more likely to believe him?

Had it been a lie? Had William slept with someone else the eve of their wedding day? Had Clay felt nothing for her? Simply acted to gain her trust on his brother's behalf? She didn't know what to think, what to believe. Just when Cassie had gotten to a comfortable point after the Vegas incident, just when her mind seemed to filter everything through and make some sort of sense in her head, this was revealed and everything seemed to explode.

Did the revelation really mean anything? Friend or brother, would it have made a difference? Cassie made coffee, it was the only thing she could think to do, and with each second that passed her fears and anger grew. Her mind had to decipher again the events. Consider any meaning their true relationship might have in the scheme of things, and she kept returning to one crucial point. Was their bond so strong Clay would have done anything to save William the heartbreak of surely losing her?

Pretend to care for her? Gain her trust? Had it been a game for Clay the entire time? Had it all been a game the two of them had won? Had they laughed afterwards at how easy it had been for them to dupe her?

Cassie compared it to her relationship with Mel. Even though they weren't as emotionally close as they'd once been, would she lie for her? Would she deceive another if Mel begged her to? Cassie couldn't answer the question for herself. Different circumstances perhaps, maybe the same circumstances, she couldn't honestly be sure. And she couldn't answer the question for the two brothers. The only thing she knew for sure at that moment was that she was mad as hell.

She couldn't look at William and not want to throw something. How dare he put her in this position? Just when she thought everything would come off smoothly, a beautiful day planned to begin their married life and he threw this at her. Uncertainties now overwhelmed her.

William found her in the kitchen making a pot of coffee. She almost broke the glass container when she shoved it under the coffee maker and she didn't look at him when she spoke.

"Don't expect me to talk to you for a few days. Right now I feel like the both of you laughed behind my back when I ran off with him thinking it would make you jealous. And I'm trying to figure out what was real and what wasn't? How am I to be sure it wasn't all planned from the first day for him to set it up so that I'd believe him when he told me it was his girl? That you hadn't been unfaithful."

"Cassie, this shouldn't change things. Everything that happened was as I said, what Clay told you. Having him there with you was the only way I survived that grueling week. I knew he'd watch out for you and not let you do anything stupid." William still felt the pang of guilt when he thought about that week, still owed Clay everything for making it right.

"Shouldn't change things? I'm beginning to think it was your girl in that room and it was all a set up for you to hang on to me. He's your brother, he would have lied for you."

"We've gotten past all this." William saw the look in her eye, the hesitation and question that haunted him and scared him now.

"Right now I feel like I was manipulated."

"Cassie," he tried to put his arms around her but she jerked away from him.

"Don't talk to me." She went into her small office and slammed the door.

Cassie's mind whirled. What angered her more? The thought that it was possible William had been unfaithful? Or the thought that Clay, someone she felt she'd grown fond of, represented nothing but deceit and lies. And it was so short a week, so little time, what made her think she would know anything about him at all? As she thought back now, it could have all been a sham. The way he ingratiated himself to her, the way he came to know what she wanted with her breakfast, knew she liked the cinnamon syrup with her pancakes. She had discovered it was him that sent the orchids to the suite and not Hernandez. The way he'd covered her with his shirt to protect her from the sudden rain that appeared one day, or seemed to know instinctively when she was chilled.

There were other little things that she once thought meant Clay cared about her more than he wanted to admit to himself or her. Now the realization it was all a farce, a lie to coerce her, sent her into a fury.

She'd been in a vulnerable position and his attention to her needs set him up to be the perfect gentleman. One she could trust who looked out for her best interests, it's the way she'd come to think of him anyway. Maybe the way he'd planned for her to think. Then the intimacy, she desired him, wanted him desperately. Even now, remembered the way his naked body felt against hers, the way his eyes filled with the same desire when she touched him.

Cassie felt duped. She'd thrown herself at him like a desperate, needy woman, only to be rejected because he'd played her, set her up, and she fell for it. He probably now laughed to himself how easy it had been. Clay had experience with women, knew the right buttons to push, the right things to say and do. Like strumming a guitar he pulled strings and women thought they heard music. She'd been led exactly where he wanted to lead her, and she'd followed along without a second glance backwards.

But she remembered catching the look in his eyes as he stared at her when he thought she didn't notice. She wasn't a stupid woman, Cassie knew he truly yearned for her also, she was sure of it, even if only sexually. Her vivid memory let her think of it then, the tender way he'd touched her, the way he gazed at her, and she was confident it had been a look that was one of sincere desire. When it came to sexual attraction, it was difficult for a man to hide true emotions.

Knowing what she did now, it was only because he was William's brother he didn't act on his desire for her. So he had a blood loyalty to William, one could commend him for that, but it didn't stop his want for her. He simply didn't act on his want for her, had he been only a friend as she believed, she knew he wouldn't have held back, even if it would have cost a friendship. But that wasn't the case and he didn't risk losing his blood tie, had the morals and values to know where to stop.

The thought of it forced her to go shopping and purchase a few new dresses, a little more revealing than what she'd previously packed, the kind she knew Clay liked, the kind that took his breath away.

Let him desire his brother's wife, a woman he'd never have. Where William was concerned, she'd have to trust him, either that, or live the rest of her life with question which she wasn't prepared to do. So she took it as truth he hadn't been unfaithful, and the wedding would go on as planned. But in her own way, she prepared to get back at Clay for what she believed he'd done to her, a small quiet revenge.

CHAPTER FOURTEEN

A small wedding and reception would take place at Crystal Lake Resort. The days passed quickly as the wedding loomed directly in front of her, and Cassie didn't get nervous when she thought about the wedding day, she got nervous when she thought about being face to face with Clay. The thought caused anger, pain, regret, hurt, all kinds of emotions ran havoc inside.

Maybe it wouldn't be revenge at all, maybe it wouldn't matter to him one way or the other, but for Cassie, it was a small thing to make herself feel better. Show him how happy she was in spite of his betrayal, so she looked forward to his arrival, even as she wondered how her emotions would react and survive.

With everything prepared, Cassie arrived in Lakeview a week before the wedding and checked into the Crystal Lake Resort with nothing to do but relax. It was a beautiful place on the banks of the water where the wedding and reception would take place. She spent time with family then out of town guests as they eventually began to arrive and check in also.

Her guests had taken over almost every room, and she reveled in the few days before the nuptials. Caught up with everyone and it was perfectly planned so she wouldn't have to stress about doing so on her wedding day when so little time would be available. Even William's parents were impressed with what the small town had to offer.

"I had my doubts, but I think this is impressive."

Cassie had never known his mother to admit being wrong about anything. She said nothing else, only smiled in triumph. Cassie's mother and William's seemed to be on the surface from opposite ends of the earth, but when they met, you'd have thought they were two of the same. She'd previously worried about how the two would get along, worried more about her mothers feelings getting hurt over something, but the two women could have been old friends instead of new.

William's mother seemed sincerely interested in tales of Lakeview and its slow paced life as Cassie's mother droned on about things even she found uninteresting. But his mother absorbed every word with earnest attention.

"I came from a small town myself." Jill said with fondness.

Cassie hadn't known that about her. Thought she was the type born and raised in the city life. Just went to prove her point that she wasn't an expert on people.

"Of course Redman loves the city life, so I've settled into that." Jill continued and looked around. "But maybe I could talk him into summers here. I think he'd like it if he gave it a chance. He'd rather fly all over the world to strange countries though, when we could have something like this."

"Have you been to many different places?" Cassie's mother Helen questioned with interest. She'd only been to a few places along the east coast, nothing exotic.

"Redman loves to travel. Most of the Caribbean, we go to Europe on occasion, always someplace different. If I didn't know better, I'd think somehow Clay got his traveling fever from him, but they had different fathers and we didn't travel much when the boys were young."

"Clay travels a lot also?"

Helen asked the question with innocence and Cassie wished they could pick another subject, but she appeared interested.

"Works all over. Wish he'd settle down somewhere and make me a grandmother, but I think that's going to be up to William and Cassie."

Great, she thought to herself. It would be her responsibility to make his mother happy. "In time, we're not rushing it." Cassie said with a smile.

"What does he do that he works all over?"

Cassie wished her mother wouldn't be so genuinely interested in someone she didn't know, wished they would change the subject but they went on and she was about to make her escape.

"He builds houses, fixes them, rents them, sells them. I don't know, something to do with houses, I think a little of everything. He's very successful at it." Jill said it with a proud smile. She loved both her sons equally even if she saw him quite a bit less than William.

"And he's your older son? Not married and no children?"

Helen droned on and Cassie was about to leave when Jill got a wonderful idea and grabbed her arm. "Cassie dear, surely you have a nice young single friend you invited to the wedding that would be interested in a handsome, wealthy man."

She pretended to think about her question. "I'll have to think about that one, most of our friends are married."

"He's a pretty irresistible catch, but it would take the right girl to catch him."

Yeah, she thought, he was irresistible all right. And any girl who could catch him should stay out of Vegas where she imagined Clay looked at the city like a candy store.

She finally got away from them and the conversation and joined Redman at the banister overlooking the lake. Cassie had never felt close to him, William's father was the type of man who kept his distance, held his pretenses high and mighty. She suspected he liked her, but he wasn't the type to display much emotion, so she was never really sure how he felt about her.

Whereas she felt comfortable calling Jill by her first name, she always addressed him properly. "Thinking about fishing tomorrow, Mr. Sampson?"

"I'm not going with the others, I'm taking in a round of golf."

"The fishing should be great this time of year." She smiled but his face remained like stone.

"I've never been fond of the sport." He stood tall, close to six feet, but seemed much taller than that. "When are William and the other one arriving?"

"The other one?" Cassie's mistake was made honestly, she thought it an odd choice of words, didn't understand who he spoke of, then it dawned on her. "Clay?"

"When will they be here?"

"They should be here in about an hour or so."

William had explained more of Clay and his stepfather to her even though she hadn't asked about it. He felt his father held it against Clay because his mother always held such strong feelings for her first husband. Then Redman took it as a personal affront when he'd tried to help him go to college and do what was expected, told Clay he'd never make a decent living and Clay proved him wrong.

With nothing but a high school education and hard work, he was probably worth a ton more than Redman Sampson. William thought that was what was so unacceptable to him more than anything. Redman called it luck, waited for him to blast through his money foolishly and come crawling back to him for help.

Most of the guests that afternoon were the older generation and Cassie was delighted when Susan and Mark arrived after she'd gotten someone to cover for her at the deli for the rest of the day.

"My, my." Mark whistled when he approached her. "Can you take Susan shopping with you?"

"Susan knows how to shop, she looks beautiful." Cassie defended her friend but knew Mark just teased.

Susan hugged her in greeting. "Beautiful is one thing, you look like a knock out. How can you take an afternoon party dress and make it look so sexy? Simple white linen has never looked like that on me." Susan held Cassie's hands outward, as she seemed to inspect and nod her approval. "Its simple linen, but the way it's cut, the way it fits on you, how do you make it look like that?"

"I just slipped it on, but thanks."

"William is one lucky groom." Mark commented and hugged her. "If I hadn't of fallen in love with Susan when I was eight, you would have been second place, but since I fell in love with her, there is no other place, she fills them all."

Her dress was cream colored and fitted to every curve just above her knees, wide straps at the shoulders, then plunged down her chest just enough that she looked completely covered, yet a hint of her sexiness was revealed. She'd worked on a tan and her bronze skin was moisturized and soft.

"I can't wait to see what the wedding dress looks like. Even Mel said it was the most stunning thing she'd ever seen on you."

"Mel paid me a compliment?" Cassie raised her eyebrows.

"Of her own free will."

"So where is the lucky groom? I want to finally see if he's up to my standards, you know this wedding won't take place unless I approve of him, don't you?" Mark teased and looked around. "I have to have someone to fish with when you come to town to play with Susan."

"He should be here shortly." Cassie looked around but didn't see him yet and she glanced at her watch, knew it shouldn't be long.

"I can't tell you how anxious Mark has been to finally meet him."

"And how angry I am that I haven't met him before now. This hurts me, Cassie, I'm like your big brother, shouldn't I have had a say in this big decision of yours?"

Cassie laughed and put her arm around him. "You had a say that time you talked me into racing you on the lake when we weren't supposed to take the Sea Doo's out by ourselves, I was on restriction for a year."

"I think we're even, you got me back many more times, I think you enjoyed that restriction for a year just to think of the ways to get me back." Mark kissed her cheek with affection then kissed his wife with love. "You two beautiful ladies carry on, I have fish to talk about," then he was off to the group of guys who were going fishing the next day.

"This is so exciting, this is how the rich and famous do weddings. They party all week and it culminates on the wedding day." Susan exclaimed as she looked around.

"Well we aren't rich or famous. It just happened to work out well this way."

Cassie looked out to the crowd also. It had been a good week so far, several luncheons, dinners, outings. She enjoyed meeting and getting to know some friends of William's family she hadn't before. She enjoyed watching her family and his intermingle and truly enjoy each other.

"Even Mel is excited by all this."

"She is?" Cassie looked at her.

"Seems to be. Every time I talk to her she mentions something about it, but it isn't in a nasty way. I think she's really happy for you."

Cassie wondered why she hadn't seen it. Then again, she'd automatically assumed Mel would be her bitchy self throughout the whole affair and didn't get around her much, didn't want her to bring down her mood, she already had enough on her mind.

"Maybe because you asked her to be your maid of honor." Susan continued. "Maybe she realized how much she does mean to you, since she probably feels like she means shit to her husband. I think she was really surprised. It was actually her idea to have our little traditional boat party tonight."

Cassie laughed. "Yeah, she probably wants to throw me over."

"I think something's going on with her, I think she might be waking up." Susan took a glass of wine from the offered tray when someone came around. "Like Rip Van Winkle. She'll wake up, divorce Eddy, and be a new person in a new world."

Cassie looked over towards Mel who talked to a few people, seemed to be enjoying herself, but she always did with others, it was only their private moments that seemed strained.

Others joined them and as Cassie slipped out of the crowd, she whispered to Susan. "You're in charge of the wine for the boat party. I'll have to mingle so if I don't see you again, we'll meet at 11:45."

When William and Clay arrived, she noticed Redman leave. A quick moment of sympathy for Clay passed before she greeted them with her arms open to her fiancé'. "Hey you." Cassie put her arms around him and kissed him tenderly. "Did you have to make me wait all day?"

"I couldn't get out any earlier." He pulled away a little and admired her. "But I should have."

"We've been without each other a few days now, did you forget what I looked like?" She teased, noticed Clay glance at her then away.

Cassie kissed William again then approached Clay when others joined them to welcome her fiancé'. She greeted him with a kiss on the cheek, just as she did others, but lingered against his chest for just a brief moment, her voice a soft whisper so they wouldn't be overheard. "Hello, Clay. Just to start the festivities out right, I want to say there are no hard feelings. Everything turned out for the best after all."

His eyes bore into her soul but she could read nothing in them. "Looks like they did."

Cassie wasn't prepared for the sight of him, the emotions that surfaced, but she easily smiled unaffected. "Grab a drink, there's much to celebrate."

Jill, their mother, was ecstatic to see him. Cassie thought she saw tears in her eyes when she hugged Clay but she turned away before it softened her hatred for him. On the other hand, when Redman returned to the party from somewhere unknown, he made it a point to greet William and made it a point to stay away from Clay.

Both men were equally as handsome, but in so many different ways. William was tall, dark blond hair, brown eyed. Quiet in his manner, mostly dressed in pressed clothes, suits for most occasions including work. He now created an impressive presence in a black double-breasted suit with black tie.

Clay was equally as tall, dark hair, blue eyes. He looked more rugged and muscular, tan skin from working outdoors and was opposite in personality, there was a charisma about him, open and conversational with anyone. And his choice of attire that evening was a nice pair of black pants with only a crisp white shirt. His sleeves now rolled up and the top few buttons undone.

She heard his laughter as he stood with a group of older men and looked up at the same time he glanced up. His smile faded slightly and he went back to his conversation. It seemed Clay had made quick friends of those there, both young and old, and William seemed to center around most of his own business friends.

Cassie found herself subconsciously comparing the two. For what purpose she didn't know, other than she found it interesting and odd how opposite they seemed to be now that she saw them together in the same atmosphere.

She'd been sitting with Marie at a table, discussing her latest crush that happened to be the son of friends of hers who would be at the wedding and he would attend also.

"How should I wear my hair? I wonder if mom will let me wear a little makeup." The girl worried already about how she would look.

"Of course she will." Then Cassie realized she hadn't seen Eddy all day. Not that she missed him not being there, but she wondered where he was. "Where's your father?"

Marie shrugged her shoulders. "Who knows? How about I wear my hair up? Maybe with curls?" She pulled her hair up and looked to Cassie for opinion.

"Marie, we will have someone to do all of our hair, and our makeup, those aren't things you have to worry about."

"Really?" She squealed.

"Absolutely." Cassie laughed at her pleasure.

"This is the coolest wedding. When I get married, I want to get married like this. All my friends are jealous, they all want a cool aunt like you. The whole town is talking about this."

"Of course they are. It's a small town, there's not much to talk about with tourist season over."

"Hey, Cassie." Susan's husband Mark shouted to her from the crowd Clay was a part of. "Remember that time you got your tongue stuck on the freezer case?"

"Mark!" She exclaimed. "Why are you telling my embarrassing moments to everyone?"

"We were just talking about old times."

Marie looked up to her and laughed. "You got your tongue stuck on the freezer case?"

"I was reaching in the back for something and my tongue came out while I was stretching and it got stuck there," she explained herself.

The group seemed to congregate towards them now to hear her explanation, they laughed and continued to talk of it, and Cassie glanced up to see Clay enjoying it as he leaned against the deck railing.

Mark acted out how she stood there with her tongue out. "I can't remember, how did we get it unstuck?"

"I think you poured a gallon of water on me," she leaned back with a coy smile. "If you're going to tell my moments, have you told everyone about the time you got your pants stuck on something in the lake and had to take them off to come out of the water?"

"Oh yeah." One in the group recalled it also. "And you had to sneak home. Old Mr. Kerry saw you behind the bushes in his yard and thought you were a pervert after his daughter. Chased you three blocks with a broom."

"Straight down Main Street, there was Mark in all his glory." Cassie laughed so hard she almost fell out of her chair, leaned against Susan who came to stand next to her.

Several others went on with their own childhood stories they remembered, it wasn't often all of them got together, as most had families now that needed their attention. The group of them talked and laughed well into the night, and it was only the younger crowd that remained outdoors. The older generation had gone inside to relax on the comfortable sofas in the library. Some played chess, read books, enjoyed a cigar or a few more glasses of wine as the fall night air began to get a chill.

When Cassie looked around for William she remembered seeing him go inside earlier, and she was about to rise to find her light sweater when she saw an arm to her side that held it, and she looked up to see Clay.

"Need this?"

"Thanks." Cassie took it from him and wrapped it around her shoulders.

"Hey, Aunt Cassie, mom said I could go with Clay and some others tomorrow afternoon on the Sea Doo's."

"She offered to show me around." Clay said.

"Mr. Mark's bringing Ellie." Marie smiled at the prospect of such fun after school.

Cassie became uncomfortable with the thought that Clay made himself right at home as if he belonged, but she didn't say anything, just smiled as if it were a great idea. Then Mel came over and gave Marie the bad news that her evening was over.

"Just a little while longer, Mom?" She pleaded but was denied.

"Not tonight, maybe tomorrow you can stay up later."

"Good night." Marie said and kissed Cassie before she left then turned to Clay a few feet away. "I'll be here at three, you won't leave without me, will you?"

"Not a chance," he assured her with a broad smile.

"That's nice of you to take her." Cassie said when they walked away.

"I'm looking forward to it, Marie seems to be a great little girl, and the invitation from Mark was an offer I couldn't refuse."

"She's the best. You seem to have made quick friends, I should have known you'd be one guest I didn't have to worry about fitting in." Cassie wasn't sure why it irritated her, but she kept the irritation from her voice.

"I adapt well." It came from his moving around and becoming comfortable with strangers and new places. He didn't elaborate on how comfortable he felt there, how at ease he was with these people he too could have known for all his life.

"Mel, you're going tonight, aren't you?" Judy, one of the women in the group asked when she noticed Mel leaving, and Mel answered with a smile.

"I'll be there."

"Be where?" One of the men asked.

Mark looked to Susan. "I knew it. I knew it when you said it was going to be a late night for you. This is the night, isn't it?"

"The night for what?" The man kept asking for answers to his confusion.

Mark answered as he shook his head with confusion. "No one knows. A secret tradition with these women, every time there's a wedding these girls go somewhere, but no one knows where, all I know is they come home drunk and smelling like fish."

"Probably down at Boater's." Someone mentioned a bar they frequented at times.

"Nope, it isn't any place public. No one ever sees them out, believe me, we've scoured for answers to questions the next day and it's like they literally disappear for the night." Mark answered and looked to Susan who smiled. Knew she, nor the others, would ever reveal it.

Eventually, everyone wandered to the inside and Cassie found William in conversation with his father and a few of his friends whose wives had gone to bed. Cassie tried to make them feel a part of everything, but the business wives tended to stick together in a pack. She sensed they didn't particularly feel comfortable around a boisterous crowd that talked of naked kids being chased down Main Street.

She sat on the edge of his chair and put her arm around him, he looked up and smiled and she stopped herself from kissing him. His father didn't believe in open affection of any sort. She'd never seen he and Jill even put their arms around each other, or hold hands, and William was a firm believer in his father's ways. When Redman's attention was drawn to conversation she whispered she was leaving and kissed him anyway.

Cassie changed into a pair of jeans and a black shirt then finished wrapping her gift box and saw no one as she stepped quietly outside, off the deck and stood in the grass area for awhile. She was a little early, would take a few quiet moments, then would go out front to meet Mel and Susan when it was time, then they would pick up the others along the way.

She looked out over the lake she'd grown up on and took a deep breath. Cassie remembered herself as a child who once worked at the Resort busing tables one busy summer. Often saw weddings and parties there but never dreamed she would be like one of the beautiful people one day. As a child, it was too grandiose to imagine, the most expensive place on the lake, but as an adult, she and William could afford to begin their life there. It would have to be her compromise since she couldn't live there.

"Nice night." Clay said from behind her and Cassie swung around.

"Usually is in the fall."

"One of your favorite times of the year here, isn't it?"

Cassie looked at him in the darkness but his eyes remained focused across the calm lake. "Maybe."

Clay wondered if William knew her like he did, if he could sense the things he could about her. "Thinking about what you're giving up?"

It angered her to think he knew what she was thinking, but her voice didn't reveal displeasure, only calm sweetness. "I'm not giving up anything."

"No? Did William decide he wants this little town life after all? Congratulations for convincing him. I didn't know you bought that house at Cape Point, I thought he said you purchased in Virginia."

Cassie smiled casually. "Don't pretend to know me, Clay. We spent a week together and I voiced some ideas, some notions that I once thought about. But if you knew me at all, you'd know how happy I was to marry William and live our life the best way possible for both of us."

"You mean the best way possible for William," he stated. "So you've officially joined the rest of society. Cast aside what others classify as foolish notions for the safe, boring life."

"What have those foolish notions got you? You move from place to place, woman to woman, and you want to make me feel guilty for wanting something secure in my life?" She turned to him fully now. "Does that make you happy? Running from town to town?"

"It's irrelevant."

"Is it? You want to tell me what's right and wrong in my life, how I'm feeling, yet you don't want to talk of your own?"

"Fair enough," he said. "Yes, it's made me happy, and it's the way I've chosen to live, that's the difference in us. It's a conscious choice I've made for myself, and yes, I've been extremely happy with it." He didn't lie, and he thought at one time it was everything he would ever need until he'd met her, the one thing he could never have and couldn't even pursue.

"I have what I want, Clay, William makes me happy."

"Are you sure about that?" Clay had moved close as he talked, now he placed his mouth to just within her reach, tested her.

"Of course I'm sure."

"Then why is your hand in mine?"

Cassie hadn't even noticed, didn't even know how it had gotten there but she quickly pulled it away. William didn't have to be there, it was as if he was physically there between them anyway, and she felt a tinge of guilt.

She was like jelly on the inside, but her voice solid. "If I weren't sure, the two of us wouldn't be standing here right now, would we? We are here for my wedding, or had you forgotten? And it won't be a safe boring life. Didn't you learn anything about me? I would think you'd know that I might be able to find a few ways to spice it up on occasion."

"That I have no doubt of."

They stood dangerously close and Cassie felt like she had to remind both of them the roles they would serve in their lives now. "You're to be my brother in law."

"A fact I'm well aware of."

They'd been in complete darkness, there was no fear of anyone seeing and she'd put up a solid stone front. But as she walked away, clutching her beautifully wrapped present of her past, only she knew her inside was jelly.

CHAPTER FIFTEEN

The woods were quiet as six women stealthily moved along an old path towards the water. Hardly a branch cracked, all of them adept at moving without a sound. No one said a word as they reached their destination, climbed into the large old wood fishing boat that belonged to Susan's father with their supplies of blankets and wine and easily rowed out to the middle of lake.

When they stopped, in unison, they all seemed to let out a giggle. Wine was poured and blankets dispersed to ward off the chill.

"It's cold tonight." Judy said as she took two blankets.

Cassie teased. "No complaints from you, you got married in the very middle of winter and all of us were still frozen when we walked with you down the aisle."

"We drank hot toddy's that night." Judy defended.

"But wine tonight." Susan cheered.

"Well, Cassie, this makes it official, are you ready?" One of the women handed her the first glass.

Cassie looked to the beautiful gift on her lap, her thoughts still a jumbled mess inside after the encounter with Clay, and thought she'd be more ready after she threw it in. It was a tradition, the intended bride would pick something of her past, weight it so it would sink, and wrapped it. What was inside would remain a secret as it was thrown into the lake.

Cassie remembered Mel revealed what hers was many years ago and they all laughed. It had been her birth control pills because she was already pregnant.

"I guess I'm as ready as I'll ever be." Her voice sounded unsure.

"Sounds like it's starting to hit you. Everything's fine for so long, you run around planning, doing things, don't even think about it. Then when time slips away and it gets close and you stop to think about it, that's when the reservations come."

"All of you had reservations?" She asked, shocked. "No one ever told me about reservations. It's normal to think you might be making a mistake?"

"Is that what you're thinking?"

Cassie sighed. "Well, not exactly a mistake, making the change is a better term."

"Of course it's normal. He's thinking it too. Not only is it normal, it's natural. You're changing your entire life and it's the biggest step you'll ever take. Not thinking about it and just leaping in is irrational."

Judy raised her glass. "But I have to say, you're doing it with class. This week has been so much fun I don't even want the wedding day to come."

And it would be here soon, Cassie thought. She'd felt in limbo during the festivities, as if life could continue in the same manner. But it would culminate only two days from then. In the darkness, no one noticed when Cassie quietly held her hand over the side of the boat and watched as she let her little pretty box with silver bow slip out of her fingers and disappear into the murky unknown of the water. She knew it was foolish to think some magic was performed by it, but the action seemed to give her strength.

Then she raised her glass. "A toast, to an official goodbye to the past."

"You let it go." Susan exclaimed and looked to her empty lap where it had previously been. "No ceremony, no hoopla, you just let it go."

"Seemed to be the easiest way to do it, if not, I might have made it more important than it was." Cassie thought about the dried flower from the Ohia tree in Hawaii that represented new life. She remembered clearly, more vividly than she cared to, the day he placed it in her hair on top of the mountain in some other dreamlike world. Remembered with great detail how tenderly he'd placed it there behind her ear, how his eyes unknowingly pulled her in to him, and the way her heart and stomach lurched at his mere gaze. It seemed the most appropriate thing to use, put her farce honeymoon behind her, put Clay behind her, let it all rest in the murky waters at the bottom of the lake.

Mel held her glass in the air. "Now a toast to what lay ahead."

The two sisters locked eyes and looked to each other. Cassie seemed to read sympathy intended towards her, there was a look of sorrow for the road she was about to embark upon and it confused her. Mel was jealous of her life, now looked to her with pity.

"There's kind of a freedom of letting go of something of the past, isn't there?" Cassie sipped the wine and looked out over the lake towards the distant lights of the resort.

"It's liberating." Mel commented. "Was for me when I let go of my birth control, nothing I could do about it then, and it was kind of like an official acceptance."

Cassie thought of it with sadness, Hawaii was like a different life to her, her attitude then was of a different person, one who had freedoms before her, choices to make. How was she to know at the time it had all been make believe?

The woman drank, laughed and talked quietly of their lives. Their past as children growing up together, their futures, and how their lives had changed. Responsibility of families, or distance in miles had separated them and though they no longer gathered on a frequent basis, it only made their time together that much more special.

No one wanted it to end but at the first sign of changing sky, they knew they had to get back to shore before sunrise. Judy and Susan rowed as Cassie concentrated on carving her name and the date among the others who had before her. As she looked to each one she remembered every night over the years.

"This would be easier to do if I'd done it before all the wine." Cassie finally finished and looked to Susan's carving and laughed. "Mine looks better than Susan's though, you'd have been better off putting a big X, your name is spread out over the entire bench."

"I had to write big, I could barely write at all." Susan remembered with a laugh.

Then she noticed both of Judy's, due to divorce, she had two. Mel mentioned it and told her if she ever got married again, they might have to get a new boat, and Judy promised it wouldn't happen, her husband wouldn't be able to get rid of her if he tried. Which they all knew he wouldn't, Ben was so in love with her it made them all jealous at times. As they got out of the boat, Cassie fell face first into the muddy shore of the water and rose looking like a swamp monster. Mud covered her head to toe and everyone doubled over in laughter. They used the blankets to get as much off as they could then saved a dry one to wrap her in.

Everyone had been dropped off back at their homes, only Mel and Cassie remained as Mel would drop her off at the Resort and return to her own home.

"Want me to help you inside?" Mel asked when she pulled up to the front. Cassie had consumed quite a bit of wine, more than she'd ever seen her drink before, and still held the last remaining bottle in her hand, even swigged it along the way.

Cassie laughed. "I might be able to manage, I just hope William is asleep so I don't have to explain why I look like I was mud wrestling."

Mel giggled. "At least you'll be able to sleep all day if you want. I'll only have till noon."

"Can I have until noon next week?"

"You'd miss your wedding." Mel looked at her with a serious expression. "You okay? I've never seen you drink this much."

"Probably because I've never drank this much before, then again, I've never gotten married before. I'm fine, other than just the thought of the hangover I'll have tomorrow is already making me ill." Cassie opened the door and almost fell out of the car, just as she did the boat and they laughed again. "I'm already anticipating my hangover tomorrow and I only have one bottle of aspirin. Can you bring me more when you come?" She stood with the door open and leaned back inside across the seat, took the opportunity for a sentimental moment. "You know I love you, don't you Mel?"

Her sister looked at her softly. Wanted to joke she said it because she was drunk, but she knew it was truth drunk or sober. "Yeah, I know, Cassie. I love you too."

Cassie's voice got so low Mel almost didn't hear her. "Bring aspirin, lot's of aspirin."

She was about to go in the front door and decided against it. Not only did she see some staff preparing the continental breakfast table through the salon window, but her journey up to her room would be longer and she would track mud along the way. If she went to the back, she would only have to go down one hall and up the back stairs, besides, she figured the walk along the grass would probably remove the majority of dirt from her squeaky wet tennis shoes.

She didn't see anyone as she crept up the back steps and onto the large deck, hadn't noticed Clay sitting at a table with coffee in his hand until she heard his soft laughter he had tried to hold back.

"If I didn't know any better, I'd say you were a swamp thing that crawled out the lake," he said.

She walked over to him with all the dignity she could muster. It was difficult with her squashy shoes, ratty old blanket, mud dried and caked along her face and mottled in her hair that stuck up in places, now stiff. She held out an offering of her wine but he declined with a shake of his head and she took a swig.

"I don't want to know what I look like, I'm going to finish this bottle of wine so when I look in the mirror it won't scare me so bad," she laughed easily and took another swig. Cassie pulled a chair around to face the direction of the lake, plopped in it, and then put her feet up on the table.

"I'd offer you coffee, but I only have one cup."

"I don't want to sober up, let me enjoy my drunkenness, and the hangover I'll have tomorrow. It will be a long time before I'll drink again, I know that already."

"I know what you mean, I used to enjoy whiskey on occasion, now the smell of it makes me violently ill."

Cassie laughed. "I guess I'm better off than you were, I can still walk without assistance."

"A matter of opinion, I saw you stumble up the steps."

Cassie remembered he was an early riser, liked to be up at dawn. It angered her she remembered so much about him and her mood shifted slightly as she took a sarcastic jab. "Sorry this little ole town isn't as wild as Vegas, guess it makes it kind of hard for you to find someone to bed when your pickings are so slim."

"Why are you so angry at me?"

"Who said I'm angry at you? I've been nothing but the most proper host, hostess, hostesses, whatever I am, I've been nothing but the most proper kind."

"That's what it appears to be on the outside, but it's not what I see on the inside."

"You can't see my insides," she quipped, then gave him truth to his words. "Besides, why shouldn't I be angry at you? You led me along, flirted, and pretended you were concerned for my well being only for the purposes of gaining my trust so I'd believe you when you told me William hadn't been unfaithful."

"Is that what you think I did?"

"Isn't it?" She looked at him and raised her eyebrows.

It hadn't really been planned that way, but when he looked back he could see how she would think so. There was no sense explaining, let her think what she would.

"You haven't denied it." Cassie pressed.

"Would it make a difference whether I denied it or not? You're still going to believe what you want."

"Is there something else I should believe?"

"No," he said softly, with William first in his mind. He pictured the way he looked at Cassie, the way he talked about her, he loved her there was no doubt.

"You could have disagreed, pretended I meant something to you, at least as a friend. I won't remember in the morning anyway." She rose from her seat, finished the last swig of the bottle and set it on the table with much pomp and circumstance as her arm flew out. "Ta Da. Now I'll go officially start the process of my hangover."

"Goodnight, Cassie."

"Yeah, a good night, with hell to pay in the morning," she mumbled and scuffed away, her squishy wet shoes the only noise in early dawn.

Cassie passed a few of William's friends who would be going fishing that morning. They'd been told of the secret tradition of women and knew she'd been out, now stood with gaping mouths even more perplexed than before.

"Have a good day boy's." She smiled broadly as if she looked her best.

****

Cassie slept a good portion of the next day. William only laughed when he saw her that morning, started to ask about her appearance, then thought better of it, he knew she wouldn't tell him anyway and he went off to play golf. Most all of the guests would take the day to do as they pleased. There were no parties, no luncheons, and Cassie thanked Mel silently, would remember to thank her in person for choosing the evening she did.

By early afternoon she was ready to shower again and get dressed for the day. Cassie chose a simple pair of black capri pants and a black top. Nothing but gold earrings for jewelry and her hair was just as she'd blown it dry, she hadn't the strength for more. When Jill mentioned her and a few others were going for a late lunch, Cassie realized she was famished and joined them. Her errands would have to wait until later but it worked out perfectly, she lunched with them, and then had the water taxi drop her off in town as the others went back.

Instead of going straight up the hill to Main Street she stopped at the Marina Deli to see Susan first and found Clay and Mark casually sitting on the pier in the chairs in front of the door.

"Well, don't you two look like you're having a productive day?" Her sarcastic tone mixed with laughter.

"Looks can be deceiving." Mark answered as he leaned back in his chair. "It can be tough work taking two pre-teens on an outing, especially since they had to fly by every boy's house on the lake, and this is a big lake."

"Ah, I'd forgotten you were taking Marie and Ellie out. Yeah, now I have much more respect for what you accomplished."

"It wasn't as easy as it sounds." Clay piped in. "What did you do today, Cassie? Spa appointment? Mud mask treatment maybe?"

She stuck her tongue out as she passed him and went inside.

"If you've come for Marie, they're gone. She's spending the night with Ellie, didn't Mel tell you?" Susan asked from behind the counter where she was cleaning out the stainless steel bins.

"Actually I hadn't. I stopped in to see if you could pick up Ms. Nellie for the wedding, she needs a ride. Called me in hysterical tears because she thought she wouldn't be able to get there, you know how she won't take the water taxi, and she doesn't drive."

"Of course I can pick up Ms. Nellie." Susan threw her a dishrag. "Can you finish this up while I clean out the register?"

"Yeah, give me the dirty job. You have two loafers on the pier, should have had them holding this dishrag."

Susan laughed. "They offered but I refused. You know how Mark needs constant direction for anything close to domestication. They've been out there since they came back. Like two old friends since they met each other, if I didn't know any better, I'd say you were marrying the wrong brother."

Cassie closed her eyes for a brief moment and took a deep breath Susan couldn't take notice of. She didn't need verification for thoughts that crossed her mind more often than she liked and she didn't let the comment alter the tone of her voice. "Well, I guess Clay will settle down one day, if he stays in any place long enough to find someone to settle down with. Course, maybe he's looking for a wife to hit the road with him. Lot's of women like to travel, shouldn't be a problem." Her voice was casually disinterested and Susan was none the wiser to her emotions.

"He was in town all morning. Marge works at the new boutique across from the bank and said he was in there for a few hours it seemed."

"Hmm." Cassie pondered the reason and could think of none, continued to work as if she didn't think of it at all. "You still haven't told me what you're wearing to the wedding."

Just then they heard Mark's voice from outside. "Hey, Cassie, remember that time you tried to take your father's old pick up to town?"

Susan laughed and Cassie looked to her. "Why does he insist on telling all my embarrassing stories to everyone he meets?"

"Because you're the one who has the most interesting one's to tell. You were always the one who dared to do anything, while we all sat back and watched."

The window was open and Cassie took good aim before she flung the wet dishrag out of it and it landed smack against his head. They laughed, but she heard him tell Clay the story anyway of when she was ten years old and decided to take the truck for a ride. She could barely see over the steering wheel, almost stood to reach the pedals and see at the same time. She got out of their driveway, across the main road, and down the other side right into the lake. It was still there to this day.

She helped Susan clean up as quickly as she could and slapped Mark against the side of his head on her way out but didn't stop or turn around. "You'd better be careful, I'll have to tell everyone about the time you walked down Main Street in six inch spike heels. Hot pink to boot."

Clay chuckled and Mark winced as he spoke. "It was ugly. I lost a bet." Then he motioned his head towards Cassie who hadn't stopped, her back to them as she walked down the pier. "To her."

Cassie spoke loud, could easily be heard as she continued on her way. "Or how about the little puckered red lip's on your ass. Not that I'm keeping count, but don't you have three of those tattoos now?"

"You're not playing fair, you're fibbing, delirious from all the champagne you've been drinking this week." Mark tried to act as if she'd been mistaken but it was no use. Clay looked at him and he confessed. "She won again. It's ugly, don't ask."

CHAPTER SIXTEEN

Cassie did a few errands. Picked up some last minute small items for the honeymoon and stopped into one of the newer boutique stores and purchased a small book for any beach reading she might do. No parties or festivities had been planned for that day or evening, everyone had it to enjoy as they wished and she knew William was probably not back from golfing so she decided to walk to her parents to say a quick hello. Then she almost literally ran into Clay in the town square.

"I thought you'd already gone back to the resort," she said.

"Had to pick something up but I'm going back now, taking the next water taxi across." He held a large envelope in his hand but there was no indication of what it was and he didn't say. "You headed back now?"

"No, I'll be a little while longer."

Clay noticed the streetlights coming on. "It's getting late, want me to wait for you?"

Cassie laughed. "If you're worried about me, I'll be fine. This isn't the city, there are no muggers lurking around the corner. This is my home."

He looked around as if he took it all in. "It's a great place, but it won't be home for much longer." He reminded her and turned away.

"Why do you do that?" She stopped him, her voice showed her irritation. "Why do you keep bringing that up?"

"Because I don't think you understand what you're giving up. You think you'll marry William and can have both. The city life with him and your life here, it won't happen, Cassie. Maybe I just want you to see that."

"I don't expect to give up Lakeview completely. I'll come back, it isn't like I'm moving out of the country or anything, I've always made it a point to visit."

"How often do you think you'll visit once you're married? It will mingle down to a few times a year, then maybe once a year, and only for a long weekend or two."

"I'm starting a new life with William, maybe that will be enough for me." She didn't believe his words, but acted as if it wouldn't matter anyway.

He laughed. "You honestly think that? Lie to me, but don't lie to yourself."

"What makes you the authority on my life? We spent a few measly days together on the other side of the world, that doesn't mean you know me."

"I know it won't be enough for you. You'll have your career, your life with William and it might even be enough to fulfill you, for a while. Later, when you're sitting in your beautiful condo in the city and your children have no place to play but a 6 x 6 balcony, you'll think about the people here sitting on their porch and passing a lazy night away."

"I'll take them to the park," she countered.

"Where you'll have to walk overtop homeless wino's and hope you don't step on any used needles along the way."

"Highly exaggerated."

Clay shrugged his shoulders. "Maybe, but you get my point."

"Actually I don't." Cassie threw her hands in the air with exasperation. "I don't get the point to any of this. What are you trying to do, Clay? Why is it that at every turn you remind me how my life will change, how I'll be leaving Lakeview behind? Maybe it's what I want to do, did that ever cross your mind?"

"This little town is in your blood, but more important, it's in your heart. I know what I see, you belong here."

"What do you know about belonging anywhere? You've moved so many times you have enough maps to start a world archive."

Clay knew she was right. He also knew that if he found a place like this to belong to, a place that made him feel welcome and at home, he wouldn't be so restless. In the back of his mind he knew it was more than the location, it would have to include the person who stood in front of him with black hair that blew around her face as she stood with fierceness in her eyes, hands on her hips as if ready for battle. It wasn't him she actually felt angry at, but her emotions she battled, the truth of having to give up this part of her life.

He wanted to wait, had just completed the business transaction but maybe if he waited he wouldn't go through with it. Now couldn't have been more appropriate so he took her hand and led her through the square.

"Where are we going?" She protested.

"This won't take long." He pulled her along the sidewalk until they came to the vacant building where he stopped in front of the door, removed a key from his pocket and unlocked it, then held out his hand for her to enter.

"What the hell are you doing? Why are we here? And why do you have a key?" Her face and words puzzled.

"Just go inside."

When she did, he entered behind her and locked the door again. Cassie walked to the center of the floor and looked around. It was dark and dusty, had been vacant for quite some time but she didn't see the gloominess. For a brief moment she allowed herself to see bright paint, gleaming counters, and people milling about, just as she'd done the first time she peeked into its dark windows. Then she stopped the visions from coming.

"What is going on?"

"It's yours for the taking." Clay said with such a soft voice it was barely audible.

"What are you talking about? Have you gone mad?"

Clay walked over to her and held out the envelope he had in his hand. "In here are papers you need to sign within a year from today. Once you sign them the place will be yours, not free and clear, this isn't any sort of hand out. All you have to do is pay the mortgage but there's no down payment or anything, so that gives you more capital to work with."

Cassie's hand came out slowly and her fingers touched the envelope as she looked at her name written across the front, and nothing made sense. She couldn't think, couldn't speak.

"Consider it a pre-wedding gift."

"Oh no." She quickly pulled her hand back.

"All you have to do is accept it, Cassie. And you'll have a year to decide."

"I can't take something like this. This is... it's foolish, it doesn't make any sense, why would you do something like this?"

"Because you won't. Are you going to live like your sister the rest of your life? Yeah, you might have better circumstances than she, William does love you, but it will be the same. Stuck in something that's bearable but doesn't make you happy, does that ring a bell?"

"It isn't like that."

"Isn't it?" He pressed.

"So you don't want me to marry William?"

Clay looked to her and spoke the truth. It didn't matter one way or another where he was concerned, Clay would still never be able to pursue her. Loyalties to his brother would still be there and it would never be appropriate to go after his ex fiancé', no matter she had gotten hold of his heart and wouldn't let go. "I'm not saying that. William loves you, he'll make you as happy as he possibly can, but I know he doesn't fit in here enough to make it his home. I know you'd give it up for him and that's commendable, but it will only make you bitter in the long run."

"Why do you have to do this to me? I'm getting married and you think you can just step into this town and hand me my dream on a silver platter. It isn't that simple, Clay, I take this and I might as well stop everything now. Call the entire wedding off because William could never make it his life. I give up William and I risk the happy life and family I could have with him." Cassie kicked at a piece of wood on the floor and it made a clunking sound that echoed in the empty space. "In case it hasn't crossed your mind, I love William."

Clay was quiet before he spoke. "I do too, Cassie, and I don't want to see him hurt anymore than you do. But I know what it's like trying to live a certain way, trying to fit into the mold other people have made for you. Thank God I found out early that I like the view from the clouds because I couldn't imagine having to go through life that way. Give up your dreams because other people say they aren't possible."

"So maybe one day I can have both. Maybe William will come to like this place and want to settle here."

"In a perfect world." Clay sat upon a broken table, actually leaned against it, afraid it would crack and break any moment.

"So if I decide later on I want to give it a shot, I'll do it. I don't need your handout."

"It's far from a handout. I simply purchased it because when I saw it I could envision your dream myself. Everything you told me about it in Hawaii, from the awning and sidewalk tables to the back deck..." Clay laid the envelope on the table and got up. "This would be the perfect spot for a cafe', there couldn't be a better place in town, but I knew it wouldn't stay vacant forever. Once you sign those papers, the bank purchases the mortgage from me and I'm out of it completely, you pay them." He placed the key on top of the envelope and moved to the door. "You have a year to the day. Think of it as a year to talk William into it. If that happens, you can have everything."

"And if it doesn't happen?" She turned to him and questioned.

"Then I guess you'll have choices to make."

"I don't want choices, I've already made my choice, why make me question it now? Why are you doing this to me?" Cassie was still confused and befuddled over what he'd done.

"I've been there, Cassie, I've tried to fit the mold and it doesn't work. It's like trying to force a piece of a puzzle into a place it doesn't fit. Maybe I care for you enough to at least help you not make the same mistake."

"If you cared for me at all you wouldn't..." she stopped herself from saying things she shouldn't. "You wouldn't be doing this to me. You'd give us a nice silver plated tea set, or a set of china, if you cared for me at all you would drop all this talk of all I'm giving up and understand it's what I want to do."

He noticed her words were loud and forced as she tried to believe them herself. His voice was a sad resignation at his reality. "This wedding will take place, I've accepted that. You're to be my sister-in-law, I've accepted that. I'm not trying to confuse your life or change your plans, I'm trying to make you see it won't be as easy as you think to try and fit yourself into something. In the long run, you'll be miserable, you'll pretend you aren't, and you might even force yourself into that mold and be somewhat happy, but it will never be enough, not when you have to give up so much. Marry William, I understand if you think he offers you things you want in your life, but do so with the clear understanding that you aren't being true to yourself."

Her heart was as confused as her mind and she couldn't listen to it right now because it sent her emotions into a turmoil. She wanted more than that from Clay, she wanted him to say he didn't want her to marry William, she wanted something else, more than he seemed willing or able to give her. But did she? She was to marry his brother, why did she want more from Clay? What was it she expected from him? When he left her there alone, Cassie stood in the middle of the floor, leaned her head back and closed her eyes with a heavy sigh. He perplexed her around every turn. Just when she thought she could keep an even keel he tilted her again.

****

Cassie walked to her parents and stored the envelope secretly in her room. She'd give it back to him, take it back to the bank, do something with it, but it was impossible to consider. It was preposterous. How could she do such a thing? How could he do such a thing? With everything on her mind and he had to spring something like that, wanted her to be as foolish with her life as he was with his.

What was wrong with the safe journey? She'd be content, her and William would have children, she was ready for children, wanted them in her life, her nice stable life. Decisions of beginning a business did not work into her plans. There would be no time for anything, she would have to use all of her savings and more, and... Cassie stopped herself from thinking such thoughts. Had to turn her mind back to the present and her wedding, her marriage to a man she loved, one who would give her everything she wanted.

Cassie stood at the window and looked out to the lake. She didn't know how long she was there when her father came in.

"Hey, your mother told me you'd come in."

"Hey, Daddy." Cassie smiled sweetly.

"I know you're smart enough that you haven't changed your mind, but your mother said you've been up here for quite some time. She didn't want to disturb you but she started to worry."

She looked at her watch and realized she'd been there two hours. "I didn't even realize how long I'd been here. I was just... I don't know."

"Something wrong?" He moved closer and asked with concern.

"Nerves I guess, just needed a little quiet time and this was the only place I could get it."

"Big step in a few days. I'm proud of you Cassie, the life you created, the one you'll have now with William. I couldn't think of a better road for you."

"Why dad?" Cassie looked to him for answers, looked to him for something, something more than he wanted to give.

"William is grounded. You need someone like that because otherwise I'd worry the rest of my life away. Alone, you'd take chances you probably shouldn't."

"Without taking risks we don't discover new things."

"That applies to sky diving, or jumping from a bridge on a rubber band, bungee jumping maybe, but not your life." He put his arm around her shoulder. "By your first anniversary, you'll see how nice it will be for you. You'll be glad you made the choice you did."

Nice? Glad? Whatever happened to words like phenomenal? Wonderfully exhilarating? What was wrong with those words to describe one's life? Her father would be proud because she would have a nice little life. Cassie looked out of the window again to the old pickup truck route from the side of the house, up the drive, across the road and to the lake. Whatever happened to that little girl behind the wheel? When had she given back the keys? Turned over the reigns? She couldn't remember.

****

"I was about to send a search party till your mother called and said you were on your way. Where have you been all afternoon?" William took her in his arms and pulled her close when she returned to the Resort.

"Few last minute things from town. Time got away from me." She pressed closer. "How was golf?"

"Great. Father won, that always makes him happy so he's in a good mood tonight. He took mom out to dinner with another couple. I think the Baker's or something?"

"Good, and what about you? You look nice, did you plan on taking me out too?"

Before he could answer, Mark spoke up. "Boy's night out, Cassie."

She looked to him as he stepped to their side. "With you? Oh, that's not a comforting thought."

"Come on, you know I won't get them in too much trouble. Susan would have my hide." He put his arm around her when she stepped away from William who only smiled. "I thought it would be a good idea to show these city boys a thing or two." Mark looked at her and sighed as if she'd say no. "You owe me, my secrets are way more embarrassing than yours."

"Yeah." Clay said as he patted Mark on the back. "I wouldn't argue that one."

"Come on, Cassie, you had your secret tradition night, Susan still smells like fish."

Clay laughed and when she looked to him she knew he didn't laugh at Susan, the look in his eyes was for her, the sight she'd made with mud caked all over her and squishy wet shoes. He hadn't said a word about it to anyone and she knew he wouldn't.

Of course they only teased, didn't need to ask permission and she wouldn't object. Despite what reservations she would have had previously, she had to trust William, had learned to. Either that or it would drive her insane. Cassie was confident with herself, and him, it was a place she had to get to before she agreed to marry him again.

She held onto William just before he left, needed to feel him close to her and her body pressed to his as she kissed his neck then his lips. "Are you sure you want to go?"

"Are you trying to get me to stay here? That wouldn't be a hard choice to make."

"Go and have a good time. I just wanted to say thank you."

He raised his eyebrows. "I guess I should remember if I've done something to deserve your gratitude but I can't. Why the thanks?"

"For all of this, this week in Lakeview. I told you it wasn't as bad a place as you think, you seem to enjoy it." She kissed him softly, didn't move her lips far.

"I never said there was anything wrong with the place, I just always said it was a place I certainly couldn't live. You know the old saying... nice place to visit, but wouldn't want to live there." He rubbed her back and if she hadn't started pulling away from him, he probably would have stayed there.

"We can't have a bachelor party without the groom." They'd all wandered out and now Mark came back in to search for William. "Come on, William, Lucy Lee is the only stripper in town and she's eighty five. Goes to bed at 9:00, we have to hurry."

"I love you, Cassie." William said softly before he let go of her.

She kissed him once more. "I know you do, but you're going to love Lucy too, better hurry."

He laughed as she reinforced Mark's words and actually wondered in his mind if they were for real.

"Mark, you'd better bring my boy's back in one piece." She called out to him as the door closed.

She hadn't realized what she said until a few seconds later. In her mind she sounded like Jill when she talked of William and Clay, but that wasn't what Cassie intended. She intended it to mean the crowd of them, all of them. Hadn't she?

CHAPTER SEVENTEEN

Cassie had dinner with the wives of William's friends, actually looked forward to it, as it was seldom they really sat down together without the men. She'd become friends with them, but not too close a friend. Not because she hadn't made attempts to bond with them, but all of them seemed distant, not only to her but also with each other as well, possessed an attitude that emitted they didn't care one way or another whether you were in their life or not.

She didn't feel it was a materialistic thing, all of them were on the same level of financial stability, and she didn't view them as snobby, merely unhappy people. There was never an animated conversation, never a joking and teasing atmosphere, they all seemed clones, Stepford Wives that had been manufactured.

As Cassie looked from one to the other, Jenny Livingston and Kerry Hence, she realized they could have been the same person. The two discussed the different brands of dry cleaning products you could buy at the store and do it yourself at home.

"It's great to use in a hurry, when I don't have time to wait."

"I'll have to try that brand, but I really like the other kind."

Then use the other kind, Cassie wanted to scream. The conversation went on for more than thirty minutes and when another mentioned a completely different brand, it started all over again. The evening gave her a description for these women she hadn't been able to figure out. Boring, it was plain and simple right there in front of her face, these ladies were boring. They said nothing interesting, certainly nothing to laugh about and she classified it as menial time filling. She would have had a better time sitting in a dentist chair and getting a cavity filled. It droned on and on and on and on.

"... sometimes Craig can't even tell I use it. Can't tell the difference between..."

"Are you ladies happy?" Cassie broke in and put a stop to the conversation. Right in the middle of words, right in the middle of Jenny's open mouth which gaped open now in the same position, frozen there. Then she repeated the question none of them seemed to have an answer to. "Are you ladies happy? What about you Kerry?"

"Well... I... I'm not unhappy."

"And you? Jenny? Do you ever wake up on a rainy day and say 'Screw it, I'm going to lie in bed and read a book all day long and Craig can clean his own shirts'."

"Craig doesn't clean anything, but that doesn't make me unhappy."

"What makes you happy? I'll start." Cassie said as if it were a game they would all play. "It makes me happy to walk through the park alone after a long day at work and stop for a quick minute and play hopscotch with some little girls... or to leave work in the early afternoon for a matinee... or skip work all together on that rainy day and lay in my pajamas and read until the sun goes down."

Jenny was the one who spoke up. "Well, that just sounds like you're childish and irresponsible."

They'd all lost themselves. Somewhere along their lives they gave up a piece of themselves bit by bit and now lay stagnant, and the sad part was they didn't even care. It didn't escape her that Jenny used words that came from her father's mouth before... childish and irresponsible. Who ever said growing up meant giving up things that made you happy?

Cassie wouldn't be like them, she couldn't be like them, she would surely die a slow painful death. Of course it wasn't but a few moments after that the ladies talked of what a long day it had been and were ready to retire for the night. She hadn't been so direct to specifically run them off, but she wasn't sorry it happened.

When she went into the Salon she found Jill and Redman returned and were enjoying a nightcap so she joined them. It was mostly Jill she spoke with, Redman always put up with her, but just barely so as not to appear rude. He was pleasant enough, maybe more so that evening since he'd won his golf game, and as William said, that always made him happy. But they too turned in soon after. The festivities of the week must have caught up with everyone because Cassie couldn't find anyone around, and all of her other friends, including Susan, were all busy with one thing or another. She went out onto the deck to sit alone with her book in the beautiful night air but wasn't there a short time before William came through the door on his return home.

"I was wondering if you boys would get back before morning, you're actually way earlier than I expected. Everyone just went to bed less than a half hour ago."

"We..." William began laughing and could hardly get his words out. "We were drunk early and... had to... "

As he laughed Clay had come out behind him and just looked at him. When William could control himself and catch his breath, he came over and gave her a kiss that smelled strongly of liquor.

"I have to... to go to the bathroom, I've been laughing for hours and I have to go before I explain. I won't be able to get through it. You stay here. I'll go." His last words were a whisper, as if they were a secret.

She smiled as she looked after him and shook her head. Clay leaned slightly against the wall, very unsteadily.

"Have a seat, you look like you're going to fall over." Cassie pushed out the chair she rested her feet upon but he remained standing.

Clay wobbled and winced a little. "I don't think so, maybe tomorrow."

"Are you okay?"

He cleared his throat. "I... I lost a bet with Mark." He leaned against the wall with one side and looked a little awkward.

"What happened? Or do I want to know?" She asked.

"It was somewhat of a contest. I agreed to it before I knew what it was going to be, then Mark came up with the idea of who could drink the most shots of whiskey in the shortest amount of time."

"Oh God." Cassie put her hands to her face and laughed, knew exactly what was coming.

"Loser got red lips tattooed on the behind. I thought I had to give it a shot, because if I won, he said he would officially retire from the sport of drink betting. One that called for per... permanent embellish... ments on the body anyway. Said his butt was only so big." Clay mumbled on his words and Cassie chuckled at the state he was in. "The three you gave him are on one cheek and he promised to get one big one on the other cheek if I won. Like a retirement flag." Clay took another swig of a bottle of water he held.

"And obviously, you didn't win."

"I don't know what came over me. I'm sorry, Cassie, no offense, but I guess I underestimated you, didn't mean to. I thought if you could do it and win... three times at that... well... maybe I stood a good chance. I just said 'Hey'... to myself I said that, not out loud... I said 'Hey, I've done this before, I have some sperience under my belt.' Remember? I saved you from beef and beer." Clay's mind began to wander. No Clay, don't go there, stick to what you're talking about, nothing else. "Then..." He paused for a moment. What was he talking about? "Where was I?"

"You decided to go for it." She got a kick out of his struggle to stand, talk and drink at the same time.

"I wanted a legacy."

"What?" Now he really didn't make sense and she wondered if he was off on another subject.

"Some people have the legacy of children, grandchildren, businesses here in Lakeview. Things they leave behind, people know they've been here and don't forget. My legacy would be a big ole' pair of red lips on Mark's butt."

Cassie burst into laughter again.

"Stupid, huh? People here have roots. I like that. Know who they are and where they come from. I don't have any roots. I've never been anyplace where I wanted to plant myself and grow any. I leave one place for the next, just pick up and move on without looking back. But this place... with all its... water." Clay couldn't think of the right words. "It's different and I wanted to leave something before I left and didn't look back. I could hear them talking for years to come about Mark's ass. Makes a more interesting story than a tree carving, and if I couldn't be here, at least my name would be mentioned." Clay finally struggled enough in trying to stand that he sat in the chair but leaned to one side. "An odd legacy from a passing stranger, I couldn't resist. I like this place, I've lived everywhere but... I don't know... just wanted to leave something, even if it was on Mark's behind." Clay rubbed his face. God, give him strength, he was saying too much, feeling too much, dammit, he hated whiskey. "He said you started it on your 21st birthday. What is it with you and your fascination with whiskey?"

"So now you have a nice little souvenir to take home with you."

"Yeah. Home." He laughed cynically. "Should have bought a magnet, a key chain or something. I don't even know where home will be next. Maybe Wyoming. Nebraska. Hell, maybe I'll go really up, Canada... no Mexico, they have tequila there, and it can be anyplace that doesn't serve whiskey. I used to love whiskey until one fateful, innocent day when I was minding my own business and it tossed me into months of pure hell."

Cassie could see the pain in his eyes. He didn't want to be there anymore than she wanted him there, and for the same reasons, they sent each other into a tailspin of mystifying abyss.

Clay focused on her and tried to stop himself. No, look away, two more days and you could leave her behind you and not look back. Two more days of hell, then many more ahead but don't think about that now. Don't think about her. Don't look at her. It will all go away soon, it would all be over soon. He finished what was left in his water bottle, it helped to digest the whiskey, he told himself that anyway.

Out of nowhere, Clay started laughing.

"What are you laughing at?" She chuckled, it was contagious.

"I was thinking it would be easier to sit here with you if you had all that mud and gunk all over you. I think you had something growing out of your hair." He paused and looked as if he thought seriously of something. "I think I've seen movies like this town. Strange things and all going on. Women out all night and come home looking like swamp creatures. Red lips on butts. Jimmy... Jetty... Jet... Jimmy Jet..." Clay struggled to remember the name and Cassie helped him.

"Jimmy Johanson."

"Yeah, you know him too? Nice guy. He showed me his red lips. Pulled his pants down before I went into the tattoo parlor, and they told me about others too, seems most of them lost to you. It's like a club or something. Are there any club dues?" Clay shifted in his seat, leaned hard on the table to take most of the weight off his backside. "And swamp things. Maybe I'd do better if you looked like that... well... it wouldn't make a difference. You still looked..." Stop yourself Clay. Do not proceed forward. Keep your mouth shut, better yet, get up and leave. You can't be near her sober and not go crazy, it was extremely difficult when you were drunk. "You looked like shit."

Cassie chuckled and rose. "As much as I'd love to sit here all night while you lavish me with compliments and praise, I think I'm going to have to help you up to your room. I thought William would be back, but he must have passed out in bed. Not that he'd have been much help, I would have ended up trying to get both of you upstairs. Come on."

Cassie reached for his arm and though he used her as a little support when he got up from the chair he insisted he didn't need much more. She simply stayed beside him, her hands close in case he faltered and after a few bumps into the wall, tripping on the stairs only twice, he made it to his room. She reached into his pocket to get the key when he couldn't find it, he said he couldn't feel his fingers, said he didn't have any fingers.

When he got close to the bed, Clay immediately fell face forward onto it. His mumblings before sleep made her pause and listen. "You have roots, Cassie. You're planted here. You'll just look for it somewhere else, but it's not there... never there... it's here. Don't let your tree die... your tree Cassie... don't let it die..." His voice faded off and she knew he was asleep.

CHAPTER EIGHTEEN

Cassie watched him quietly. William looked so vulnerable as he lay in deep sleep, and she wondered what he would look like ten years from then, twenty years, and knew he'd still be just as handsome only in a more mature way. When she met William, it wasn't an immediate attraction. She thought him too straight laced, not spontaneous enough for her. But when he began helping her with some classes in her freshman year of college, then again her sophomore year, Cassie found herself thinking about him with feelings other than just a good friend. Possibilities of being with him crossed her mind but neither one acted on anything their entire college career. They graduated and went their separate ways with nothing more than a deep friendship.

It wasn't until quite some time later they ran into each other again. It was a time in Cassie's life she'd tired of the dating scene and vowed to never date again but it only took her a few months of his persistence to cave in. When a job opened at his firm and she applied, as it would mean a substantial position upgrade along with more money than she would be able to refuse, they became even closer.

As Cassie thought about it now, she couldn't even remember why or when they moved in together. It wasn't discussed but she woke up one morning in his bed and never seemed to leave after that. They had a past, they knew each other, loved each other, they were comfortable.

William moaned and opened his eyes to see Cassie beside him. "I don't have a tattoo, do I?"

"It's awfully nice, you broke tradition, got a little pink heart instead of red lips."

"Oh please, Cassie, that isn't even funny." His voice sounded worried, the way he felt, he wouldn't have known otherwise.

Cassie rubbed her hand along his back and onto his behind. "Don't worry, it's still a blank canvas."

Then he chuckled. "I can't believe Clay went through with it."

Cassie didn't need to hear the name first thing in the morning. "I'm sure he'll be saying the same thing."

She went to rise but he pulled her back. "Don't get up."

"Both of us have to get up, breakfast at my parents, remember?"

"Oh no, I can't think of breakfast, I can't think of food." He rolled on his back and pulled her to him. "All I can think about is you. This is our last day as an engaged couple, it's been a long week. Tomorrow we'll end the day as man and wife."

Cassie hadn't really noticed the time that passed so quickly. Gone along as if she had months, maybe that's why she appeared so calm and collected when people said she should be much more stressed and worried. She pushed it to the back of her mind when she got out of bed.

Breakfast had been served as if it were Christmas morning. The dining room table set instead of eating in the kitchen and her mother's best china and silver, champagne in her crystal glasses she saved for special occasions.

"Why all the fuss?" Cassie asked her.

"Dear." Helen sighed as if she'd know. "It's your last day in the role you've played all your life, and you'll become something else now. Your role as daughter will be backseat now to your role of wife."

Her mother had to be so melodramatic about it all. Cassie thought she was just so excited she was finally getting married and took it to the extreme, her mood was as if she was moving out of the country and wouldn't see her for years. Nothing would change. It would be the same as it always was, why did she have to be so sentimental about it all? Cassie wasn't, or hadn't been until she left her mother's house.

William insisted on driving instead of taking the easy water taxi across and walking, so on their way back she took the opportunity to drive around a bit and told him to take a right or take a left and guided him to Cape Point where she pointed out a few houses where friends lived, then almost at the very end of the point stood an old decrepit house that had seen a better day.

"That's my dream house." Cassie said and he laughed as if she joked. "I'm serious. Ever since I was a little girl I've loved that house. Course it used to look a little better but no one's lived in it for years."

"I can see why. It would cost a fortune to make livable. Best thing to do would be to demolish it and start over."

"Look at the perfect spot it sits on. It belongs to old Morty Canton. Used to live there with his wife and family, but when she died he built a smaller house over there behind the trees. His kids all moved away and don't want it, but he won't get rid of it." Cassie paused for a moment. "Why don't we see if he wants to sell?"

William laughed again. "What for?"

"Maybe one day we'll want to live here." Cassie said it casually as if she thought he would be thinking about it too.

"And do what?"

"Start a family, raise our kids. Maybe we should think about Lakeview as a possible home."

"I can see me now trying to convince your friend Susan to run a commercial ad about them having the best bait in town. We're in the marketing and commercial production business, Cassie, not that much of a need here."

He didn't know her dreams, she'd never told him, and she didn't fully explain then. "So maybe we'll do something else."

"Even if I changed careers, I can't imagine this place having anything to interest me." He drove to the dead end of the road where the lake was and you could go no further, and then turned around in the drive to head away.

Cassie looked up the hill and saw the house not as the run down ugly home it presented itself as. Instead, she saw white pristine paint, new porch railing, a porch swing, maybe bright red shutters and door. It didn't matter. Why had she come? There was so much Cassie wanted to say, so much she wanted to discuss, maybe plant in his mind the possibilities of how their lives could be here. But she knew her words would mean nothing to him, knew her dreams were not his. As with the vision of her café, she let this too fade into the distance of her mind.

****

It was a beautiful early evening along the lake for their rehearsal and dinner, perfect for one last evening of relaxation before the wedding day. Dressed in a clingy red dress that hung to her ankles, with fringes on the bottom, Cassie looked radiant in the setting sun. The wedding party was important, but minimal. Mel was her maid of honor, Clay the best man, Ricky the only groomsman and Marie her only bridesmaid. Their parents joined them, watched from the sideline as the minister and the resort's wedding planner walked them through it.

"Cassie, you and the girls will come from back here." The planner said as she walked them towards the inside.

Cassie looked to William and waved before she disappeared. The minister took Williams arm and led them down where the aisle would be. "You'll come from inside when instructed and simply walk across this portion of the deck, down the stairs and to the end of the white rose petals that will be spread for the aisle."

They walked quietly, followed the minister, and William began to chuckle. "Am I supposed to be this nervous at rehearsal? I feel like my stomach is going to come out of my throat."

Clay felt nauseous himself but didn't say anything about it. "A big step, are you ready this time?"

"I've never been so ready, Clay. We might as well say the last time didn't really happen at all, it's out of our minds now."

Clay looked straight ahead, across the lake to the deli on the other side, the place she'd worked as a child. Then beyond that, he could see the backs of the stores on Main Street, the place her dreams lay. "Yeah, out of our minds."

"Thanks for being here, I really mean it. I know it's hard for you to put up with my father, and I appreciate it."

"It's hard for him, not me." He spoke the truth, it certainly wasn't William's father that made it difficult for him to be there, it was looking at his beautiful bride to be and wanting to take her in his arms.

His feelings only got worse as they stood for a moment then watched the door open, watched Marie walk through, and then Mel, then Cassie as she stood for a moment with the red dress that hugged her curves and the smile that Clay pretended was just for him. It was at that moment, when he thought about the next day and how she would look, the new life she would begin, one she didn't belong in, that he wondered if he'd done the right thing in coming.

Clay took an inward deep breath and smiled at Marie who looked nervous, and then Mel, who tried to look happy, but his smile faded as Cassie only had eyes for William as she walked in the arms of her father.

"That's a long way to walk, I don't know if I can wait that long tomorrow. Think you can run down the aisle?" William sighed when she reached him.

"Just for that, I'll take even more time and make you wait even longer. Maybe I'll walk all the way around the lake before I get here." She teased and smiled, noticed out of the corner of her eye that Clay couldn't look at her, maybe she was having a small affect. She liked to think so anyway. "Think we could do that, Dad? A little stroll around the lake?"

"If my hip can hold out, we can stroll around town too."

"We'll go through the service quickly. I'll start by greeting everyone then I'll read..." The minister explained the order of things to come.

Her father went through the motions of answering when asked who was giving the bride away then took his seat. Clay was lost in his own deep thoughts, had to be nudged by William to pretend to give him the ring when he and Ricky were laughing about something. Then Mel was talking to Marie when Cassie pretended to hand her a bouquet to hold.

"Is it just me, or is everyone distracted?" She looked around and it seemed to be only her and William who paid attention.

They ran through it once more with quick speed then dispersed. Some went back inside with others who gathered in the salon to wait for tables for dinner to be set on the deck. Cassie walked down to the water and Mel came when she asked her to.

"You seem odd this evening." Cassie commented on her mood. "Anything in particular wrong?"

"What's always wrong with me?"

"Other than me?" Cassie knew her moods and didn't think it was her this time. "Your husband."

"He hasn't been home the last two nights." The lake was calm as Mel gazed over it, there didn't seem to be one ripple on its smooth surface.

Cassie looked to her sister, debated the conversation she would initiate but knew it would come as no surprise. "Some people have said there's a reason he spends his time away from home, have you confronted him?"

"A million times."

"Mel, I know you've been thinking about leaving him, why don't you do it already?"

She seemed to have a smile on her face, although it was more of a small cynical smirk directed towards Eddy. "You could say he'll get the hint when he does come home. All locks have been changed and his clothes and every single item he's ever owned are in the front yard."

Cassie laughed. "Knowing Eddy, he'll just think you've been fall cleaning."

"I've been stupid and passive way too long, it's what's best for me and the kid's and it's about time I used what little brain I have left. It was getting rusty."

"That's an understatement." She laughed jokingly and Mel didn't take offense, she always knew where Cassie stood on her miserable marriage.

"I'm a little smarter now. One morning I woke up and realized I was being unfair to the kids. I was willing to stay because I thought they needed the stability of a two parent home. Few people get divorced in Lakeview, they'd be like an oddity of nature or something among their friends."

"You're doing what's best for them. And you." Cassie put her arm around her and hugged her for support she needed now and would need to get through it.

Mel began to cry. "I have more news, Cassie. This doesn't change me leaving Eddy, as a matter of fact, when I found out, it's what made my decision to leave him. I can't do it again, I can't do it for all the wrong reasons."

"What are you talking about?"

"I'm pregnant." Mel cried and laughed at the same time. "I'm not upset about it either. I'm crying because of the hormone thing going on. So I'll be a single mother of three children and that's fine, not like I plan on dating anytime soon. Not for a long time, if ever."

Cassie wasn't quite sure how to take the news but Mel truly seemed fine with it so she was too. It would take time to digest but her sister beamed. "And you'll be a wonderful single mother of three."

"It's what's best for us." Mel wiped her eyes and paused. "What about you, Cassie? Are you doing what's best for you?"

Cassie raised her eyebrows. "Of course I am."

"I know I've had my head buried in the sand far too long, and I'm not an expert on marriage, I think I've proven that. But I've missed out on so much because I thought he made my life easy. I never thought I'd take the easy road but it's like I fell into a pit so deep I felt like I couldn't climb out. Aren't you doing the same thing?"

"What do you mean?"

"All you talk about is Lakeview, how you'd love to live here, make it your home. And yet you're following a path you didn't choose, it's one dad chose for you, one William is choosing for you. Won't you be in the same pit? The circumstances might be different, but the pit is the same black hole."

Cassie didn't say anything as Mel's words and Clay's words mingled together. She'd never seen it that way, never compared herself to living the kind of life Mel had, and didn't want to now. It was different, it wasn't the same, she told herself.

"I'm sorry, Cassie, I didn't mean to open my mouth. I am happy for you and William, if that's what you want. I guess I've lived a farce so long I'm a little cynical."

Cassie was glad she wouldn't have to say anything when Marie ran up to them with excitement. "They're almost ready to serve dinner, hurry up, they have four kinds of cakes for dessert. Mom, can I have two pieces?"

"Why stop at two, why don't we have three?" She smiled at her daughter.

"Why stop at three? I think maybe four, one of each kind." Cassie included.

After dinner it was as if it were a preview of the wedding. There was a small band and the champagne and wine flowed as guest mingled about and enjoyed the evening. Cassie saw Clay alone and approached him.

"I didn't think it was proper dinner conversation, but how's the ass?" She laughed, unconsciously touched his arm and rested her hand there for only a second.

"Better. I forgot to put the private sign on the door last night though, I think the maid came in when I was passed out naked. My newly tattooed bottom was face up for the entire world to see. She smiled at me a little funny this morning when I saw her in the hall."

"You were clothed when I left you, I..."

Clay laughed. "I remember getting up and undressing, I knew it wasn't you. I didn't even remember it was you who took me to my room until William mentioned it this morning."

William joined them, put his arm around Cassie and pulled her close. "Discussing Clay's induction into the celebrated branded butt club?"

"I think it's a strange, sadistic Lakeview tradition, all the men are tattooed like a gang or something. Is it actually for identification?" Clay asked with a look as if he was serious.

William looked to Cassie and knew she would understand what he would reveal. "It isn't only a men's club. Cassie is the only woman, but that's only because no other woman has ever participated in the little friendly bet. Mark got her back a few years ago, she finally lost."

Clay's laughter resounded in the air, boomed clear across the lake and she blushed even more.

"I still don't think I lost, I think I was just so drunk I believed him when he told me I did." Cassie said in a playful huff and walked away.

Clay watched the red dress cling to what they spoke of and imagined it there. Surprised he hadn't seen it on their 'honeymoon' as many times as he'd seen her naked.

William too had been looking at the same thing. "I think she's embarrassed more at the loss than she is that she has it. A mark of defeat so to speak, but I think it's sexy as hell."

I bet he does, Clay said to himself. He'd seen her naked, with or without tattoo she was sexy as hell, but as many times as he'd seen her naked on their 'honeymoon', he hadn't seen that side of her, only her naked back lying in bed, the sheet covered her behind.

Clay turned his eyes away from her. "I wanted to let you know, I'm leaving right after the ceremony tomorrow."

"Tomorrow night?"

"No, right after the ceremony, my flight is at 6:00. I have a meeting I've already postponed that I have to get to. If I don't catch the flight tomorrow, there isn't another until two days and I can't delay it any longer."

"I guess I can't complain, you've spent a couple of days here and that's more than I thought I'd be able to get out of you. It's been great, hasn't it? A long time since we've done anything together, let's not wait so long to do it again? Plan a visit soon to the new place before it's full of kid's and all I have left to offer is the sleeper sofa."

Clay knew it wouldn't happen, just the thought of it was unbearable. "Yeah, that'd be nice."

"You've never really said what you think of her." William watched Cassie stop and pick up Marie's arms and they playfully danced a few moments.

"First impression was a crazed lunatic, but I guess she grows on you." He too glanced in her direction, heard her laughter, had to smile himself at the fun she was having.

"And after tomorrow, she'll be all mine. I didn't really think a marriage certificate meant much, but I understand now. Guess after almost losing her, the commitment means that much more to me."

Clay looked William directly in his eyes, his face stern and unwavering, and his voice embodied how important it was for him to listen. "Make her happy, William. Cheat on her again and you'll not only lose her, but after what I've been through, after what I've done for you, I can't promise you won't lose me also."

"I can guarantee that if anything happens to us and we don't work out for some reason, it won't be because of me. I can't even begin to try to explain the feelings I have for her."

Clay felt as one with his brother.

****

The eve before her wedding, Cassie didn't want to see the night end. Surely the clocks were wrong, but the evening did wind down and come to a close. She planned to leave and stay at her parents for the night until the wedding the next day. William didn't want her to leave but there was nothing he could do about it because she was insistent.

"I'm being banned until tomorrow. Do you know how hard this will be for me?" William sighed and shook his head.

"You're not supposed to see the bride."

"I know, I know." William sighed, wished she wouldn't stick to that tradition but he couldn't change her mind as he watched her pack just a few things.

She would return the next day and dress there, but he would be out of their room by then and into Clay's. William would spend the evening having dinner with his parents, spend time with his family and friends, and he would go to bed early. It was what Cassie planned for herself until she was too restless to stay put and decided on a quick visit to Susan's and maybe a glass of wine or two.

Cassie didn't knock, never had, and walked in the back door to find Susan in the kitchen helping Ellie with homework so she wouldn't spend the weekend on it.

"An exciting night in Lakeview." Susan said when she saw her. "You must be counting the days to get out of here and back to your exciting life."

"Not hardly." Cassie sighed.

"What are you doing here? Everything's okay, isn't it?" She asked with concern.

Cassie kissed Ellie atop her head. "Hey girl," then turned her attention back to Susan. "Everything's fine. Just a little restless this evening, thought I'd stop and have a glass of wine, or two, maybe even three," she laughed.

"Sounds better than this math I'm working on."

Cassie had brought her own with her, already chilled, and knew exactly where the glasses were and got two of them down. "Where's Mark? Think he wants a glass?"

"Hey Mom, since Cassie is here we're done, aren't we?" Ellie asked hopefully. "I can finish tomorrow. Or Sunday. I promise I'll be through before Monday."

"Go on." Susan encouraged. "Take a bath and get ready for bed. You can watch television for a little while." Then she turned her attention back to Cassie who waited for an answer. "I'm sorry. No Mark's not here, he won't be having one."

"Where's he this evening?"

Susan laughed. "It seems your soon to be brother in law can't get enough. They're out again and Clay warned me he didn't plan on losing this evening. I don't think his pride will take it, so they may be out until he wins."

"I hope Mark beats him twice."

"I don't know, he looked pretty confident when they left."

"Was William with him?" Cassie asked.

"No, just him. I think those two can get into enough trouble on their own, I'd be afraid to add William to the mix. Even as wholesome as he seems."

"Wholesome?" She laughed at Susan's description.

"What's a better word? Proper? Polite? I know he likes to have fun, but he seems more reserved I guess would be the right word."

"It's a good thing, he keeps me grounded." Cassie said words her father used and almost cringed, was she so brainwashed she couldn't think for herself?

"Yeah." Susan said softly. "I kind of picture you as a hot air balloon, and he's on the ground holding your string."

Cassie laughed. "That's what you get from knowing him such a short time?"

She shrugged her shoulders. "I don't know why, but I do. It's not anything bad, I like William, I really do."

Cassie pictured it in her mind and laughed again. Didn't take offense at her friends words, there was no offense to be taken. It was her honest opinion and she appreciated hearing it. "Maybe I need someone to hold me down from the clouds." Cassie said the words as she thought them. Then all of her conversations with Clay entered her mind, the way he used the words and talked about the view from the clouds. Is that what she was thinking of William? He was holding her away from Clay? Or the way the words were intended, he was holding her from her dreams?

"What?" Susan asked.

"Huh?" Cassie looked up.

"All of a sudden you got serious on me. I didn't mean..."

"No." Cassie stopped her. "Nerves hit me when I least expect it. I was just thinking about something."

"He'll make you happy, I can see he loves you." Susan said the words without elaborating more, didn't want to admit she didn't see the same from Cassie.

Happy? Was that all there was for her? She wanted to be delirious, wanted to be mad with joy, consumed by passion and love. In that moment Cassie pictured Susan's vision and willed William subconsciously to hold on tight, to hold her from the clouds. They talked for a long while and Cassie watched a television show with Ellie then felt she had to be getting home. A good night of rest was what she needed. Sleep, without William, without anyone. It was as if Cassie could hear the tick of her watch with every second, and with each second that passed, thoughts permeated her mind.

She gathered her few things and heard a car outside indicating Mark's return, and wanted to leave and not be faced with Clay if he were with him. It was the last person she needed to see that night.

"You're coming over early, aren't you?" Cassie asked Susan about the following day, her wedding day, before she left.

"I'll be there as early as you need me."

"If that's the case, you can come back and sleep with me tonight. I'm going to need all the help I can get."

Susan stood in front of her, took her hands. "You need no help. You'll be a beautiful bride, Cassie."

"A beautiful bride indeed." Clay's voice came from the back door, he spoke with spontaneity, now realized his mistake. "Speaking as a proud brother in law."

"You two at it again?" Cassie asked and looked to Mark who walked funny, then laughed. Clay would leave his mark after all.

"My final drinking bet. No more for me, I have no more room on my ass." Mark put his arm around Susan, more to use her to hold him up. "I have more art now, it's a big one this time, the entire cheek of my butt. That's it, I'm officially retired."

"I'm so glad to hear that." Susan held him and laughed then looked to Cassie. "You heard that, didn't you?"

"I heard it." Cassie said as she looked to Clay who smiled proudly, she was actually happy for him he'd accomplished what he wanted.

One of the men, who remained sober to drive, waited for Clay as he helped Mark inside the house, though he couldn't have been much help, both of them smelled of whiskey. It was Cassie to walk with Clay back outside after they said their farewells.

"Hey, Cassie." Bob McDermott said from the open window of the driver's seat. "I didn't expect to see you here."

"I didn't expect to see any of ya'll here."

"I think Clay must have practiced, never thought he'd do it, but he was determined." Bob laughed.

"I can leave a happy man." Clay smiled broadly, satisfied with his accomplishment. "On to Mexico now, where tequila will be my drink, I've drunk my last whiskey."

Cassie knew Bob would have to go in the opposite direction to take Clay back to the resort, and then return home afterwards. Against her better judgment, she promised to drop him off so he wouldn't have to go out of his way. "No sense you running all over town, it's out of your way, I'll take Clay back."

"You sure? That would be great."

"I'm sure." Her voice didn't reveal the doubt she felt, being alone with Clay was the last place she wanted to be.

"Thanks, Cassie. We'll see you at the wedding tomorrow."

"The wedding." Clay mumbled sarcastically as he got into her car. "The big day, I can't wait."

"Put your seatbelt on, Clay."

"Oh yeah, I forgot you ran a truck into a lake." He fumbled but eventually latched it and sat back and sighed. "Nice little life here... you have... one day... ah." He waved his hand as if to dismiss his thoughts. "What do I care what happens one day, I've left my legacy, I can die a happy man now."

She drove in silence. The eve of becoming his sister-in-law, she didn't need to be alone with him, didn't want to talk to him, feel things she shouldn't be feeling.

"Congratulations, Cassie." Clay finally said to break the silence that had enveloped them.

"Are you telling me early so you won't forget tomorrow?"

"No, not for the wedding, Congratulations on your courage to ascend to the clouds," he said sarcastically.

"I don't want to argue with you, not tonight."

"I..." Clay was going to tell her he was in love with her. How stupid whiskey made him. It's what got him into this mess of his emotions he couldn't get out of. He'd never drink again, swore to the statement under his breathe. "I don't want to argue with you either, I hope you're happy. Have your babies, have your nice little family."

"You know, Clay, I hope one day you can find something too."

"Something? I don't want what you'll have, I'm happy and satisfied from right where I am, thank you. I don't like to make sacrifices, not on things so important." Clay probably shouldn't have ridden with her. The confines of the car, the two of them alone, he didn't need to be alone with her as his erratic thoughts ran rampant. Had it been a simple case of passion, he could have dealt with that, but he didn't just want to make her his lover, he wanted to make her his life. He saw in Cassie everything he ever wanted for his own life, everything he'd ever searched for. "Do you ever think... do you ever think about Hawaii?"

Did she tell him the truth? Would he even remember what she said in the morning? "I try not to. It wasn't such a good time in my life."

"Miserable, wasn't it." It wasn't the answer he wanted.

"I've tried to put it behind me."

He'd tried too, and predicted he would forever be trying to forget things. "William will make you happy. Not delirious, as you should be, but he loves you."

"Yeah," Cassie whispered. "He loves me."

****

When she lay down that evening there were so many things that went through her mind. The envelope Clay had given her was in her nightstand drawer within reach. She didn't have to look at it to think about it. Off the wall things popped into her head, and all she could think about were roots, trees, trucks, keys, hot air balloons... and red lip tattoos. What did it all mean? Did it mean anything? Cassie looked for reason and rhyme to her jagged thoughts.

Nerves, jittery nerves caused by thoughts of her changing life, a life she wanted, a life full of promise. Wasn't it? A family, children, all those things were about to happen for her and William's face loomed into her mind, then the sound of Clay's laughter interrupted thoughts of him.

What was she doing? What was she thinking? When she let her feelings for Clay take any sort of control, he took over and her gut wrenched with pain, with heartache, with love for him. But he promised nothing and committed nothing. Had given her a dream in a brown envelope and yet nothing of himself. It was infatuation, nerves, anything but love. Wasn't it?

Everything she'd pushed aside, all the feelings she held locked somewhere not to escape, all came rushing at her as if like a giant wave as it fell over her and pushed her underwater. Surrounded her and she couldn't breathe.

CHAPTER NINETEEN

Cassie woke early the next morning before dawn, actually, she hadn't really slept and when she looked into the mirror her face revealed it. This was her wedding day, she shouldn't be looking like this, she thought to herself. Maybe Susan could perform some miraculous cucumber or mud treatment for the puffiness of her eyes and the dark circles under them.

She felt lifeless, had all day to wait and lay back down in bed but knew she wouldn't be able to sleep, so she just lay there as the sun came in through her window. Why couldn't she have picked the morning to get married, get it over and done with and have the rest of the day, the waiting all day was going to make her edgy and impatient.

The house came alive as she listened to doors that opened somewhere, heard her mother in the kitchen getting coffee and breakfast and her father's mumbled voice when he joined her. She couldn't make out what they were saying but she knew both of them were there. Then the phone rang, she heard her father talking a little, then the back door opened and closed and silence followed.

"Where did Dad go so early?" Cassie asked as she stepped into the kitchen after throwing on a pair of jeans and t-shirt.

"Raymond Briggs called and needed some help this morning, that old rotten tree hanging over his house finally fell on his roof. He won't be long, Raymond already has a crew coming to fix it, and your father is just going to help him throw a tarp over it in case it rains."

Cassie looked out the window and looked above to the clouds that were beginning to tinge with a little gray. "It isn't supposed to rain, is it?"

Helen put her arm around her daughter. "It's going to be a beautiful day, just a few clouds but they'll blow over I'm sure. The sun will come out brilliant again in a little while for your wedding day." She saw the hesitation in her daughter. "I promise it will be a beautiful day."

Cassie didn't think about it again as she got a cup of coffee and took it out onto the back porch. She wanted to talk to her father, was going to do so that morning, but she wouldn't have a chance to either drink her coffee or talk to him after the phone rang.

Raymond's wife had called and frantically told them to meet them at the hospital because Cassie's father had fallen off the roof. They didn't change or pamper just jumped into the car and left. Cassie's hands shook as she drove but she remained calm to keep her mother calm.

"She said it was his legs, he probably sprained them, even if he broke one it isn't a big deal. A broken leg is nothing, just means he'll be under your nose every minute while he heals."

"If he broke his hip…"

"Mom, let's not jump to conclusions until we know exactly what's wrong with him. Maybe it's just an ankle, it could be anything minor."

"And it could be major." Helen still worried, her face was a twisted expression as she thought of all it could be, it was the unknowing that plagued her.

Cassie was right with one aspect, it was a broken leg, but not just one, he'd broken both his legs. He immediately pulled Cassie to him when he saw her.

"This doesn't change today, it's still your wedding day."

"Daddy, I can't…"

"You can and you will." His face and voice were insistent.

"You have to be there, we can change it and…"

"It was the first thing I asked the doctor's about, they said they'd set my legs and I'll be in a wheelchair, but I can be there."

"I… it's no problem to…" Cassie was on the verge of tears and her father cleared the room of everyone.

She'd wanted to talk to him that morning, but the talk they had wasn't the talk she had wanted. Her father was insistent, talked to her again about how proud he was she was beginning this new phase of her life, how happy he was about it being her wedding day and how disappointed he would be for it not to happen that day, especially because of him.

As Cassie sat silent and listened to his heartfelt pleas that her plans didn't change, the courage she'd accumulated overnight began to fade and reality set in again. This was reality, this was her wedding day, and everything else faded into the distance as always.

She listened as her father talked for a long time, even through the pain he was still feeling after they'd given him some medication. When the doctor's returned with a final x-ray to be able to set his legs, and her mother entered the room again and fussed over him, Cassie disappeared into the background then from the room altogether as she left quietly.

Helen had called everyone there was to call and as Cassie glanced out of the window from the second floor she saw Mel running into the building. She took the stairs down so as not to have to face her, she didn't want to see Mel, didn't want to see anyone for fear they'd be able to see the guilt on her face for having second thoughts about getting married that day.

She knew Mel would bring their mother home, so Cassie left the hospital, drove home but didn't go inside, and then walked over the hill to the lake. From the view there she could see the truck she'd run into the lake, just a small top corner of the roof that protruded out of the water. If one didn't know what it was they would think it was a simple piece of log or perhaps a stone.

Then she looked further, beyond that to Cape Point and the house there. Old, decrepit, and rundown after years of neglect, but she used to vision it so perfectly, could see the potential in her dreams, but now as she stood there and stared, she could only see the old and decrepit place it was.

She wasn't sure how long she stood there, but when she turned and saw Clay, she knew he'd been there standing in silence for quite some time also.

"You okay?" He asked as he tried to see her face but her head was bent down.

"My father will be fine." She answered as she tried to walk past him.

Clay wasn't going to let her walk by him and took her arm, pulled her to stand in front of him. "I wasn't asking about your father, I went to the hospital and I know he'll be fine. I was asking about you."

"It's my wedding day, of course I'll be fine," she tried to hide her emotions, tried to wipe her eyes and keep her head down but he took his finger and lifted her chin.

"I don't think potential brides are supposed to look so miserable on their wedding day."

"And how many brides have you seen on their wedding day?"

"One, but I've seen her twice, and you don't look much different than you did on your first attempt at this. That can't be a good sign."

"How did you find me anyway?" Cassie tried to look strong as she changed the subject.

"I listen. I remembered you telling me something about coming here when we were in Hawaii."

Cassie huffed. "A man who listens, probably only one in America and it has to be you." She tried to pull away but he wouldn't let her. "Leave me alone, Clay."

"Don't be angry at me."

"I am angry at you, I'm angry you're here, I'm angry you're... I'm angry, okay? Leave me alone and let me be angry for awhile. Then I'll show up for the wedding looking the radiant bride I'm supposed to be, but let me be angry right now. I'll get through it."

"Maybe it's fate, Cassie, maybe its life's way of changing your plans. Maybe this ought to tell you something."

"It tells me fate doesn't want me to have second thoughts."

"Are you having second thoughts?"

"Of course I'm not, I meant..." Cassie was flustered as she brushed past him. "Leave me alone, Clay, you're the last person I need to talk to about this."

"You need someone, you're miserable."

"Mel is still at the hospital, she was when I left anyway, do you want me to take you over to Susan's?"

"I don't need anyone, Clay, I didn't get enough sleep last night, my nerves were already bad and then my father had to fall off a roof, and now I'm feeling guilty again for making it sound like he's to blame for my nerves and my problems when all he…"

She rambled on as Clay gently placed his finger over her mouth. "Shhh… Cassie, listen to you, you don't seem to be in any shape to get married today, everyone will understand if you postpone the wedding, and William will certainly understand. You may marry him one day and no one can stop what you do, but it doesn't have to be today. It isn't me trying to tell you something, its fate this time that's trying to tell you something."

"I'd like to know how to get hold of this fate person you keep talking about and tell them to call my father." The words lashed out, she'd unknowingly revealed things she wanted to keep to herself.

He looked at her eyes closely with her revelation and now knew what drove her, now knew her reasons for going through with this wedding, reasons she hadn't admitted before. "You're doing it for your father?"

"I'm doing it for me." The events of the morning, her father's words, made her obligation to make him proud that much stronger. She looked out over the lake and tried to appear strong, tried to appear as if her words were true.

Clay tenderly touched her cheek and turned her to face him again. "Cassie, your father would understand if you'd changed your mind, he's your father, he loves you."

"He loves me, but he wouldn't understand," she'd been crying but she wiped her eyes and pretended she hadn't.

"At least postpone the wedding."

"I can't. It's all he wants to happen today, wants the wedding to go on as planned and refuses to listen to postponement. He'll be there but he won't be able to walk me down the aisle." That fact almost sent her into tears again, if she had to get married, she always dreamed of her father walking her down the aisle, but she'd always dreamed of other things also, hadn't she?

Who was the person responsible to instill dreams in people? Whoever it was, whoever the Lord had put in charge, wasn't doing a very good job and should be fired.

She tried once more to be on her way, to get past him, to get away from him, but he held tight. "I'll be okay, Clay, really I will."

"You won't be okay, you're doing this for reasons you shouldn't, you're doing this to make others happy and not yourself. I'm not trying to complicate your life, Cassie, I'm not trying to talk you out of anything you don't want to do, but you don't want to do this. I'm just trying to make you see things how they are, and I know deep in your heart you don't want to do this."

"You don't know me, Clay, quite pretending you do."

"Whether you like it or not, I know you. I knew where you were, I know what you're feeling, and I know what's making you do this now. That makes you angry too, that I know you better than William does."

"Stop."

He grabbed her arm to stop her again and pulled her close to him. Clay forcefully stopped himself from kissing her, stopped himself from wrapping her in his arms and telling her what he felt about her. He wanted to comfort her when he saw she was in dire need of someone to comfort her, could see the torment she suffered in her eyes, the torment of doing something she didn't want to do, yet feeling obligated, especially now with what had happened to her father.

"Clay," her voice was a whisper as she pleaded with him, tears on the verge of her eyes at what she had to do. "Don't make this anymore difficult for me than it already is, please."

He had to let her go and watch her walk away, Cassie suffered battles he couldn't help her with, they were battles she had to deal with herself and nothing he said or did would change that.

****

Cassie didn't talk to William all that day, he'd been frantic to talk to her, but she kept sending messages to him that everything was fine and she'd see him at the appointed wedding time. She was afraid to talk to him, afraid of what she might reveal in her vulnerable state. She hadn't slept, hadn't eaten anything at all, and was concerned with all that had happened, though her father was in good spirits.

Cassie looked breathtaking as she stood before the full length mirror and was mesmerized by her appearance. Her wedding dress was a cream colored simple gown that had the appearance of an heirloom from a bygone era. Beaded with small pearls around the bottom in a lace pattern, around the waist as if it were a belt, and just slightly at the neckline that scooped down in a V shape. It fit tight to her body. Nothing plumed out, no crinoline, no bows, simple and regal in appearance. She didn't wear a veil and the only other accessory was a string of pearls her mother placed around her neck earlier.

"You look perfect now." She'd said and cried when she looked at her. "You're going to be so happy."

Why did people assume to know she was going to be happy? Everyone kept telling her that, how happy she'd be, what a great life she was going to have, could they guarantee her that? Would there be anyone to apologize if it didn't work out? What if she gave her dreams up for nothing? Would there be anyone there to tell her how sorry they were?

Cassie had been alone for awhile but was constantly kept abreast of everything happening and she knew everything was going smoothly and everything was on schedule. There was one task left that hadn't been ironed out and it wasn't long before the knock on the door came.

They'd set her fathers legs and he only took a mild dose of pain pills, wouldn't take anything strong. He smiled proud when he saw her in her wedding dress when Mark wheeled him into her room.

"The most important job of the day, bringing the father to see his lovely daughter, and I almost broke his legs again coming around the corner." Mark laughed and so did George.

"He isn't a very good driver, of course I knew that the first time I saw him come barreling down our driveway to pick you and Susan up the day he got his drivers license." Then George swatted him playfully. "And this isn't the most important job you're going to have today."

"It isn't?" Mark looked confused.

"No, leave us alone a minute and then you'll find out what your next job is."

Mark left the room and Cassie smiled broadly for her father. He looked happy and tired at the same time, it had been a long day for both of them and the clock seemed to move in slow motion.

"I knew you'd be beautiful, but I didn't know you'd be this beautiful. You don't look like my little girl anymore."

"I'll always be that, Daddy. I may be many things in my life, a wife, one day a mother, but I'll always be that. That's guaranteed." There weren't many things she felt sure of at that moment, only that statement.

"I have someone to take me back to your mother, she's having the best time watching people come in." He patted the armrest of his wheelchair. "At least I don't have to sit in those stiff uncomfortable chairs." He kissed Cassie when she leaned down to him. "You made a good choice with Mark. I can't think of anyone else better to do my job."

"I had to wait until the last minute to tell him, I was afraid he'd think of some prank to pull if he knew ahead of time." She laughed and they both knew she was probably right.

Cassie opened the door and Mark and another man were standing in the hall laughing. When it was the other man to take her fathers chair Mark looked confused as his hands came out with palms up and a perplexed look on his face. He immediately began to object.

"Hey, he's taking my job. I didn't hit the corner, I said I almost did, you didn't have to fire me."

Cassie motioned towards the inside of the room with her head. "Get your red lipped tattooed ass in here."

He walked inside and she closed the door. He immediately tried to defend himself from something he didn't know anything about.

"Whatever it is, I didn't do it. I know anything that happens and you blame it on me because most times it is, but I swear I didn't do anything. This is your wedding, I've been nothing but…"

Cassie took his hands in hers and stopped him. "Shhhh, whatever was done I know you did it because you're already jumping to the defense. But I obviously haven't discovered what that is."

"Good," he stated, then laughed. "Not that there is anything, just the car thing, but that's expected, you…" he stopped himself from digging deeper into a hole, noticed she'd been staring at him with eyes that began to water and a strange look. "I can clean the car up, I can…"

"I'm not worried about the car, as long as there is a car I don't care what it looks like."

Mark winced a little. "Oh, it has to specifically be a car?"

"You can't be serious." Cassie groaned, was thankful for his comedic relief, and hoped he only joked with her.

It got quiet and she looked to his face with nothing but pure emotion in it and she felt the tears as they threatened to come, her eyes stung for a moment and she laughed at the worried look on Mark's face.

"I'll put the car back, I promise, I have a back up and…"

"This is hard enough, will you let me get it out."

"When I get nervous I talk a lot, you of all people know that, remember when I got married and you had to duct tape my mouth because you got tired of… okay, I can't help it, but I'm nervous right now because I don't know what you're about to tell me and you look," he stopped and smiled as if he'd just noticed. "You look gorgeous by the way. You look like you did when you and Susan dressed up that time and, well, Susan looked better than you but that's because… okay, I'll stop, but you have to hurry because I don't know how long my mouth will stay closed."

Cassie held his hands in hers and looked to them, saw the scars from their childhood, most of them she was witness to when they happened, or she'd caused them herself. Her voice almost cracked when she spoke, she wasn't aware how emotional this was going to be for her.

"Mark, you know I love you."

He waited, wasn't sure what was to come but squeezed her hands for support. "Is this bad? I'm not used to you being emotional on me, that's always Susan, and I love her for it, but I'm not used to you being emotional, this is a little weird. Should I brace myself for something?"

"I need someone to walk me down the aisle."

Mark sighed with heavy relief. "Oh, that's all you're worried about, jeez Cassie, you scared the fool out of me. Of course you need someone to walk you down the aisle, and you called me in for my opinion? All you had to do was say something."

"Not your opinion, Mark, I need you to walk me down the aisle."

"Me? You want me to... Cassie I... you... Me?"

She laughed. "Of course you, who else? You're the next closest male in my life, you're my brother I never had, my best friend, and my best friend's husband, who else would I want at a time like this?"

Mark wiped his forehead of the sweat that had formed. "Maybe Uncle Bob, don't you have an Uncle Bob?"

"I do, but," Cassie paused, this wasn't the reaction she expected. "I see my Uncle Bob once every two years, he's here for the wedding but just because... what is the matter with you?"

"Cassie, I..." he was flustered, relief swept through him that it wasn't something more serious, wasn't something wrong, and yet he instantly felt worried.

"I thought you might be a little shocked, but at least maybe a little happy?"

"Yeah, I, well..." Mark turned away from her. "I'm honored you want me to, I'm just worried, it puts a whole new perspective on things."

"How is that?"

"I'm a friend. I have no job here, no job other than to show up and have a good time, now I feel obligated to..."

"To what?"

"No, I told Susan I wouldn't say anything, I promised her, but this changes things."

"Mark, what are you talking about?" Cassie was worried, didn't expect all of this to a simple request, and wasn't sure what 'all of this' was going to be and it concerned her.

He turned to her and quickly blurted out his concerns. "I don't like William."

Cassie looked at him and talked softly. "Okay, that's fine, I never said you had to like him, I never forced you to like him, or threaten to beat you up about it, so you don't like William." She shrugged her shoulders. "It's no big deal."

"How am I supposed to walk you down the aisle to him when I don't think he's the one for you, I can't see you being happy with him for the rest of your life," he sighed. "As a friend I was going to keep my mouth shut, that's what Susan told me to do, and by the way, she doesn't think he's right for you either."

"And I respect your opinion but..."

"But you also expect me to be hypocritical and walk you down the aisle to him? Maybe anyone else wouldn't see it as a problem, but," Mark paused. "But I don't know if I can do that."

She sighed and threw her hands up in the air in frustration. "Why can't things be simple? Can I just get through this day without a battle with everyone? You're not the one marrying him, I am, so let me make the decision on who I'm going to marry without your stamp of approval across his forehead. Mark, please, I have to put up with it from… from other people, I didn't expect to have to put up with it from you."

"Would you like it better if I kept my mouth shut? Is that being the friend you see me as? Obviously I'm important enough for you to ask me to do this, aren't I important enough to listen to?"

Cassie took a deep breath and turned away from him and he felt bad for revealing his feelings, for having reservations about doing the job she asked of him. He walked over to her and placed his arms around her.

"I'm sorry, but you know me, my mouth comes open and things come out. I care about you Cassie, you know Susan and I love you dearly, there's nothing in the world we wouldn't do for you." He turned her around to face him.

Cassie could see the struggle he had with it, he struggled with her choice possibly as much as she was struggling with it. All she'd wanted was a simple day, a simple ceremony, maybe they should have hopped another plane to Vegas.

"Just be here for me, Mark. Don't try to understand, just be here for me."

He fought with his emotions, as one of his best friends, second only to Susan, he didn't think she was doing the right thing, not for her and not for William. He could see in her eyes she tried to hide a hesitation she herself experienced, tried to push aside any qualms that she might be doing the wrong thing.

"I'll always be here for you, Cassie." He felt sorry for her as he took her in his arms and took a deep breath, he too felt the pain she was trying to hide, but he knew it wouldn't matter what he said, Cassie was going to do what she thought best for herself. And if that was to marry William, then he couldn't talk her out of it.

She backed up and looked at his handsome face, a face she knew she could always count on. "You don't have to agree with me, just support me, literally, because I'm a jumbled mess of nerves."

"Oh," he laughed. "So you only need me beside you because I'm strong and will be able to hold you up."

"Yeah, that and because I do love you as one of my dearest friends, Mark, you know that."

"Yeah, Cassie, I know that." He kissed her forehead. "Did you tell Susan you were going to ask me? Is that why she's been so edgy?"

"I made her promise not to tell you."

"That's why she's crying already, every time I look at her all she can do is cry."

"Yeah, she started blubbering and crying when I told her, but that's our Susan, its part of her sentimentality that makes us love her. She's the one that has always kept us out of really deep hot water." Cassie touched his face. "So what do you say? I have no escort down the aisle and I could think of no other person than you. Feel sorry for me and do it."

"Why feel sorry for you?"

"Because you're all I've got, how pathetic is that?"

They laughed together at her statement.

"Yeah," Mark agreed. "That's pretty pathetic." He kissed her again on her forehead. "Now, since I have the most important job of the day, I think I have time for a shot of whiskey. Care to join me? Or should I bring one back for you, for old times sake."

"Bring one back." She smiled as he left the room. She should have been prepared for that battle but it caught her by surprise, she didn't know he had such strong emotions or objections to what she was about to do.

Cassie took a deep breath and sighed, then looked at her watch, she had less than thirty minutes. Why was this day dragging on so?

****

Clay was walking through the foyer and noticed Mark standing at the bar that was through the card room so he joined him. He was the only one in the room other than the bartender who was setting up for the day.

"Festivities have started before the wedding?"

"A special drink," he held up the shot of whiskey.

"Whiskey? Isn't your behind still sore from the latest tattoo?"

"The last tattoo ever, but I have one for me and one for the bride, my last shot of whiskey I'll ever have, and this one is just for old times sake, and because I need it."

"You okay?" Clay could see a tension in his face and hear it in his voice.

Mark shrugged his shoulders, would have liked to confide in Clay, he liked him immensely, but had to remind himself he was William's brother after all. "Sure, I'm just fine."

"Care to make confession? Because I don't buy that." It concerned him a little that it might have something to do with Cassie, he said he was getting her a shot of whiskey, maybe she wasn't holding up well.

"I've just been handed the most important job of the day, and it makes me a little nervous," he laughed. "And I'm actually afraid to drink this shot of whiskey for fear I might trip and fall, taking Cassie on a roll down the hill and into the lake."

Clay looked confused and Mark went on to explain.

"She just asked me to walk her down the aisle, her father can't do it of course, so she asked me."

"A great honor, I would have thought you'd be happier about it."

"Yeah, maybe I would be if..." he stopped himself just in time.

Clay could see what he struggled with. "But you don't think she ought to be marrying my brother, you can fess up, I won't take offense."

"I like your brother, I do, but," Mark paused and turned to face him. "But I guess my main concern is making Cassie happy, and I'm not sure he'll do that."

"He'll spend his life trying really hard, but he never will, and there's nothing you or I can do about that."

Mark stared at him for a long time and a slow realization came. She had mentioned having to put up with objections from other people, and he realized then Clay was one of them. "You've tried to talk her out of it too."

"Cassie has a mind of her own."

Mark squinted his eyes a little suspiciously, "I'll be honest about why I don't want her to marry him, I don't think he's right for her, I don't see her truly happy with someone like him. So what are your reasons?"

"The same, William loves her, but I think in the long run, she'll regret not doing certain things she wants to do with her life."

Mark still looked at him suspiciously, stared at him for a long time before he motioned to the bartender. "Can you get me two more shots?"

He then held out one of the already full glasses to Clay and took one for himself and they each downed the contents. He set his on top the bar and turned to him again. "You're in love with her, aren't you?"

Clay didn't bother to avoid the question, and didn't lie in his answer. "Yeah, I am."

"And she's to be your brothers wife."

"Right again," he chuckled. "And I thought you liked me, are you trying to make me feel more miserable on purpose?"

"Does your brother know you're in love with her?"

"No, hell, Cassie doesn't even know."

Mark felt sorry for him, knew his situation had to be pure hell. "The ultimate sacrifice, you're giving up someone you love, because of family loyalty to your brother."

"Yes sir."

"Would William do the same for you were the situations reversed?"

"That's irrelevant." Clay answered.

"You're a good man, Clay." Mark patted him on the back. "A stupid man with morals, values and loyalties that are commendable, but I still like you anyway."

****

When Susan entered the room, she was crying, and Cassie laughed as she hugged her. "Susan, you've been so emotional today, I'm not sure you're going to make it all the way through."

"I'm not. How can you be so calm? Didn't you even cry when you asked Mark? I saw him come out, I've been out there hiding in a corner crying, this is all so much."

Cassie handed her a tissue. "Actually, it was very emotional, and I did tear up, but it was over quickly and he went to get us whiskey."

"Whiskey." Susan shouted, immediately object to the idea. "How could he…"

"Calm down, it's only one shot, just one for old times sake."

"You know Mark, he'll bring back ten."

"I promise, we're just having one, both of us need it."

"Need what?" Mel asked as she entered.

"A shot of whiskey, you're going to join us, aren't you?"

"You're not…" Mel too began to object and Cassie stopped her.

"I am, but just one, I promise."

"If Mark's going to walk you down the aisle, I don't think he should be allowed to have whiskey just before he does."

"It's because he's walking me down the aisle, that he needs it." Cassie commented and saw the confused look on Mel's face, but the knowing on Susan's.

When Marie entered her face glowed and she was as excited as Cassie had ever seen her. "Aunt Cassie, it's time. They're taking Granddad out now, you should see how happy he looks."

Mel laughed and teased. "That's the medication he's on honey."

Cassie smiled, he was happy, medication or not, and she felt she owed him this, her obligation to make him proud was strong and unwavering as she put her arm around Marie.

Her voice was calm when she spoke. "I tell you what, you and Mel and Susan tell anyone that needs to know that I'm ready whenever they are. And if you can send in my handsome escort, we can get this thing over with."

"Did someone call me?" Mark stood at the door with two shots of whiskey, one in each hand.

Mel rolled her eyes. "You two hurry up, if anything goes wrong Mark, you'll have hell to pay."

Susan gave her husband a kiss when she left and when they were alone, Mark walked slowly over to Cassie and handed her the small glass, then they clinked them together in toast, drank the liquid, and she slipped her arm through his.

Everyone was seated outside on what had turned out to be a glorious day after the morning clouds, and the foyer was quiet as Cassie watched Marie go out with a smile over her shoulder, then Mel kissed her cheek before she stepped out the door and then the door was closed as they had to wait a few moments. Cassie took a deep breath as the wedding march began. It was her cue to appear and begin her new life.

CHAPTER TWENTY

Two Years Later

When Clay received the call from William, he packed very few things and made quick arrangements for the next flight. Their mother had a slight heart attack, it wasn't serious, she was in stable condition, and doctor's assured him she would be fine with a few changes to her lifestyle. She'd have to give up the rich foods and decadent desserts she'd come to love, but she would pull through in grand style.

William picked him up from the airport and they went immediately to the hospital where he was reassured she would be fine by looking at her. But it was obvious she would milk it for all it was worth in dramatic style.

"Oh, Clay, you're finally here. I couldn't have died without seeing you."

"You're not going to die, Mom, one of these days, but not now," he kissed her forehead and she smiled.

"I feel better just seeing you."

"You are better, the doctors say you'll be fine, we're even taking you home this afternoon." He looked around the room at all the flowers and plants that had been sent. "We might need a separate truck to carry this stuff home."

"Aren't they all lovely?" She perked up. "So many beautiful flowers, it's been like living in a florist shop. There's even a bouquet from the Dickson's, I hadn't heard from them in ages."

"How are the Dickson's, Mom?" Clay asked merely to hear her voice, to see if there were any affects he couldn't notice on the outside.

"They just had their sixth grandchild, can you believe that?"

It figured her response would have something to do with grandkids, it seemed the only thing on her mind, as if it were a race. "I'm glad for them." Clay rolled his eyes to his brother when she wasn't looking. "They also have a family of five girls."

"William?" She looked to him standing by the door. "Speaking of grandkids, didn't my heart attack scare that wife of yours enough to go into labor?" She smiled at the thought of her first grandchild on the way, excited at the prospect of the new life that would bless them soon.

"If I didn't know any better, I would have suspected you did this to make her go into labor."

"She's due any day, I guess I can wait if I have to." Jill huffed.

"You're going to have to, but I'll see what I can do."

"Where is that wife of yours anyway?" Jill asked.

"She wasn't feeling up to the airport ride."

"She's okay, isn't she?" Jill asked with immediate concern. "Here I am worried about myself and..." she began to get flustered and William stopped her as Clay looked on intently.

"She's fine, just wasn't up to the ride."

"The pregnancy is going good, isn't it?" There was concern in Clay's voice.

"Perfectly. She has a doctor's appointment later this afternoon so we'll stop by afterwards."

"I worry about her, I hope everything is okay."

"William said it was."

"But he probably just doesn't want me to worry."

Clay looked towards the closed door. "I'm sure everything is fine." He kept his own concern from his voice so his mother wouldn't worry more.

"You know," she spoke to Clay when William left. "I could be on my death bed, I'm not going to be around forever, it would be nice to see you settled before I'm gone."

Clay laughed. "Oh no, you're not on your death bed and you're not going anywhere, you'll be around for a long time. Don't try to guilt me into anything."

"I shouldn't have to guilt you, you should have your family by now. Look at William, married and settled with a new baby on the way, that's what I want from you."

"William and I are different people, Mom, and right now it's not what I want for myself." Clay busied himself by walking around the room and looked at the cards attached to the flowers. Read the names of friends and family he knew or heard her speak of and was familiar with.

"Well if you..."

"Mother," he spoke playfully but with a serious tone. "I didn't come here to be badgered about my life."

"I'm not badgering you, I'm worried about you. Look how happy William is, don't you want that for yourself?"

"I'm happy with my life, free to do as I please when I please. How lucky is that? Some people don't need others to make their life complete, a person can be happy on their own."

"They can, and you can say what you want, but I see something missing in you."

"Then put on your glasses." He walked over to her and sat down in the chair next to the bed. "Can I get you something?"

She didn't want or need anything so he sat next to her and read the paper out loud. Articles he knew would be of interest and articles he knew would initiate a debate of their different opinions. By the time the doctor's released her Clay was satisfied to know she would be fine, just as they said.

When Redman came in, Clay was as polite as he could be, shook his hand like a gentlemen would, then left the room. He was in the hall when he saw William from the far end with his large pregnant wife as they got out of the elevator.

He stood and watched as they came down the hall, she looked good, an extra large, due any day now belly, but she looked healthy and good.

Clay smiled broadly and greeted her with a warm hug. "Hello, Anna, you're looking great."

"Yeah," she huffed and placed both hands on her large belly. "As well as any whale can look but this baby should be here any day now, the doctor said if I don't go into labor within the week, they'll have to induce me and force this baby out."

They didn't have to wait much longer. Jill was released that afternoon and early that evening they were back in the hospital when Anna's water broke just before eight. Clay stayed at his mother's home, even if he knew it bothered Redman for him to be there, but when William called with the news and wanted him at the hospital he took off. Jill was sound asleep and doing well so she would hopefully wake in the morning to the news.

William paced in nervousness as they prepped her for birth and Clay tried to calm him as he waited in the waiting room. Assured him everything would be fine, her screaming and pain was normal, it was labor. His brother's face was beaded with sweat and Clay knew Anna would make it through with flying colors but William would probably end up passed out on the floor and his prediction came true when the time came. Just as the new baby boy was delivered, William hit the floor.

"It was unbelievable." William said when he was finally able to tell Clay about it. "All of a sudden there he was, and then all kinds of stuff... never mind about the other. It was unbelievable." He sat next to him in the chair as they waited until Clay could see the baby.

"You can calm down now. Take some deep breaths." Clay encouraged.

William did eventually calm down as they waited and it wasn't long before the doctor came in. "Anna and the baby have been settled and they're waiting for you. Christine will take you."

William shook his hand boisterously. "Thank you, Dr. Adams, thank you. He's healthy and all, isn't he? And Anna is fine, no problems? She looked a little rough there and..."

"Everyone is fine, William. However, I might have to prescribe you something." He joked and had to pry his hand loose before William shook it out of socket.

Clay didn't want to go in initially, thought William would want some time alone with his wife and new child, but his brother insisted, wouldn't take 'no' for an answer. Anna held the baby who was now clean and wrapped tight in a blanket with a stocking cap on his little head. The smile on her face gave no indication of the pain she'd just endured.

"Come see him," she whispered. "He's amazing."

Clay had to admit he was. Holding the newborn only hours old was the first time he'd ever been that close to new life. So many things the little guy would have to learn, to endure, so many things yet to live through and Clay didn't envy his road ahead. Afterwards, the both of them were whisked away as Anna needed her rest and they decided they still had time to have a celebratory drink before returning home. It was around midnight when they stepped into a bar a block away and ordered a beer.

Clay raised his bottle and the two came together. "To new life, to your new son."

"A few years ago, I never thought I'd feel this way, hard to believe my life worked out like this after being stood up at the marriage alter, I've never been happier than at this moment."

"Guess it's true what mother always says. Life has a way of working out." Clay sipped his drink and placed it on the bar. Wondered why the phrase 'never' seemed to apply to him, his could be 'Life had a way of never working out.'

"After Cassie, I thought I'd missed my chance to ever be happy. How was I to know I'd find the one I was truly meant to be with?"

Hearing her name still caused his heart to jump. His mind wandered to the last vision he had of her, standing in her wedding dress in the foyer of Crystal Lake Resort. It had been a beautiful day for a wedding. William, Clay and Ricky stood with the minister, watched as Marie and Mel made their way down the aisle, but when the music began for Cassie, she never appeared. It stopped for several moments, then repeated again then stopped when only a member of the staff came from the door, walked down the aisle and whispered something in William's ear. He informed the audience to hold on a moment and asked Clay to come with him. They entered and saw Cassie by the door with sadness in her eyes.

"I can't do it, William. I have to go," she whispered.

"No, Cassie, you can't do this. Its nerves, everything is fine and our guests are waiting, you're just having a panic attack, take a few deep breaths and..."

"No. Since Vegas I've been going through the motions, I've been convinced it's what's best, by you, by your family, by my family, but I never listened to myself. Never listened to my doubts and fears I was doing it for all the wrong reasons. You can't offer me the life I want."

"We'll have a family and children, it's what we both want."

"I want more than that."

"What more is there? We love each other. I'll give you the life you want, whatever you need is yours," his voice was desperate and pleading.

"You can't, I know that now."

He looked frantically at Clay who said nothing. In his shock and growing fear he began to ramble when he should have taken a deep breath and calmed down. "Did you tell her? Is that what this is all about? Cassie, I..." Then he stopped, knew he'd been mistaken and said things he shouldn't have.

"Tell me what? What are you talking about?" She looked back and forth between William and Clay but neither could look her in the eye and the truth slowly dawned on her. "That was your girl in Vegas."

"No, Cassie, I meant..."

"Stop, William, don't lie to me now, at least give me that," she spoke softly and opened the front door. "It doesn't matter, that isn't the reason I'm leaving. I'm leaving because I know what's best for my life now. I'm listening to myself and no one else. Maybe I'm not the smartest one to listen to, and if I'm making a big mistake, then at least I only have myself to blame."

To the shock of everyone, Cassie left that day, left William and any life he offered. The very day her option to purchase the commercial building from Clay was to expire the bank called him and told him she'd been in and signed the papers. He thought of her now, thought of her life, and was happy she'd found her way. He had settled himself to the fact that he'd never see her again, could only hold onto the distant memory of what little they were able to share.

"This is an incredible feeling, Clay. You should settle down and try it." William said, could see a distant look in his brother's eyes.

"You're starting to sound like mother now, and you wonder why I don't come more often, I can't take the pressure," he teased.

"I still can't figure out what you're waiting for."

"Nothing. When it happens, it happens, I just don't spend my time looking for it."

"Maybe as crazed as Cassie was when she dragged you onto that ship, left you with scars that makes you leery of all women." William laughed and Clay pretended to also, he knew the scars were far different than what he spoke of.

They were silent for a few moments. Clay tried so hard not to say anything, didn't want to bring her up or mention her name, nothing. He wished they would change the subject but William was being sentimental in his new fatherhood mood.

"Cassie and I are great friends by the way. As painful as the breakup was, I got past that and we're at a good place now. Anna even invited her to the wedding, she didn't come, but she stopped in soon after. Anna likes her."

"I never would have expected that." Clay laughed. "Not that I can't see it, I can actually picture the two of them being friends, just in the sense that I'd have to move out of town if my girlfriends ever met one another."

"She's doing great, moved back to Lakeview, opened up some little shop. I guess that town is okay for some, it was way too small for me."

Clay listened intently but his eyes scanned the room. Why did they have to talk about Cassie? Why did she still have to permeate his thoughts? Couldn't she just go away?

But she wouldn't go away as William continued. "You know, you and her have a lot in common. Rebellious. Strong willed. Probably should have been you two to hook up instead, would have worked out better than we did. I guess if you two felt anything for each other, it would have come out spending a week in Hawaii with her."

Clay had never lied to him and wouldn't start now. "I was physically attracted to her, it was hard not to be, but she was your fiancé William. I never would have done something like that to you."

William set his beer bottle down and looked to Clay who seemed to have a distant look in his eyes. As if an invisible outer shell appeared to protect him. "So what's stopping you now?" The words came from his mouth and William didn't know why he hadn't thought of the two of them together before. Was sure Clay felt something for her, something more than he was willing to admit because they were brothers. He was protecting him, William was sure.

"Stopping me from what?"

"Maybe you still feel something, maybe that's the perfect one you've been looking for."

"I spent a week with her and the majority of the time we hated each other. She hated me because I was a man and I hated her because I felt like I was being held against my will."

"Kidnapped by a beautiful woman and taken off to Hawaii. Yeah, I'm sure it left you with psychological problems." William said it sarcastically and they both laughed.

"Okay, so it ended up not being that bad."

William's voice was serious. "I know you didn't like lying for me, but I was so desperate I couldn't think straight. I realized later it was something I never should have asked you to do, I should have taken responsibility for my own mistake."

Clay shrugged his shoulders. "You were in love, who is to say I wouldn't have asked you to do the same for me? I've never faulted you for that."

"I owe you, Clay, if you think you need permission of some sort to contact Cassie, you have it. I'd want nothing but the best for you, and her."

"It was a physical attraction, any man who wouldn't admit to that is crazy, she's beautiful, but there was nothing more, William." Clay looked at his brother who listened intently.

"Don't let me stand in the way because you think it isn't ethical. I loved Cassie once, but not in the way I love Anna. She did what ended up being best for both of us. But if you two had something and I stood in the way then, I don't now. I'll hand over my blessing if that's what you need."

Clay laughed. "She has the life she wants, what makes you think she would want me to be part of it?"

"I don't know that she does, I'm guessing, for all I know she could be involved, even married, I haven't talked to her in quite some time now. But it just dawned on me that you two could have made a good pair," then William laughed. "And maybe I'm being selfish. If you settle down, mother won't bug me to be the only one to give her grandchildren. She won't stop on the first, he's less than a day old and I can already hear her tomorrow morning asking when we're having another, and another. I'm trying to save myself from working until I'm 100 just to pay for college educations."

It was quiet between them, Clay wasn't sure what he was feeling or thinking at the thought there was nothing that stood between them now. It was obvious William's words were true, he wasn't saying them to make Clay feel better, he was truly happy and content with the life he'd found and wanted the same for him.

"I don't know, William, like you said, she's probably married by now."

"And if she's not? I don't know what you've been looking for out there but obviously you haven't found it yet. Do you think you could live with yourself knowing it might be waiting for you in Lakeview and you won't go get it?"

Too much time had passed, it had been two years, for all he knew she was settled and content just as William was. Married with a child, living her dream with everything she ever wanted and what made him think she would even want him to be part of it? Cassie had never contacted him, she'd walked out the door that day in her beautiful wedding dress and he set his mind into never seeing her again, tried to forget about a woman who'd impacted his life in such a short amount of time.

He tried to forget with many other women. Moved from place to place as if he'd find what he searched for. He'd run all over the world trying to find something that wasn't out there, thought he'd find a place that felt right, but nothing ever did without her. He got out of bed every day and did the same things he'd always done, but at the end of every day, he was always faced with another lonely night. He'd encouraged her to pursue her dreams, now felt as if he should take his own advice to heart.

As Clay sat in the airport and waited for his plane, William's words rang in his ears. He continued to ask himself the same question William had, what stopped him? If he thought it was William who stood in the way, his brother officially stepped aside, gave his blessing. When his plane began to board he found himself sitting there until the last passenger walked through the doorway, then rose from his seat in the boarding area, went back through the airport to the ticket counter, and changed his flight to North Carolina.

CHAPTER TWENTY ONE

Clay landed in Charlotte, rented a car, and obtained a map. It took him an hour and a half to find his way to the town of Lakeview and it's small Main Street on that early Saturday morning and the town bustled with activity. As Clay parked the car and got out, several people greeted him with...'Hello'...'Afternoon'...'How are you today?'... Strangers who wanted a response and he gave them a smile and a nod. He remembered its charm and hospitality from his previous visit for the wedding that never took place and he got the same feeling he did then, a welcome feeling.

He parked the car in a new small lot at the end of the row of stores that overlooked the lake, it was just next to the cafe' that sat at the end of the row. The parking area was the only thing between it and the Town Square and it reinforced her vision that it was the perfect location for almost guaranteed success. If he hadn't purchased it when he did, surely the opportunity would have been lost to her and he was even happier now to have been able to help in what small way he could.

Customers lounged on the deck at tables that faced the lake and enjoyed the lazy Saturday. He could see other customers at even more tables on the sidewalk in front, and then he crossed the street to view it, saw her dream just as she pictured it, exactly as she explained, with a red and white awning and gingerbread trim. Paintings of coffee and bakery items such as cakes and muffins adorned the window, white curtains on the door and the sides of the window, and it beckoned you to come in and sit for awhile.

It looked the freshest on the street and he noticed several other buildings had been renovated or were in the process. Perhaps Cassie had been the start of an entire urban renewal in this hometown. It was the middle of a busy summer tourist season and her place looked to be the busiest on the street and when he finally walked inside it was crowded. Several people relaxed on overstuffed couches and chairs in a separate room that resembled a charming library. Where the tables and chairs were located and the counter with stools, that area resembled someone's kitchen, as if he'd just stepped into a friend's home.

Beyond, he could see out the window to the busy deck again. The day was bright and beautiful and he was tempted but found a stool instead, asked for a cup of regular caffeine coffee, a simple choice, out of many flavors of espresso, cappuccino's and latte's.

"I've never seen you around, you just get into town?" The woman asked as she poured.

"Yes, as a matter of fact I did."

"Staying long?"

He thought about her question, would hope to answer he would be there for the rest of his life, but that, he wasn't sure of. "Just passing through for now."

"You must be lost. We're a dead end, no one just passes through." She pulled a small menu from the stand. "All kinds of fresh things to offer, can I get you something to go with your coffee?"

"Just the coffee, but thank you."

Nonchalantly he looked around for Cassie but couldn't see her, then heard the bell of a door in the library area, immediately noticed the business ploy to divert customers through the library onto the deck in order to browse the books for sale along their way. It was also where the cash register was located so even those who sat at the stools or tables were diverted there also. He heard her voice when the door closed.

"Ms. Nellie, you take that book home first and if you like it, then you can pay me. But don't leave yet, let me wrap up Morris's muffins for you to take."

"He'd have a fit if I didn't bring home his muffins. Doesn't like a dang thing I bake anymore, Cassie, you've spoiled him. Used to be my plain ole apple pie was all he needed, but even that doesn't hold a candle to yours."

"I've had your apple pie, Nellie, and I know better. Just think of it as giving you more time to spend with Morris on the porch and not be in the kitchen." Cassie came into view and stepped behind the counter, wrapped the muffins she took from the display for the woman who now waited in front of her.

"Oh, I do, it's more freedom for me. Speaking of porches, how's your house coming along?"

"Slowly. I thought this place would slow down a little and free up some time to do things but that hasn't happened yet." Cassie bagged them and waved to a leaving customer. "You have a safe trip home, we'll see you next summer?"

"If not before then." The woman smiled and left.

Ms. Nellie accepted the bag she was handed. "You're coming by for Sunday dinner tomorrow, aren't you? Morris is expecting you."

"I'm looking forward to it already, I'll bring dessert." She smiled broadly. Cassie never had to worry about fixing dinner, the last thing she wanted to do after twelve-hour days, and there was always an invitation she could accept, and Ms. Nellie made the best roast in town.

When the woman left Cassie grabbed a pot of regular coffee and began down the counter. "Anyone need a refill on regular?"

"I do, Cassie." A man shouted from a table and she laughed at him.

"I'll bring decaf for you Jack, your wife would kill me."

"Can't get away with nothing." He mumbled to his friend that sat with him.

Clay watched in silence. She looked magnificent wearing a pair of jeans, a white shirt, a stained apron, and her face shone, her voice like a song. Cassie was happy, of that he had no doubt, Clay had to ask himself again what he could offer to her life, she appeared to have everything she needed.

She hadn't paid much attention to the faces, looked inside the cups to see if they were empty and automatically poured more. Of all the kinds she offered, her regular's, residents of Lakeview, always drank simple coffee. Nothing fancy, nothing with foam, just plain coffee, and most of her regulars sat at the counter for a quick cup and some conversation.

She often felt like a bartender would, or perhaps a hairdresser, it was the kind of job where people came in and talked to her. Some revealed confidences she didn't think she needed to know, but they knew she could be trusted, and she gave advice or her opinion when she thought it's what they wanted.

Clay sat on the last stool in the row and she didn't look up as she filled his half empty cup and he didn't say a word, neither did she until she was done.

"Can I get you something else?" She looked up and almost dropped the pot.

"Hello, Cassie," he smiled easily and then the shock on her face made him laugh.

"Well you were the last person I expected to see." She laughed at the shock of it. God he looked good. And she thought her heart was going to bust through her skin as it became overwhelmed in emotion.

"You told me if I were ever in town to stop in for a cup of coffee," he smiled and shrugged his shoulders. "So I was in town."

She smiled as her heart rate slowed. "So I did, you could have warned me."

"What fun would that have been? It was worth the trip just to see your face."

"What are you doing on this side of the world? Last time I talked to William he mentioned you were in Oregon or somewhere." Cassie tried to get her breath back to even breathing, tried to calm her heart that beat rapidly.

"Mother had a slight heart attack." Clay saw the panic in her eyes and calmed her right away. "She's fine. Just a little warning the doctors said, with a little change in her lifestyle and diet she shouldn't have any more problems."

"Oh, good." Cassie was relieved.

"The day she came home, Anna went into the hospital and had a baby boy."

Cassie smiled broadly. "How wonderful, I'll have to send them something."

"I was kind of surprised to hear you'd kept in touch with them a bit."

"I like Anna, the two couldn't be a more perfect pair." Cassie finally set her coffee pot down before she dropped it. "Can I get you something? We're the best bakery in town."

He laughed. "You're the only bakery in town."

"Thanks to you. I would have sent a thank you note, but I didn't know where to send it."

"I didn't expect thanks, I was just glad to be informed you signed the papers and took over. I didn't know what I was going to do with it if you hadn't."

Cassie leaned on the counter with her arms crossed, a normal position she took when talking. "I probably would have sooner than I did, but I waited for Mel to get her life straightened out a bit. I had to time it perfectly for her to say yes. She divorced Eddy right after... I was going to say the wedding, but I guess it's the wedding that never took place. So by the time the year was up her divorce was final and she was at a good place, and was ready for a new life. The timing couldn't have been better."

"I'm glad things have worked out for you." He could see the happiness, the contentment at her life.

She was always beautiful but much more so now because of the person she'd become. Maybe his mother was right, life did have a way of working out. Clay knew they couldn't have had anything two years ago because of circumstances, nor soon after, now William had his happy life, had given him his blessing to free the way and Cassie had the time to find her dream. He just hoped he'd fit into it now.

"So far it's worked just as I thought. With my marketing and business and her baking skills we're a great team. And she's a completely different person now without Eddy, she's the sister I used to have. If I told someone this would be my life two years ago they would have thought I'd lost it."

He smiled at her proudly. "See? I didn't steer you wrong, I told you the view was better from the clouds."

"You also told me a lie, how was I to trust anything?" Cassie said it with a sly smile but forgiving eyes.

"You slept with me naked so you must have trusted me a little," he teased back.

"That was before I knew you lied. I guess it worked to my benefit you were William's brother, if not I'm not sure you could have been trusted to sleep with naked."

"I'm sure I couldn't have been trusted."

Cassie blushed and lowered her head shyly, the thoughts made her flush with heat. How could he walk in after two years and still have this effect on her? She'd pushed him so far back in her mind but in the instant she saw him, everything she'd ever felt rushed to surface.

She was glad she didn't have any duties she had to tend to. Cassie's job was to fill in where it was slack most times and they weren't slack today. Her main priorities were to mingle with customers, pour coffee when she thought it needed to be poured to free up someone else, act as hostess, but she was thankful she didn't have any customers who waited on items or waited for checks.

Others took care of that while she enjoyed spending time with Clay. He talked of the new baby, William and Anna, and his mother. Told her where he'd lived over the past two years, from Indiana to Oregon. Some of his favorite things about certain places he either lived or visited, how he had crawfish for the first time in New Orleans, and he went salmon fishing in Alaska, a dangerous sport when the bears vied for the same thing. As customers came and went she was lost in his eyes overtop the counter she hadn't moved from, absorbed in every word, absorbed in the memory of him and the way he made her feel.

"Ever get back to Hawaii?" She asked.

"No desire to. It wouldn't be the same."

"I still keep in contact with Lee. Remember Kyle and Lee?"

"Of course, how are they? I guess you finally told them the truth."

"I called her after my second attempt at marriage to William. Both of them were shocked of course then we all laughed about it."

"I guess we can now." Then Clay asked her a question he'd been curious about the last few years. "What stopped you that day?"

She raised her eyebrows. "Stopped me from marrying William?"

"I've always been curious why you didn't go through with it."

Cassie shrugged her shoulders. "A combination of quite a few things, but I think the main things were a shot of whiskey, and the fact that Mark refused to walk me down the aisle. That was the beginning of it anyway."

"He refused?" Clay questioned with more than curiosity, he'd seen him that day, had seen he had trouble with it, but never suspected he would have refused her.

Cassie laughed. "Shocked me too, I actually thought he was going to go through with it, then at the very last possible second, he left me high and dry in the foyer by myself, not just refused me, but left me there all by myself."

Cassie recalled the events to him. They'd been in the foyer alone and the doors had closed, the wedding march began, and Mark turned to her and took her arms with his hands.

"I can't do this," he stated.

Cassie was shocked at what he was doing to her, shocked and hurt he would pick that moment of her life, the most important day of her life, to do something like that to her.

"You said…"

"I said I needed whiskey, I said I'd always be here for you, I never really said I'd walk you down the aisle, I never really agreed."

"A select choice of words, you were lying to me? I thought…" Cassie looked to the closed door in panic, a rage began inside her. "You're going to pull a stunt like this, at the last possible second, and make me walk down that aisle by myself? How could you do this to me? What kind of friend does that?"

"If you can look me in the eye and tell me this is what you really want to do, and you're doing it for all the right reasons, then I'll have no problem with it. I may not like him, but I'll support your choice."

"Don't do this to me now."

"Listen to me Cassie, calm down a minute, that's all we have is one minute, and listen to me. I know a man that has more morals and values than I could ever dream of. I'm a pretty decent guy, but he's a hell of a lot stronger than I am. And he has deep loyalties to someone, and he reminded me that I have deep loyalties to someone also, and that's you." Mark took her hands in his. "I can say I'm a loyal friend to you, but if I don't do anything about it, what does that mean? So I'm doing something about it, you may not understand it right now, but I'm proving how devoted I am, I have a responsibility to you as a friend, a loyal friend, and I can't be a part of this. Because if I were, it would mean that I agree with what you're doing, and I can't do that."

Cassie's hands were shaking. "Mark, can you just…"

"I can't. You want me to give you away, you want me to walk you down that aisle and when the minister asks who is to give this bride away, I'm to say her family and I. That makes me a part of it, which makes me an accessory to the crime…"

Cassie was quiet as he continued.

"…Walk down that aisle if you want to, but you'll have to do it alone. Curse me, cuss me, hit me, and you might hate me for what I'm doing right now, but I know in your heart you know it's best, and maybe not today, but you'll understand one day why I can't do this." Mark placed a kiss on her cheek. "I'm going to the bar and get more whiskey, because I've not only probably lost one of my best friends, you may never forgive me for this, but this is going to piss my wife off like you wouldn't believe. I told her I wouldn't say anything, I told her I wouldn't ruin this day for you, and I know she'll understand, but that's after she gets really, really pissed. So I'm going to need to be drunk and numb when she gets hold of me…"

"There are two doors in this room, one leads out to a wedding, and one leads the other way to your car parked right out front." Mark pressed a set of keys into her hand and walked away.

Cassie stared at the keys, and in her mind it was a symbol, a representation of something, even if Mark hadn't known it when he placed the keys there. She thought of the truck she'd driven into the lake. She'd been impulsive and rash when she'd taken it, but it had been fun, she and everyone else remembered it to that day, and she could remember the exhilarated feeling it had given her. Over the week, she often found herself wondering when she'd handed over the keys. Now she stood in the empty foyer with the keys in her hand again.

Clay had listened intently to what had happened that day, and Cassie reached behind her and replenished their coffee with a fresh cup. "So,' she stated with a deep sigh. "He gave me back the keys."

"Gave you back the keys?"

Cassie smiled and waved her hand. "A symbol of something, another long story."

"So how is Mark?"

"A pain in my ass."

Clay laughed. "So I guess he's still the same. I always envied the relationship you two had."

"Yeah, even though I left, and I knew it was the best thing to do, I was still really pissed at him for awhile. Then one day when I came home, he grabbed me, threw me in the lake like he always does, and that was the end of that."

"And of course Susan forgave him?"

"Always," she smiled.

"And what about your father?"

"He couldn't chase after me of course, he had two broken legs, remember?" She teased. "But they healed fine and once we sat down to talk, you were right."

"I was right?" Clay questioned, unsure of what she meant.

"He loved me anyway, and understood. Still doesn't agree with me sometimes, but he understands me better."

As they talked more, Clay listened and watched her intently, he felt there was no doubt the connection he felt for her was still there, as real as it was the last time he saw her. It wasn't something he doubted before he'd come, and didn't doubt now. Not only had it not faded, it had grown stronger, maybe with the knowledge William wasn't between them now, it made him open to what they could have.

The only question was if it was still there for her? He wasn't sure what he read in her eyes, there was shock and wonder he was sitting there in front of her and her eyes sparkled, her smile and laugh carefree, but that's how she was anyway. He'd just seen her with customers and she'd been just as hospitable. He didn't see a wedding ring, but there was a tan line on the finger it would have been and a tan line on another finger. Did that mean anything? More important, was the question of how far she had taken her dream. Was she married? Did she have children? Was he too late?

Just as he was about to ask about her personal life, a little girl came toddling around the corner and ran directly for her with a loud playful squeal. On young wobbly feet she made her way to Cassie who scooped her up in her arms as the little girl giggled.

"Hey little miss, how did you escape?"

She was young and looked as if she'd just learned to walk. Pure innocent face with the biggest blue eyes he'd ever seen that peeked out from a head of curls. His heart sank, he'd been too late, and Clay felt an instant desolate pain in the pit of his stomach at the sight of what had to be her child. She looked like her, the same eyes, a resemblance in the face, who else could it be? Mel had divorced Eddy, and Marie was much too young for children. Cassie had the life she wanted, everything she'd dreamed, who was he to think she needed anything from him?

Then Mel rounded the corner from where the child had come from. "Sorry, Cassie, I put her down for two seconds and she took off, had to find you." Mel stepped next to her and looked to the handsome man at the counter who looked familiar but it was a few moments before she could place who he was. "Clay?" Mel said when she realized. "What on earth are you doing here?"

"Cassie invited me for a cup of coffee a few years ago, I just got around to taking her up on the invitation." He smiled as best he could, there was no disappointment that showed on his face but inside he felt as if he were falling apart in little pieces. The nightmares he'd had over the years of her life without him had now materialized and his heavy heart of before was even heavier now.

"We have the best in town," she said.

"So I hear." He looked to Cassie and her little girl then quickly back to Mel. "Congratulations on the success."

"Thanks, I never thought being in business could be so much fun. Guess that's why we're successful, we're having a good time doing it. I may have done some stupid things in my life, but the smartest was the day I let my little sister talk me into this." She looked to Cassie proudly, and appreciatively. "I never would have guessed things would work out like this, but here we are. What about you?"

"Doing well, I can't complain."

"Are you in town long?" Mel continued but was interrupted by someone from the kitchen telling her the timer she set to go off was done. "I'll be right back, won't do to have burnt pastries. Cassie, you want me to take Abigail?"

"No, she's fine." She smiled sweetly, a motherly look to the little girl who was fascinated by her necklace. Then as Mel ran off she was called to the library side where a box of books had been delivered and they didn't know where she wanted them. Her attention turned back to Clay. "I'm sorry, Clay, can you give me one second?"

"Don't give it another thought, duty calls."

Cassie saw the open box and knew they were the new releases that went in the front window and the table there. Marie came in the back door and Abby wanted nothing more to do with her, wanted her sister instead and Marie took her willingly.

"Can I take her outside a minute? Someone has a puppy and she'd love it." Marie asked.

"I don't see why not." Cassie took the little girls face in her hands. "You are too cute." Then she turned her attention to Marie and did the same. "And you are too beautiful. When did you grow up so much?"

"When you weren't looking, Aunt Cassie, isn't that what you tell me all the time?"

"I have to keep my eyes wide open from now on." She thought about her statement again when she returned to where Clay once sat but now the stool was empty. A $20 bill placed under the cup.

CHAPTER TWENTY TWO

Cassie stood there a few moments and looked around as if she'd see him somewhere but didn't. She picked up the money and took it with her onto the busy sidewalk but still didn't see him until she walked a little ways towards the parking lot and saw him about to get into his car.

"Clay!" She hollered and he stopped at the open car door and turned around as she approached. "What's this?"

He saw the money in her hand and thought that's what she spoke of. "For my coffee."

"Not the money, what's this? Why are you leaving?"

"You got busy and I'm not very good at goodbyes. On the cruise ship I just left, and on your wedding day, you just left. If you think about it, we've never done it, said goodbyes. I figured there was no sense starting now." He smiled slightly, knew it was a weak excuse all the way around.

She looked at him silently, unable to believe he could just waltz in, then out of her life with such ease. What had he come for? Surely he hadn't traveled all that way for a cup of coffee. Cassie didn't understand it, it was as if she was thrown back into the turmoil of her feelings for him two years previous. Every doubt, every emotion raged through her and it would be left undone just as it was then.

"But I... we could..." She didn't even know what to say, he confused her so. He gave mixed signals of still having feelings for her then brushed her off so casually, it confused her even more. Cassie held out his $20 bill. "If you have to leave, then take your money. The least I can do is give you a cup of coffee on the house."

He took it from her slowly with apology in his eyes. "I'm sorry, maybe I shouldn't have come. I guess it wasn't what I expected."

As she caught a glimpse of her reflection in the car window it slowly dawned on her and she misconstrued his meaning. He'd fallen for her superficial persona. The beautiful sophisticated career woman who looked fashionable and particularly put together, one he'd seen in long flowing gowns cut down practically to her navel, elegant, stylish, flowing black hair and makeup applied to perfection. Now he was faced with a woman in jeans and a white shirt stained with coffee and batter and who knew what else with her hair tied up haphazardly with escaping wisps that blew around her face, she was a far different woman than what he knew.

It was the first time Cassie realized how completely different she was from two years previous. From the time he wanted her, till now, she'd undergone a change in every area of her life and he'd come in search of the person she once was, only to be disappointed. Only to discover she was not the woman he wanted anymore. Knowing that fact about him, that he was so shallow, and not the man she fantasized him to be, would make it easy for her to forget him now. She was actually glad he'd come.

"Maybe you shouldn't have," she said as anger tinted her words. "Sorry if I disappointed you."

Cassie turned quickly to leave and Clay grabbed her arm. "What do you mean disappointed me?"

"I guess I'm not quite the woman you remember. You could have at least had the decency to politely say goodbye."

"Cassie, that has nothing..."

"I get it, Clay," she turned to him with venom in her eyes. "You remembered the beautiful career woman of two years ago and you expected to find her again but she's not here. You're faced with the person I am now and maybe that's not as attractive to you. I'm sorry to disappoint but that other woman is gone."

"You don't..." He tried to interrupt at every turn but she was hell bent on voicing what she misread as his reason for leaving.

"I guess your visit served to open both our eyes. For two years I've wondered what, if anything, could ever become of us, I've always felt it was left unfinished. Now you've made it easy, you're certainly not the man I thought you were either so I can say goodbye with no regrets and easily put you behind me once and for all."

She jerked her arm away from him with force and when he stopped her this time he turned her back against the car and pressed against her so she couldn't get away. His hand reached behind her head and his fingers entwined in her hair as he kissed her with all the passion he held in for so long. The fight she gave was not one of a married woman, the child may be hers but he knew she couldn't have been committed to someone else to be so passionate about him leaving.

He held her to him and she gave in, neither cared about the passerby's on the sidewalk who smiled or gawked at their behavior. Then she abruptly pulled away but he kissed her again when she was going to speak, he did it three times before he was sure she wouldn't talk and he could speak first.

"Cassie, I thought you were married," he said with what little breath he had left.

"Married!" She exclaimed. "How could you think that?"

"Your little girl."

Her hand flew to her mouth as she realized the mistake. "Abby? I never introduced you. You thought... oh my God, I didn't even... I wasn't thinking and..."

"I don't care if it's your little girl, she's beautiful, and I'll love her just as much as I love you. Just tell me you haven't started your life with someone else, tell me I'm not too late. Tell me you're free, that's all I need to hear."

"Free? I'm bound by many things. My business, my house at Cape Point that is always in need of repair and remodeling, and my sisters children, including Abigail, that I spend most of my time with, what little is left. But if you're asking if there's anyone who shares that life with me, the answer is a definite and loud no. It's not very appealing to most and I haven't had the time or the desire to try to talk anyone into it if I wanted to."

Clay laid his forehead on hers and sighed as he closed his eyes, the relief combined with what he'd almost done, overwhelmed him. "I can't believe I almost made the biggest mistake of my life."

Cassie laughed as her anger was released and she swelled with love for him. "You say that now, you haven't seen my house. You might change your mind because if you decide to stick around, Clay Walters, there's a list that you're an expert at. And we're going to get this straight right here and right now, if you decide to stick around, this is it. Lakeview. I'm not leaving, I'm not moving, if your life is going from one place to the next and you can't give it up, we might as well say goodbye for the first and last time because..."

He kissed her again to shut her up, her lips soft and smooth against his, the smell of her, the feel of her familiar and yet so new. "I've run from place to place trying to find something and then two years ago I found it here, in Lakeview with you. Then I've spent the last two years running from it because it wasn't mine. I'm not going anywhere, Cassie, this is the end of the long road for me."

"Clay Walters a settled man?" Her heart skipped beats as the moment became surreal, as it hit her that she woke up that morning as she had most, with her life missing only one thing, and now she held it in her arms. What an unexpected pleasure for it to become hers after all this time.

"Ironically enough, you're the only person who's ever unsettled my heart so much, and at the same time settled it. I love you, Cassie, and there's nothing between us now. If you'll have me, I want to be part of your life, I want to be the one you sit with on the porch, the one beside you as we create that place our children can always come home to."

"How many children?" She asked with a coy smile.

"As many as you want, should we start off with a dozen?"

"A little more than I bargained for. I guess I should keep in mind you're the overachiever in the family." Cassie's arms were wrapped around his shoulders, held him tight to feel him, to make sure he was real, and she was oblivious to anything else around them.

"I think if we're going to have twelve, we'd better get a move on it. Marry me, Cassie, today, tomorrow, as soon as possible."

"I've waited too long for you. Don't tell me you're a complete gentleman in every sense of the word because the way you said that sounds like we have to marry first before we start on the family." She kissed him seductively, her passion dormant for so long.

"We've waited this long, this way at least I know you'll stick around because you want something from me, even if it is just sex, and a handyman to fix your house," he joked and moved his hand discreetly under her shirt just to tease her more as he softly kissed her again, barely a touch against her lips. "You have to marry me first. I know your reputation, I've seen you run out of your last two weddings, do you think I'm going to take that chance?"

"That was different. I'd finally realized William didn't offer me everything I thought I wanted. Only you could give me that, I love you in every way possible, everything about you, everything about us together."

"Then marry me now because I won't take the chance of losing you again."

"Of course I'll marry you, but that doesn't mean we have to wait for another honeymoon." She wanted him desperately, even more so than before now that she knew he was hers and nothing stood between them, but in his eyes he stood strong, he would be the gentleman she spoke of even if it meant it would drive both of them crazy. "You wouldn't make me wait, would you?"

"Wouldn't I? Marry me today, right now."

Cassie could hear her father... foolish, impulsive, irresponsible, words that had no affect on her, hadn't in a long time. She'd be foolish, impulsive and irresponsible if that's what it took to feel this kind of joy in her heart. To feel deliriously happy and filled with everything she'd ever dreamed. She felt sorry for all the people in the world who took the safe road, the rocky one she'd traveled upon brought her to a place the easy one never would have as her heart filled completely.

They were married that very afternoon.

Books by Alisa Allan

WINDS OF CHANGE - ISBN: 0-9761480-0-5
Release Date: July 29, 2005
Cruise to Bermuda with a young woman who is forced to choose. Rekindle a past?... Or set it free?

AFTER MIDNIGHT – ISBN: 0-9761480-1-3
Release Date: August 31, 2005
Cruise to the Mexican Riviera and the Canada/New England coast with two strangers who marry and clash in a blaze of differences.

THE BEST MAN - ISBN: 0-9761480-2-1
Release Date: September 30, 2005
Cruise to Hawaiian Island paradise with a woman caught up in a tailspin of revenge after a failed wedding attempt, and finds herself in the middle of a bond that could not be broken.

BEYOND THE HORIZON - ISBN: 0-9761480-3-X
Release Date: October 31, 2005
Cruise to the Caribbean with three friends who are taken away by balmy tropical breezes and become vulnerable to its magic, then discover a web of lies and deceit underneath its beauty.

ONE LAST TIME - ISBN: 0-9761480-4-8
Release Date: November 30, 2005
Cruise to the Caribbean with a single mother and her son as they set off on a journey of adventure. Immersed in exotic ambiance, a woman lets go of a battle that threatens to drown her, but must eventually return and face it, and she must risk all she found to face it alone.

ANGEL MIST - ISBN: 0-9761480-5-6
Release Date: December 31, 2005
Cruise to Alaska as a young woman discovers a calm to the haunts of her past, but she finds she would truly have to go home again before she could find real peace.

Visit our website for more details and to join our mailing list:
www.BonVoyageBooks.com
www.TravelTimePress.com
www.AlisaAllan.com

We love to hear from our readers
Send us a review

Visit our websites:
www.BonVoyageBooks.com
www.TravelTimePress.com
www.AlisaAllan.com

Editorial questions, permissions, reviews:
Bon Voyage Books – 163 Mitchell's Chance Rd. #212 – Edgewater, MD 21037